"The best crime fiction writer in Canada."
—NATHAN RIPLEY, author of *Find You in the Dark*

"Wiebe has an incredible ability to pull you through the page." —BRENT BUTT, author of *Huge*

"A master of tone and atmosphere." —DEAD END FOLLIES

"... A great, great crime writer [who] captures the contemporary concerns of Vancouver and the Lower Mainland." —ROBERT WIERSEMA, CBC's *The Next Chapter*

"One of the most respected names in crime fiction today..." —ROBYN HARDING, author of *The Haters*

"Wiebe has a gift for place and character." —STEVE BERRY

"Vancouver's terse poet of a city in decline outdoes his own high standards." —THE TORONTO STAR on *Sunset and Jericho*

"[The] plot unfolds with absolute command of pace, tension and mood... with stellar characters, memorable settings, and clockwork plotting." —THE VANCOUVER SUN on *Ocean Drive*

"A harrowing ... and richly cinematic tale."
—THE VANCOUVER SUN on *Invisible Dead*

"A modern master of noir." —THE STRAND

THE WAKELAND SERIES

Invisible Dead
Cut You Down
Hell and Gone
Sunset and Jericho
The Last Exile

ALSO BY SAM WIEBE

Ocean Drive

THE LAST EXILE

A Wakeland Novel

SAM WIEBE

HARBOUR PUBLISHING

Copyright © 2025 Sam Wiebe

1 2 3 4 5 — 29 28 27 26 25

All rights reserved. No part of this publication may be reproduced, stored in a retrieval system or transmitted, in any form or by any means, without prior permission of the publisher or, in the case of photocopying or other reprographic copying, a licence from Access Copyright, www.accesscopyright.ca, 1-800-893-5777, info@accesscopyright.ca.

Harbour Publishing Co. Ltd.
P.O. Box 219, Madeira Park, BC, V0N 2H0
www.harbourpublishing.com

Edited by Derek Fairbridge
Text design by Libris Simas Ferraz / Onça Publishing
Printed and bound in Canada
Printed on 100% recycled paper

Harbour Publishing acknowledges the support of the Canada Council for the Arts, the Government of Canada, and the Province of British Columbia through the BC Arts Council.

Library and Archives Canada Cataloguing in Publication

Title: The last exile / Sam Wiebe.
Names: Wiebe, Sam, author.
Description: Series statement: A Wakeland novel ; 5
Identifiers: Canadiana (print) 20240525566 | Canadiana (ebook) 20240528271 | ISBN 9781998526086 (softcover) | ISBN 9781998526093 (EPUB)
Subjects: LCGFT: Thrillers (Fiction) | LCGFT: Detective and mystery fiction. | LCGFT: Noir fiction. | LCGFT: Novels.
Classification: LCC PS8645.I3236 L37 2025 | DDC C813/.6—dc23

*And I emerge from that silence
ready to live out loud again.*
—Richard Wagamese, *Embers*

ZERO

The first time she saw Budd Stack, Jan was all of eighteen, standing at the bar of the Roxy with a Seagram's and Coke and a fake ID. Jan asked her friend who was the devilish-looking guy with the tattoos.

Her friend's reply: "Not a guy you wanna mess with."

Jan had grinned, stirring her drink with her finger. "Aren't those the best kind?"

The guy noticed her noticing him. He came over, bought her a drink, paying with a fifty-dollar bill. "Jan short for Janice? That's a foxy name. I'm Budd with two D's. Never Buddy. From California, originally. How 'bout you?"

Budd-never-Buddy had good definition back then. He wore a denim vest to show off his arms. Jan liked his tattoos. This was before every college kid and barista had sleeves and a neck tat. She gawked at the pair of skeletal wings along his right forearm, ending at his wrist. A biker thing, he told her.

"That mean you're with the Exiles?" And before he could answer, she was nodding. "That is *so* freaking cool."

Jan had grown up on the Island, a good Christian kid from Campbell River. She found the city a shock. Whole neighbourhoods with no white faces, people living out of shopping carts talking to themselves, streets where you'd see two guys holding hands and even kissing. Vancouver was just too freaking much.

Bikers, though, were cool. They looked like the people she had grown up with, only tougher and with money to throw around. Nobody gave them grief. Nobody told them what to do. They kept everyone else in line. If the guy in the bar gave off a don't-mess-with-me vibe, that only made her feel safer.

Still, Jan had Budd keep his coat on when he dropped her off. Her roommate didn't need to know that the guy Jan was already in love with was pledged to the East Van chapter of the Heaven's Exiles Motorcycle Club. She kissed Budd goodbye, watched him drive off, the engine noise causing the entire block to tremble like the beginnings of an earthquake. Her man.

Hard to fathom that was forty years ago.

Budd still cut a striking figure at sixty-one, though his chest was broader, arms had a little sag. Didn't matter. He'd never hit her, never embarrassed her, and he still possessed the ability to surprise. Like tonight, taking her for dinner on the town. A reward from the Club president for completing some little errand.

If she asked, Budd would have told her. He trusted her that much. A turf war, an unpaid debt, some product that had gone missing. Jan never asked and didn't care. Her husband would help settle things. Make peace. Budd's reputation was usually enough.

Jan knew the Exiles were involved in bloody business. Knew her first dress shop had been financed with unclean cash. Knew Budd put the house and the Porsche in her name in case the government came after him. All of them did the same thing. Her best friend Darlene ran an autobody shop where at night Darlene's husband chopped cars.

What was the alternative? Look at her brother. Thirty years flying for the same airline and Junior could barely afford gas for his little seaplane. He and his wife Lori looked down on Budd, that was obvious. But who paid for the villa in Acapulco they'd all stayed at in June? Who lavished money on charities, funded college libraries?

And Budd had been home with her most nights. Junior and Lori sometimes looked at each other like strangers.

Sure, Jan was justifying a tiny bit, but look at the world. Really look at it. Nutjob politicians, trigger-happy cops, big companies shitting up the environment. Teens drowning in an online cesspool, entitled Millennials whining about justice from Mom and Dad's spare bedroom. Thank God she and Budd never had kids. And who was the Exiles' big competitor for drugs and gambling these days? The government. So who were the real hypocrites?

Jan Stack wanted to have fun and to own nice things and do a bit of good in the world. Budd wanted the same. And if the price was once in a while her husband was called to do a little favour for Terry Rhodes, well then, that was the price.

Tonight they'd gone to the Joe Fortes Chop House for tequila and a steak dinner, then taken in a Whitecaps game. Hundred-dollar shots of Clase Azul, champagne in the executive suite poured by a personal bartender. Stares of envy from the executives' wives—not bad for a gal from Campbell River.

And then home. Of all her possessions, all aspects of her lifestyle, the jewel was the two-million-dollar float home docked at Granville Island. Furnished just the way she wanted, with Budd's photos on the walls—he actually had quite a good eye—and their bedroom on the top tier overlooking False Creek. They lived in a dream—even better, a dream on the water.

"Take me to bed," Jan said to her husband.

"The lady knows what she wants."

They drove home across the Cambie Bridge through the makings of a thunderstorm. Budd had taken a couple of longnecks for the road. The only time he'd ever been pulled over, the traffic cop, instead of writing him up, had taken Budd's empties for him. That was the respect her husband commanded. He parked the Carrera near the gate to Sea Village, not worried about a ticket. Jan followed him down the gangplank to their front door, holding onto both rails. Mucho tequila, plus a bottle of Veuve Clicquot. Looking forward to kicking off her pumps, fooling around, then falling asleep with the TV on.

The TV was already on.

Had Budd left it on? Or Jan herself, in the rush to get ready? Maybe a power surge. That happened sometimes. The only drawback to a float home was the utilities, all the cords hooking you to the mainland. Once in a while the TV flickered, the clock on the stove had to be reset. So what? The trade-off was the view, the feeling of life rushing underneath you.

Inside, Budd tossed his blazer over the La-Z-Boy. A smoky sweet aroma filled the ground floor. Sandalwood and teakwood, vanilla and rose hips and lemon. Her scented candles in the upstairs bathroom were lit. All of them.

Soft music from upstairs as well: Diana Krall, "All or Nothing at All."

"Someone having a soak?" Jan whispered.

She watched her husband flip the lid off the ottoman, pulling a blue plastic clamshell out of the storage beneath. He shushed her, digging his keys out and unlocking the case. The slim, chrome-plated pistol inside smelled of machine oil. Budd thumbed shells into the clip, inserted it and racked the slide.

"Stay down and stay quiet," he said.

It never entered her mind to call 911.

Jan counted his footfalls, soft on the carpeted stairs. The storm had the water agitated. Rain slapped the windows. The house pitched and settled as if drawing a breath and exhaling. Jan thought she heard water from upstairs, the drain being pulled.

The music soared in volume, filling the house, her good sound system distorting. Jan heard a heavy splash. She moved to the bottom of the stairs, heard a baritone howl. Her husband was screaming.

Oh god, she thought. *Oh Jesus, what do I do?*

Budd was her life and yet she ran from him, booze and panic dulling her brain. Pausing at the door to put shoes on—*no—run—get out, get safe, he'd want that—Budd—*

Jan opened the door, saw the woman standing on the threshold, the broad smile on her face. A hand thrusting out as if in greeting. The world moved a little off-kilter.

The music was off, and Budd had stopped howling. Jan lay on her back, rain pelting her bare feet. The woman was upstairs now, speaking sharply to someone. "Hold it like this, dummy, keep the blade *away* from yourself."

Now the footsteps were louder and they were coming down the stairs, the woman and someone behind her, the woman carrying an axe, and Jan was eight years old again, on stage in a school play, a small child in a troll mask calling up to the other children, *who's that trip-trap trapping on my bridge bridge bridge,* and Jan thought of how unfair life was, to be together forty years and

alone here, now, at the end of the world.

ONE

The woman in 3F was having visions of broken wings and burning fuselage. She'd lasted the first four hours of the flight on costume dramas and red wine from the bar cart. Then, over the Rockies, we hit turbulence. I saw her hand bring the airsick bag to the front of the pouch. Her fingers clawed the arm rest. She gulped air and tried to measure her exhalations. The plane juddered. My fellow passenger looked over at me until I unstrung my headphones.

"What's that you're reading?" 3F asked.

I handed her the book. She admired the cover, brushed a thumb along the pages.

"Pretty good title," she said. "What's it about?"

"They're essays on faith in the modern world. Conscience, purpose, stuff like that."

"Light reading, huh? Any answers yet?"

"I still have a ways to go."

Our little in-flight book club was only a means of distraction. 3F was thinking of engine failure, of a sudden loss in altitude and cabin pressure. Imagining some disinterested stranger picking the black box out of the rubble. Not a bad reason to make small talk across the aisle with a stranger. Air travel is an adventure to some, full of luxury and peril. To me, it's the cross-country movement of easily spooked cattle. Something to be accomplished with haste and a minimum of fuss. And kindness for your fellow livestock.

"Usually I conk right out once I'm in the air," 3F said. "But today I got to the gate early and had a double-shot mocha and then realized, shoot, I left my Dramamine in my luggage. My wellness coach taught me this breathing exercise, but it doesn't seem to be working."

I nodded in sympathy as the cabin jounced again. The passengers collectively swayed. 3F closed her eyes and dug her palm into the armrest until the fasten-seatbelt lights blinked.

"What do you do for a living?" I asked, guessing corporate accounts. Warby Parker reading glasses, a knockoff Hermès handbag and a premium economy ticket—hours of eye-wrecking study in her background, business casual on a budget, flying on the company dime.

"Actually I do accounts for this ride-share company." She dug a card out of the faux-Hermès. NINA RYDELL, VICE PRESIDENT OF ACCOUNTS, PRONTO RIDES.

"You like your work?"

"I'm good at it. Not the same thing, I know. What about you?"

"Retired," I said.

"Pretty young for retirement."

"Young's the perfect age for it."

Nina Rydell scrutinized me. I'm not easy to scrutinize. Years of fieldwork schooled me in how to dress nondescript, to look like nobody in particular. Old habits. "You're not one of those billionaires who designed an app when they were fifteen, are you?" she asked.

"Premium economy," I said.

"So what *did* you do?"

Looking over her shoulder, I saw farmland rising up. The outskirts of the Lower Mainland. Soon the muddy fork of the Fraser River Delta came into view.

"The short version," I said, "I was a PI. One half of a private security firm, Wakeland & Chen. A year ago and change, I sold my share of the company and moved to Montreal."

"Why?" 3F asked.

"My partner bet me I couldn't."

"I mean, why quit?"

I wasn't trying to be evasive. My exit had been abrupt, tied to a case we'd solved—solved a little too well. At least that's how I thought about it. Jeff Chen probably saw things differently.

"It's a dangerous line of work," I said. "I had a feeling if I stayed, something bad would happen, either to me or by me. The city can be hazardous to your health."

"And yet you're heading back."

For the moment it sure seemed that way. The pilot mentioned we were beginning our descent. Nina in 3F closed her eyes, giving her breathing exercise one last shot. I re-strung my headphones and opened the book, thinking my descent had begun a long time ago, and that, yes, it *was* a good title. And apt.

What Are We Here For?

The day before, I was sitting in a park near the Marché Jean-Talon, trying very hard not to smoke a cigarette. The swampy heat of late August in Montreal made this a little easier. Occupying a bench with a St-Viateur bagel and an Earl Grey tea, sweating through my flannel shirt. Listening to the noise of the market and the power surge sound of cicadas. My phone rang. That familiar 604 area code.

"Wakeland," I said.

"I need help."

In my former career, no three words could have prompted me to action more swiftly. Other than maybe, "you owe me." Since retirement, though, I'd been practising radical indifference. Dave Wakeland *version française* was a creature of boozy idleness. He spent his days reading in parks and wandering an unfamiliar city, nights in bars with good music or sprawled on the fire escape outside his kitchen window. After eighteen months, I was only beginning to get a handle on him.

"You want, I can recommend a PI," I said into the phone. "Have you tried Jeff Chen? He's very good."

"And very busy, Dave. And anyway, this is more your kinda thing."

I knew the voice, and knew what she meant. Wakeland & Chen handled security and investigations. Jeff oversaw the larger and more profitable security division, leaving me to run the Department of Faint Hopes and Lost Causes. My kinda thing.

"I'm retired," I told the voice. "Find someone with fewer city miles on them."

"City miles bullshit. Check your email."

I did, seeing the ticket she'd already booked. Montreal to Vancouver, leaving in the morning. *Fait accompli*. Shuzhen Chen had left me no choice. I even knew the words she'd end our conversation with.

"You owe me, Dave."

And I did.

Trundling past the baggage claim to the exit, I saw her. Once upon a time, Jeff's cousin had been our office manager. After law school, Shuzhen had clerked in the Interior for an ancient, cranky judge, then returned to Vancouver, taking a job in legal aid.

"Hiya, Dave."

A sleeveless blouse, high-waisted slacks, dressy shoes you could march in all day if need be. Her nails were bitten down, and the screen of her phone looked like it had been used to hammer tent pegs. We embraced. Beneath whatever floral shampoo she used, Shuzhen smelled of coffee and concrete and rain. Of Vancouver. Maybe that was my imagination.

"Flight okay?"

"We landed in one piece. Thank you for the seat with no bulkhead."

Shuzhen nodded toward the carousel. "Do we have to wait?"

"Death before checked luggage."

"Good, we can head straight to court. The run should be in about now."

The run: the convoy of armoured vans carrying inmates or people charged with serious crimes. From North Fraser Pretrial, the sheriffs would drive the vans to court, stocking the holding cells for the trials and hearings of the day. Shuzhen's client, *my* client, would be on the morning run.

As we left I caught sight of Nina Rydell from seat 3F, waiting by the baggage chute. I waved to her. "Home free."

She shot me a grin of tension and fatigue. "Nothing's free. But home, in any case."

I felt self-conscious, shambling after my partner's cousin in my well-worn denim and plaid, a knuckle-dragger clutching a Marilynne Robinson book and an overnight bag. Welcome back, Wakeland. We do hope you enjoyed your brief reprieve. Now get the hell back to work.

TWO

We crossed the Arthur Laing Bridge. Shuzhen drove a sleek electric Merc that doubled as her office. Smoothie cannisters and coffee mugs, charge cables. A nest of parking tickets in the map pocket of the passenger door. My bag and book on the floor beside file folders and a pair of swimming goggles. I managed to slide the seat all the way back.

"How's it feel to be home?" Shuzhen said.

I couldn't answer that yet. Instead I dropped the window and drank in the breeze, saltwater and midmorning exhaust. The lack of oppressive humidity was a blessing. The North Shore mountains rose up from the other side of the city, the twin peaks called the Sisters in the Squamish language. For most of my life I'd oriented myself by the sight of those mountains. Away from them, I had to admit, I'd felt disconcerted and often found myself whipping my head around to catch a glimpse of them.

But did familiarity make the place home? That term seemed too loaded. I wasn't home, not yet, but I was here, at least for the present.

"What do I call you?" I asked. "For a while you were going by Suzie, right?"

"When I was trying to fit in at school, yeah. Never liked it. I go by my real name now. Figure if people can pronounce 'Worcestershire' and 'sriracha,' 'Shoo-chun' shouldn't be too hard."

Shuzhen drove with the aggression of someone who learned on a luxury car. We swung down Granville Street, catching every second light and stopping for most of the ones we didn't.

"I maybe should have told you about my client ahead of time," she said. "I wanted her to tell you in her own words. You read about the Houseboat Massacre?"

I hadn't. One of the pleasures of Montreal was not being barraged with West Coast news. I could sit in a park or a brasserie and hear rapid-fire chatter from all directions, too fast and too accented for my pitiful French. Cocooned in a lack of understanding.

"How about Budd Stack?" she asked. "Ever hear of him?"

"Sure," I said. Stack was a biker of the old school. A fearsome man in his day and probably no slouch in ours. Long retired, I thought. "Who'd he kill?"

"He was the victim, Dave. Budd and his wife Jan."

Shuzhen held to the right lane, taking us over the Granville Bridge. As we crossed, she pointed down toward Granville Island and the False Creek waterfront.

"The Stacks lived on one of the houseboats down there. Three weeks ago, Budd and Jan were killed in their home."

"By your client?" I asked.

"Maggie Zito is charged with it, yeah. But there's no way she did it."

Over False Creek, the water rosy and dotted with sailing vessels. Down to the law courts at Robson Square, two blocks of 1970s brutalism designed by Arthur Erickson. A steep glass roof, concrete battlements bridging Smithe Street. It resembled a greenhouse fused with a bunker.

We parked beneath the court, paid, and took the elevator up to ground level. The foyer was abustle with sheriffs and lawyers and a herd of citizens holding blue juror summonses. Shuzhen checked in with the front desk and found the room assignment, then led me back to the elevator.

"Would it matter to you?" I asked her.

"What?"

"If she did it. Your client."

"Not in terms of a defence, no. I'd still represent her."

"But personally."

"Of course. Maggie didn't do this, Dave."

As simple as that. She pointed me to the courtroom and left to change into her gown.

During the Air India bombing trial, one of the courtrooms had been terror-proofed, the blond wood augmented with bullet-proof glass and security screening. This was where *R. v. Zito* would be contested. The case was under a publication ban, meaning the defendant's name wouldn't be circulated in the press. But the hearing had attracted a few onlookers, friends and law students, a journalist or two.

I took a seat in the middle row of the gallery. In the front row I saw Natalie Holinshed, the crime beat reporter for what remained of the local papers. We'd traded information in the past.

"Thought you left?" Holinshed whispered to me.

"So did I."

Shuzhen greeted the sheriffs at the door and was permitted through the partition. She wore the black robe and waistcoat with white shirt and tabs. A heavy outfit in the muggy room. At the defence table, she shook hands with a middle-aged South Asian woman in the same attire. Lead counsel, I figured. The more experienced lawyer would argue the case when it finally came to trial. Today was one of the myriad hearings to settle on a date.

Shifting down to sit behind the reporter, I said, "What's the story with this?"

"Zito and an unknown accomplice cut up an Exile and his wife. Home invasion, from the sound of it. The craziest part, the perps took a boat across False Creek, made their getaway the same way."

"Any question of her guilt?"

Holinshed's look was wry and knowing. "That she didn't do it, you mean? Slim. Defendant has quite a record from what I hear. That the Crown can prove it, I'd say seventy-thirty. Why, what's your interest in the case?"

"Not sure yet, but growing."

The door at the back opened and a pair of nightmares walked in. Heads shot around. A sheriff called into her two-way radio for reinforcements. The two men weren't wearing their vests in court, but their size, the tattoos, the smirk they put on as they submitted to the pat-down, announced their affiliation as loudly as if they'd rode in on their Street Glides.

"Just here to watch," one biker told the sheriff. Late forties, with a dark red beard. His partner was younger and olive-complected. A prospect, from the looks of him. He gritted his teeth as the sheriff's hands travelled over his legs and chest. Both wore Carhartt tees and cargo pants and shades. Holinshed scribbled furiously.

They took seats near the back, others shifting to give them room. The smell of sweat and machine oil. The Beard extended his leg into the aisle. Steel-toed boots, the toe shiny from wear.

From inside the plastic cage, Shuzhen looked at them, then over at me.

The defendant was led in from a door to the side of the bench. She joined Shuzhen and her lead counsel. Average height, fat and wearing an oatmeal-coloured suit that looked outside of her normal wardrobe. Maggie Zito looked about forty, maybe younger. Dark hair and a nose that had been broken at least once. Murmurs of support from the crowd, which she acknowledged with a nod. She didn't glance at the bikers.

Sometimes you can tell—not guilt, which can be concealed, but whether a person is comfortable with violence. Accustomed to it. The way a defendant flops down in their seat, body language telling the judge they're bored and want to get this over with, is different from someone meekly lowering into the chair, still in shock over the night they spent in custody. Violence was written on the face of the one percenters behind me. And likely written on mine.

I watched Maggie Zito sit solemnly as her counsel instructed her and rise when Her Honour came in. I watched as the two teams of attorneys conducted their negotiations. I watched her when a friend came in late, holding up a fist in solidarity. And I watched when the two Exiles stood and crossed the long way down the aisle, forcing others to stand and earning glares from the court officers. I watched her and could only say that Maggie Zito was intelligent enough to know the gravity of her situation. She was no stranger to violence.

And I understood for the first time, since getting the call yesterday, why Shuzhen had found it so important to bring me back. Important enough to call in a favour. My partner's cousin wasn't worried about winning or losing the case. The trial itself wasn't the danger. Maggie Zito was accused of killing an Exile. Taken into custody by a court system that was capricious and cold, she was trapped in a world where the bikers held sway over life and death. Running was impossible. Before any official determination of guilt, they would move on her and kill her, in custody or out. Their presence in the court was a promise of that. It was merely a question of when.

THREE

Shuzhen led me to one of the small conference rooms on the top floor of the courthouse. I was introduced to the lead counsel. Nimisha Nair was a hair over five feet and around fifty years old. She wheeled behind her a three-storey tower of office luggage almost as tall as she was: file box, garment bag and all-purpose satchel. The effect was something between a very efficient business class passenger and a peddler carting around her wares.

"Our regular investigator booked a last-minute vacation once he learned our client was accused of killing an Exile." Nimisha opened the satchel and took out a bottle of Drixoral, giving each nostril a blast of antihistamine. "Shuzhen says you've done this work before, so you know the risks. But these are very exceptional risks."

"I'm a very exceptional PI," I said.

"Good for you. Maggie Zito is entitled to the best defence we can muster, which is being made very difficult for us. If you know these people and can work some sort of miracle, as Shuzhen thinks you're capable of, have at it."

"Any threats so far?" I asked.

"Nothing that fits the legal definition. A few shows of solidarity from the victims' friends. The kind you saw in court just now."

"And no chance for release till the trial?"

"Not with Maggie's priors. Three previous assaults."

I nodded. "Speaking confidentially, did she do it?"

"No way," Shuzhen said.

Nimisha smiled at her junior associate. "I wish I had Shuzhen's confidence," she said. "Maggie is—well, you'll meet her. In any case, she claims to be innocent. That's the case we're making."

A knock on the conference room door. A sheriff brought in Maggie Zito, who sat and leaned back in her chair, regarding me with little surprise and less emotion. We were introduced. No shaking of hands. Nimisha and Shuzhen discussed the next hearing with her. They asked if she had any concerns. Maggie shrugged and chewed her thumbnail.

"No concerns, none at all, 'sides this pesky murder charge."

"I'll head back to the office, then," Nimisha said. "The air in these old courtrooms plays hell with my sinuses."

When the three of us were alone, Shuzhen asked how Maggie Zito was doing.

"Lunch was okay. Mac and cheese. Had a nice call with my kids."

"We could bring them to pretrial, arrange some time—"

"I don't want them to see their mama in jail."

"Pretrial isn't jail," Shuzhen said.

"It's all one jail, honeybunch."

Abrasions on her hands and old scar tissue on her knuckles. Up close Maggie Zito had a toughness to her, a solidity apart from her bulk. No juror would doubt that physically she could wield an edged weapon with enough raw force to kill. Her size and her roughneck appearance—her unladylike-ness—would be a tough sell to a jury of Vancouver taxpayers.

"So what's your deal?" Maggie said to me. "Shuzhen says you're a private eye. I been picturing some broke-down ex-cop, white hair and a bad suit."

"One out of three," I said. "I was only on the job for a year or so. Didn't work out."

"What a shame. I like spending time with cops."

"You must, you keep letting them arrest you."

Maggie chuckled mirthlessly. "Only this time not for cause. I got into a few scraps over the years. Short fuse, y'know? Now they're calling it 'a pattern of escalating behaviour.' Like I been leading up to this my whole life."

"Have you?"

Her attitude immediately grew stormy. "I didn't kill anyone. You think I did, you can go fuck a fuse box."

"Problems with anyone in the cells?" I asked.

A shake of the head. "Got an idea who it'll be, though. But that's probably not the person you gotta look out for, is it?" If Maggie Zito wasn't quite as hard as she presented, she was steeling herself to get there.

"Tell Dave what happened," Shuzhen said.

"What happened is, two weeks ago I get back from walking Edie to school, and I find two cops on my porch beating their paws on my screen door. They say they got a warrant. They take me around the house to the shed and ask me to pop the lock. So I pop it, and inside they find a hatchet and machete."

"Did you recognize the tools?" I asked.

"Course I did. They're mine. I run a landscaping crew. Only both have got blood on them, which is news to me. I get taken into custody while they search my place top to bottom. The next twenty-four hours they're either interviewing me or quote unquote 'letting me get some rest.' Ever try getting some rest when you been falsely accused?"

"What else do they have on you?" I asked.

"Cuts on my hands that are 'consistent with wielding a weapon.' Only thing my ass wielded was hedge clippers. Landscaping, even gloved, your hands tend to get sliced up."

Shuzhen passed me a thick green binder. The murder book. "We don't have full disclosure yet. But the Crown has the weapons, and we think there's an eyewitness, too."

"Who's the witness?"

"We don't know yet. Confidential."

"Anything else?"

"The footage from her interview. Maggie overturned the table."

Maggie shook her head, still pissed about it.

"All night they keep asking did I do this. I tell them no so many times I get bored saying it. Cantankerous, y'know? They ask where I was the night of August 1 and I say in bed. 'Can anyone prove that?' Edie and Dominick were in the rooms down the hall, but they don't count because they were asleep. I guess putting your kids to bed first is unheard of. So yeah, I lost it a little, took it out on the table."

"It was bolted to the floor," Shuzhen said.

Maggie shrugged.

"Did you know Budd and Jan Stack?" I asked.

"Him by reputation." Maggie's features contorted in a deeper sort of anger.

"Any idea who killed them?"

"Matter of fact I do." Maggie shifted her seat with a screech. "The one-armed fucking man."

"Dave is here to help," Shuzhen said. "So am I."

The defendant looked at her hands. The anger seemed to level off. "I don't mean any offence, babe, but I think I'm pretty much past help."

Outside it was spitting rain, but warm. We bought tacos from a food truck and sat on the steps of the old art gallery, looking at the empty ice rink at the bottom of Robson Square.

"Two murder weapons won't be easy for a jury to overlook," I said. "Not that I don't love a challenge."

"Someone planted those," Shuzhen said.

"How sure of that are you?"

She didn't respond. We chewed and watched a couple of kids light cigarettes and laugh. Two old men played chess on a magnetic board, ignoring the rain.

"Are you going to see Jeff while you're in town?" Shuzhen asked.

"I expect so."

"Business isn't doing so good."

That was news. Jeff Chen was a smart and conscientious businessman. But the economy was rocky, and even Jeff couldn't anticipate everything. I wadded up the napkin and paper sleeve.

"What about your sister?" Shuzhen asked. "You going to make time for a visit?"

My half-sister Kay was in prison, serving two sentences for second-degree murder. I hadn't spoken to her since the conviction, hadn't seen her since I left town.

"I'm not inclined to," I said after a minute.

"Kay might appreciate it. Hard serving time with no family."

I changed the subject. "Tell me why someone would frame Maggie Zito for these murders. All the people in the world, why her?"

Shuzhen wiped her mouth and chin, catching a lick of ancho chili sauce. "Two reasons. Maggie has a record. She served twenty-two months for throwing a cop through a window. The officer had swatted her oldest child on the head. The court didn't see that as sufficient provocation."

"Justice being blind and all."

"Another time, she hospitalized a girl by stomping on her foot."

"Escalating violence," I said. "Could this be revenge?"

"Don't think so. The cop got compensation and the woman with the foot lives on Maggie's street. They're friends now."

"And what's the other reason?"

"Two decades ago Maggie's brother was killed up in Hope." Shuzhen held out her half-eaten taco. "Do you want this? Talking about violence turns my stomach."

I took it and finished it in two bites. "You were saying, her brother?"

"Beau Zito, yeah. He was dragged through the street by someone in a truck. No one was ever charged."

Shuzhen pulled out a vape pen, releasing a cloud that smelled like almonds. I tried it. Not my thing. I could taste peach lip balm on the mouthpiece.

"Is there any way you could convince the judge to release Maggie on recognizance?"

"Not for murder. Not given her record."

"Solitary confinement?"

"She's already being held in the refugee wing." Foreign nationals were also housed in the pretrial centre. "Maggie is at risk no matter where she is."

I concurred. This wasn't a case of justice but of preservation. The Exiles were powerful and well-established. Anyone in pretrial who wanted to earn their favour, or a bit of cash, could be a potential assassin. "Does she have people?" I asked.

"Her sister Briony is looking after her kids. A few friends in town. You saw most of them in court. Her foster mother lives in Washington state."

"Maybe there's an angle to that," I said. "Demand to stand trial as an American citizen?"

"Respectfully, Dave," Shuzhen said, "I didn't ask you here for legal advice. We need evidence Maggie didn't do this."

"A tall order," I said, wondering if that evidence existed. "I'll need a car and some expense money. And a place to crash."

Shuzhen pointed at one of the residential towers just south of the court. "I'm in that one. 707. My roommate's in Mexico till

Christmas. I'll bring your bag there after court, unless you need anything from it now."

I said no. She stood, took her vape pen back and handed me some money. I tried not to notice how the rain dappled her shoulder, or the corner of her mouth where the lipstick had been chewed away. Shuzhen placed a hand on my wrist.

"Thank you for coming back," she said.

"You didn't give me much choice, remember?"

"No choice at all, but that's your fault, not mine." Shuzhen unfurled a translucent umbrella as the rain picked up. "Next time be more careful who you get involved with."

No chance of that, I thought, watching her stroll back toward the courthouse.

FOUR

I walked through indecisive rain in the direction of the Cambie Bridge. The city had surprised me by ticking along just fine in my absence. Construction cranes loomed over unfinished towers. Pleasure boats skimmed False Creek. A shirtless man sat cross-legged at an intersection, a wet cardboard sign on his lap. ADDICTED. RENOVICTED. ANYTHING HELPS. He went ignored by the joggers and the lunchtime crowd. So did I. In an alley, a pair of kitchen workers in bandannas smoked hand-rolled cigarettes.

I had left Vancouver on a career success more bitter than any failure. Solving that case had meant implicating my sister. No choice in the matter, no right options. Call it burnout, survival or penance, but I left, no longer at home in the place I was born.

And now I was back. And didn't know how to feel about that.

At the apex of the bridge I paused and watched the Aquabus ferry people from Yaletown across to Granville Island. Looking at the double row of houseboats moored near the landing, I tried to guess which one belonged to the murdered couple.

I was here because Shuzhen Chen had asked me. Because Budd and Jan Stack had been killed, and Maggie Zito charged with their murders. Suspects who might become victims, victims who were part of organized crime. A justice system that might serve as a slaughterhouse. Nothing here was ever simple.

Whether or not Maggie was innocent, she couldn't remain in prison waiting for the Exiles' retribution. I crossed Cambie Street and walked into the brick-and-glass corner building that housed the Vancouver Police Department. At the front desk I asked for Sergeant Ray Dudgeon.

"Does *Staff Sergeant* Dudgeon know you, sir?" the desk clerk asked.

"Isn't the family resemblance obvious?"

A roll of the eyes. Dudgeon is Black and as Québécois as maple sugar drizzled on snow.

I waited ten minutes, reading police bulletins and avoiding the plaques of officers killed in the line of duty. My father was among them, the victim of vehicular homicide. The driver was never found. Every time I saw the photo, I was closer in age to Matt Wakeland: it felt as if his fate and mine were being nudged ever closer together. Death in the line of. There were worse fortunes, I supposed.

The elevator expelled Ray Dudgeon. His dress uniform bore the three chevrons and crown of staff sergeant, along with a cluster of medals. Maybe coming from a photo op. More grey on his temples. Dudgeon's handshake was still firm enough to snap a bowling pin. He head-to-toe'd me, squinting in mock confusion.

"You look like Dave Wakeland, but he left town."

"He did," I said. "But he's back, for the time being, and could use a cigarette."

"I don't smoke anymore. Gotta set an example for the rank and file. But I'll walk you to your car."

Beneath the Cambie Bridge, at a crossing near the motor pool, Dudgeon hauled out a pack of Player's Lights and a gold-plated Ronson.

"What about the rank and file?" I asked, lighting the proffered cigarette.

"All their idols got clay feet these days." Dudgeon looked down at the uniform, brushed a flake of ash from the breast. "The new improved VPD. Job has its issues, but the wife sure appreciates the salary. How's Sonia?"

"Thriving, last I saw."

"Didn't work out between you two, huh?"

I gave the requisite philosophical shrug. "When she was here, she couldn't stand that I was out risking my life. In Montreal, she was the one chasing bad guys all night, and I was home watching dinner get cold."

"So why are you back?" Dudgeon asked.

"Too many loyalty cards. I'm owed a lot of free coffees of equal or lesser value."

"This is a staff sergeant's time you're wasting, Dave. *On y vas.*"

"Maggie Zito," I said.

"Ah." No reaction to the name other than familiarity. "There's a pub ban on that case."

"I'm not publishing, just asking what you think."

Dudgeon smoked. "Ms. Zito and a scumbag to be caught later broke into the home of Budd Stack, killed him and his wife. As much of a sonofabitch as old Budd was, they didn't deserve that. After a tireless and thorough investigation, we determined Maggie Zito did it."

"She says she didn't."

"Doe-eyed innocent, huh?"

"This morning two Exiles showed up at court to watch her. She won't last inside."

"Easiest way to stay out of prison, Dave? Don't commit crimes."

"It's not impossible she didn't do it," I said.

"No, that's true. But it's impossible's ugly younger brother." He ticked off the reasons with his free hand: "Both murder weapons found at her place, the victims' blood still on them. The wounds on her hands. She can't account for her whereabouts the night of. Plus there's Ms. Zito's violent priors, including assault on a cop."

"So she's not in danger of sainthood," I said. "That's not beyond a reasonable doubt."

"And I'm not on her jury, Wakeland."

"What about a witness?"

"The Stacks lived right on the water. Anybody could look through their front window."

"So who did?"

Dudgeon shrugged. "Any other minor miracles?"

I felt tired. It would be early evening in Montreal, the heat beginning to settle. Part of me was still there. "You said Maggie had an accomplice."

"Evidence suggests," Dudgeon said. "She hasn't given him up yet. My bet, once we get closer to the trial she'll suddenly start remembering things, tell the Crown she's ready to make a deal."

"Maggie could be dead by then," I said.

"So could we. Forest fires, super flu." He looked down at the burning filter in his hand. "Cancer. We're all fucked and who cares anyway. *Tant pis.*"

"Should be the new department motto," I said. "Any chance I can walk the crime scene?"

"Find all the clues us real cops missed?"

"I just like overpriced real estate."

"Good a reason as any to come back." Dudgeon brought out the pack again. "I'll see what I can do. One last smoke for the road?"

Who was I to turn down generosity from a public servant? As we parted, Dudgeon pointed his index and middle fingers at me, slicing the air sharply back and forth. I couldn't tell if it was a salute or he was shooting me with an invisible gun. *À la prochaine.* Till next time.

He'd shrugged when I mentioned a witness. But he hadn't denied it.

FIVE

It was a twenty-minute walk along the waterfront to Granville Island. Dudgeon had texted that an officer would show me the crime scene at six. Quarter to five now, leaving me time to examine the area where the victims' home was moored.

Constructed atop a sandbar, Granville Island was joined to the False Creek riverfront. The area had been quaint and hippyish at one point. A market for produce and homespun crafts, a fine-arts college and enough quirky little bistros and knickknack shops to fill a cozy mystery series. Artists had carved totem poles in the open-air workshops, while nearby, boat owners repaired hulls and tuned motors. People here once built and crafted and created. Now the shops were more expensive and on-the-nose cute, selling the Granville Island Experience. Artisanal brooms and the thirty-dollar fish sandwich. No more smell of cedar shavings and turpentine. A criticism of the times as much as the place.

Ocean Concrete was still in operation, its large silos painted as alternating Bert and Ernies from *Sesame Street*. North of the cement plant was Sea Village, a triple row of floating houses, flat roofs and glass, pastel-painted wood, strung across the island and facing the elegant emptiness of Yaletown.

You'd be on display living here, but that would be part of the appeal. The exclusivity another part. Less than a thousand float homes in BC, and fewer than a dozen in Sea Village. A pocket of old-fashioned cool nestled among progress. The drawbacks were obvious, nothing money couldn't solve.

I bought a smoked salmon sandwich and a packet of organic Earl Grey at the market, and found a bench near the entrance to Sea Village. I ate my sandwich and contemplated the area. Granville Island at late midday: cyclists looping the banks, tourists lined up for the Aquabus. Security and the odd police cruiser roving around. Maintenance vans. Families and pairs of shoppers leaving the market hall, feeding gulls from cardboard boats of french fries.

At night the area would be quiet but not still. To gain entrance to the Stacks' home you'd have to first get past the locked gate at the top of the gangplank. From there you'd make your way down all those creaking boards and handrails. Past the windows of the neighbours, people who know when someone doesn't belong. All this would have to be done in view of the walkway and benches on the edge of the island. Motion-sensor lights. Neighbours' pets. Surveillance cameras hither and yon.

Arriving by boat had seemed audacious to me, but viewing the layout, the decision would be practical. Load up somewhere, chug across the water in the dark, betting that the sound of an outboard motor wouldn't carry over traffic noise from the bridge. Tie up at the edge of the home. You'd still risk being seen, but you'd have surprise on your side. Maybe Budd and Jan had even left the back door open.

"Pretty unbeatable view, isn't it? I'd almost forgot."

An elderly Korean woman stood behind me carrying cloth grocery bags, a striped scarf around her neck. I moved out of her way, and she set the bags down on the rail with a clink of glass.

"My hubby and I knew when we saw it," she said. "Neither of us had even spent much time on the water, other than the ferry. But there was something about the lifestyle."

"I can imagine." While I was slouched against the rail, I probably seemed smaller and harmless. Now, standing beside her, the woman re-evaluated. Miscreant, snoop or admirer of the view? She unlocked the gate and stepped through, closing it partway.

"Have you been to Granville Island before?" she asked.

"Once or twice," I said. "Guess with so many windows you see a lot of your neighbours, huh?"

"When we're home," the woman said, deciding I wasn't here to pillage. "We just got back yesterday from Madrid. We haven't seen much of anybody."

So she didn't know what had happened to the Stacks. That worked in my favour. "Are houseboat communities pretty tight-knit?"

"Float homes," she corrected. "A houseboat is still a boat, designed to move through water. A float home can't move unless it's towed."

"Pardon my ignorance," I said. "The float home community."

"I would say we are a little tighter, probably. There aren't a lot of us, and we tend to have problems our landlubber friends don't."

"Like leaks?" I asked.

"Rarely, but yes. Boats in the harbour making noise at odd hours. Waterfowl. Otters." She laughed. "Playful creatures, but they can get into all sorts of places they shouldn't."

"Do you know Budd and Jan Stack?"

"Sure do," the woman said. From her tone she didn't know about his extralegal associations. "Jan likes her music on the loud side, and Budd's not too considerate when he grills. But they're generally quite nice. I shouldn't complain. Do you know them?"

"Mutual acquaintances," I said.

She took up her groceries. "Well, I should get dinner on."

A tight smile and a nod of the head as she hurried down the gangplank. I turned at the sound of boots. Behind me stood an officer in uniform and department-issue slicker, holding her cap in her hand. Her arrival had probably hastened Mrs. Float-Home-Not-Houseboat's exit.

"Detective Temple," she said. "Ray Dudgeon says I should humour you."

"I'm not hard to humour," I said. "I'd like to see the house."

Temple shrugged. She was taller than me, solid but narrow at the shoulders, her hair in a knot at the back. As I followed her down the zigzags of the gangplank, she said, "Just so you know, I have a very low tolerance for bullshit. I'm not impressed you spent five minutes on the job or that you're on speaking terms with my superior. And I'll tell you just once: I don't do hypotheticals. 'What if some other lady matching the defendant's description parachuted down from the bridge?' That line of shit you can save for the court."

"Fair enough," I said.

The Stacks' home featured more wood than the others, a bit less of that postmodern chill. Three storeys, fish-scale shingles painted cerulean with white trim around the portholes. The side that faced the water was almost exclusively glass, with long gold curtains. Staggered decks. A propane grill and a pair of weathered Adirondack chairs. We went around the side, the platform bobbing with our steps.

Temple broke the seal on the sliding door and opened it. She led me through the galley to the living room and front hallway. She pointed to where a rectangle of wooden flooring had been removed.

"This is where Mrs. Stack was found." Temple sighed as she crouched. "Floorboards showed two separate gouges made by a sharp instrument. Hatchet or axe. These were the blows that didn't find the victim."

"How many did?" I asked.

"Enough. She was stabbed in the abdomen while standing, and then struck with the axe twice while on the ground."

"You ever think, detective, you're in kind of a gruesome line of work?"

No reply. The foyer smelled of old blood mixed with solvents and preservatives. The forensic techs had been thorough in processing the scene. Detective Temple traced a hand along a peculiar swipe mark close to the door.

"Mrs. Stack was in nylon stockings—seems they'd just returned from dinner out. From the location of her body and the spatter here and here"—she pointed at the clusters of dried blood on the wall—"one of the assailants intercepted her at the front door. Likely the perp snuck around the exterior when the Stacks came home."

The interior of the home was all treated lumber, the ceiling beams low, with viewing portals every few feet. Leather couch and ottoman. The galley's island was outfitted with hammered brass cookware. The overall impression was of elegance.

What gave the property the feeling of a home were the photos on the walls. A study of Jan in sunglasses and bathing suit. An aerial view of False Creek. Animals. Beach debris. Most were in black and white, with simple wooden frames. Several were striking. I wondered who had taken them.

"What kind of person chooses to live on a float home?" I asked, mostly to myself.

Temple's response was direct. "Someone with millions of dollars who doesn't get seasick."

The top floor was the bedroom suite. Diaphanous curtains shrouded the bed, and the glass was tinted. Making love here would give the feeling of exhibitionism without actually showing off to the world. The second floor held an office, with a bathroom close to the stairs. Temple opened the bathroom door. The high-edged soaker tub had been scoured with bleach, yet flies buzzed along the lip, one crawling over a smashed section of tile.

"Mr. Stack's body was found here. Multiple stab, cut and chop wounds. Impossible for the ME to tell which single wound was the cause of death."

Chips in the porcelain, runs of pink in the grout. "Walk me through what happened," I said.

"An ambush. The assailants gained entrance through the back door and waited for the Stacks to come home. Budd went upstairs and was shoved into the bathtub and repeatedly stabbed. A pistol was found, unfired, which likely belonged to him."

My image of Budd Stack came from news footage. Imposing, long-haired, rarely captured in his colours. There were bikers who lived to be outlaws and others who used the club to run elaborate criminal enterprises with all the efficiency of a Subway franchise. From what I knew, Stack had started as the first kind, a hellraiser, and entered middle age as the second. Getting the drop on him was impressive. To kill like this was a message—to the Stacks, to the Exiles or to the world itself.

I had far less of an idea about Jan Stack. Could she have been the real target? Often with a gangster and spouse killing, the spouse was considered a collateral victim. That could be a mistake. I'd known gangsters' wives who were far more brutal and vindictive than their husbands.

We climbed the gangplank. The area was busier now, more foot traffic, people off work and heading to dinner. I tried to put together my next step.

"Anything stolen?" I asked.

"We don't believe so."

"Fingerprints?"

"None matching the defendant."

"Footprints, then."

"Indistinct. A few partial patterns in the blood."

"So the weapons are the only connection with Maggie Zito."

"No," Temple said.

"But you don't have the boat."

"Not at present."

"And you haven't ID'd the accomplice yet. Is your witness helping you with that?"

"As it happens, he—ah." Detective Temple's smile was begrudging, laced with self-recrimination. "My slip. You're sharper than you look, Mr. Wakeland."

"He must be a hell of a witness if the Crown is heading full steam to a trial."

"Two murder weapons and a defendant with an escalating history of violent altercations. Most Crown prosecutors would give their eyeteeth for a case like this."

"You do have a witness, though."

After a moment, Temple nodded.

"Ms. Zito's counsel will receive full disclosure in time. And I'm only saying this much because Ray told me you turned in your own sister for murder. I respect that. Shows you're not without a sense of right and wrong."

"Does it?" I asked. I wasn't sure about that.

The detective started toward the parking lot. "Some of us still believe in keeping good people safe and holding bad people accountable. Not exactly en vogue these days."

We few, we happy few, I thought.

SIX

From the Granville Island dock I caught an Aquabus, sharing the vessel with a honeymooning couple from Mexico. They took photos of the float homes at Sea Village. So did I. The Stack house seemed no different from its neighbours—a glossy green pearl in a strand reflecting the falling sun.

I speed-walked through Yaletown, all luxury towers and gastropubs abuzz at the cocktail hour. A test kitchen advertised ancestral corn tortillas, jicama slaw and Margarita Mondays, two for one. At an urban parklet, a man sat on a tire swing, head bowed, smoking crack as discreetly as he could. Trash bags on the rubberized turf by his feet. I wondered if he preferred ancestral corn or the regular kind.

A friend once put it perfectly: Vancouver has lost the smell of sawdust. The days of an honest living were over. The new frontier involved corporate pillaging, jicama slaw, and the view of construction cranes from a 300-square-foot microapartment. Don't care for a million-dollar mortgage? You're free to leave. Again.

I suppose it wasn't much different in Montreal, but the lies were in French, and I lacked the sense of history to appreciate the loss. Here, the loss was all I felt. What was the opposite of déjà vu? That was Vancouver now. I had already never been there.

The Wakeland & Chen offices are on the seventh floor of the Royal Bank Building at 675 West Hastings. My key still opened the door to the lobby. The familiar antique brass and tile greeted me, though the far wall now sported a painting of a distorted chess match. Not a poor metaphor for the job.

You're still retired, I told myself in the elevator. Private Detective Emeritus. This was a friendly visit. Friends could greet each other, shoot the breeze, perhaps borrow a surveillance van, maybe a stun gun or two.

Jeff Chen hadn't changed the company name or the lock on the outer office. I let myself in. The lights were off in the reception nook. A banker's lamp burned atop the desk. Beneath it, Jeff's wife Marie punched figures into a desk calculator. She looked up at me with baleful recognition.

"What are you doing here, Dave?" she said. "Jeff isn't around."

Marie and I had never cottoned to each other. Maybe we were too alike in our differences. She pursued growing the brand the way I'd focused on casework. I disliked the way she courted corporate clients, and she detested my tendency to find cases that paid little and risked everything. It didn't help that Marie Chen was right more often than not.

"In town to do a favour," I said. "How are you?"

A squeal of castors and a wheeze from the seat cushion. Marie stood up and turned on the overhead lights. Redheaded and noticeably pregnant, she settled back into her seat.

"Busy," Marie said.

"The kids?"

"At my mother's for the week."

"And how's Jeff?"

"I don't know where he is," she said. "What do you want, Dave?"

"I was hoping to borrow one of the vans."

"Sold them off," she said. "They cost too much to maintain, and what does a security company need with two surveillance vans?"

"They came in handy for surveillance," I said. "Anything else with four wheels I could use?"

"Why? I thought you took your ball and went home."

"Left home would be more accurate," I said. "Shuzhen asked for help with a client. I stopped by to borrow some equipment and to see my friend."

"In that order." Marie shrugged. "We don't have much to spare."

Minutes passed. The small desk fan whirred, and her computer blinked into screen-saver mode. Cascading ribbons that changed colour and seemed to fold into each other.

"Jeff isn't here all that much," she finally said. "The market is oversaturated. The bigger companies are undercutting us to hell. Anyone can throw a nylon jacket on a teenager and call him a security guard. Jeff was running himself ragged, trying to keep us afloat. A contract came in for a realty company called Stoddard. He thought that was the solution. But they kept putting off payment, deferring it one quarter after the next. Then they stopped returning our calls. After that Jeff started going out. Leaving me to mind the store."

"What about the others?" I asked. "Ryan Martz? Tim Blatchford?"

"Ryan's wife got a sergeant's position with the Surrey PD. They moved maybe six months ago. Tim picks up the odd shift, but he knows we can't pay him. And you know where Kay is."

The client couch had once been plush, now replaced with hard plastic folding chairs. Looking at them, I had the urge to walk out. A nest of problems that no longer concerned me, that didn't speak to my strengths, and likely couldn't be solved.

"How bad are things?" I asked.

"Seven figures' worth of bad."

A million dollars in debt. I made an appropriate noise of shock. No doubt there were companies that happily carried that much and more. Some people view debt like a high score in an arcade game, something that can change with the next drop of a quarter. Jeff and Marie didn't think like that. At least they hadn't a year ago.

"Someone must be willing to lend him the cash," I said.

"Maybe, if he was here long enough to ask. You'd be surprised how quickly credit dries up once the word is out. The industry knows we're dead in the water."

Marie wasn't usually fatalistic. And Jeff wasn't usually absent from the office or his home. What bonded Jeff Chen and myself, other than our shared love of the Hanson Brothers, was an addiction to our work.

"I'm in town for a short while," I said. "If there's anything I can do to help."

Marie leaned back, letting the chair take more of her weight. Six months along at least. Her expression wasn't kind but it wasn't hostile, either.

"You mean well, Dave. I respect that, even if I don't always understand your priorities. And believe me, I'm not too proud to accept help. But unless you can cut me a cheque with a one and six zeroes, really, what can you do?"

SEVEN

Jeff didn't answer his phone or reply to my texts. It was nine o'clock but my body believed it was midnight. I was tired, hungry, still carrying around a packet of overpriced tea, and my phone's battery was just about exhausted. I headed for Shuzhen's apartment.

She buzzed me up and made sure I left my shoes by the door. The flat was small and felt even smaller with the clutter. Case files, legal texts, piles of mail. The furniture was student-quality IKEA. On the kitchenette counter, three external hard drives fed into her laptop amid a web of cables. Shuzhen was eating from a takeaway bento box, an iPad balanced on her knee. She pointed at the kitchenette.

"Got you some tempura and a spider roll. Your bag's on Anthea's bed."

I filled a saucepan from the tap and set it on the stove, then showered. To spare us any awkwardness I dressed in the steam-filled washroom. When I came out I made tea and had dinner.

Shuzhen alternated between iPad and television, at ease in drawstring sweats and an off-the-shoulder shirt. A surly orange tabby poked out from beneath the television stand, glowered at me and went back into seclusion.

"That's Anthea's cat," Shuzhen said. "George Eliot takes a while to get used to people."

"Makes two of us." I perched on a corner of the couch and ate some of the sushi. "I stopped by the office and saw Marie. They're in financial trouble, and she doesn't know where Jeff is. Any ideas?"

Shuzhen turned off the TV. She thought about it. "No clue. I could call him?"

"Worth a try."

She got through immediately. So Jeff was only selectively incommunicado. I tried not to take that personally. Their conversation was in Mandarin and lasted all of twenty seconds. He hung up first. Shuzhen seemed upset by the call.

"He wouldn't say where he was. Said not to bother him. I could hear people in the background."

"Any other sounds? Think it over."

She closed her eyes, replaying the conversation. "Bells," she said.

"Church? Sleigh? Tubular?"

"Like metal."

"Bells *are* metal."

"No, like electronic."

"A casino," I suggested.

She nodded. "Think so. But why's he hanging out there?"

"A bodyguard job for a high roller, maybe." There were other possibilities, none very pleasant.

Shuzhen yawned, triggering my own. The flight and the day's tribulations were catching up. "I'm going to do some laps before bed," she said. "Want to come swim?"

"I didn't pack my trunks."

"You can keep me company."

In the building's basement I lay on a chaise and watched her cut back and forth across the lap pool. After a while Shuzhen rested her elbows on the tiled coping of the pool and adjusted her goggles.

"We need to talk about your case," I said. "The trial isn't for, what, another six months?"

THE LAST EXILE · 39

"Early next year. February."

"A long time to be in custody."

"That's why you're here," Shuzhen said. "So we can get Maggie out. One sec."

She pushed off from the wall, darted through the water to the shallow end, then back to me. Smoothing her damp hair away from her face.

"What makes you a hundred percent sure your client didn't commit those murders?" I asked.

"I've seen Maggie with her children, Dave. She's not like that."

"Maybe that's true, and maybe you can prove it next February. But we can't disprove her involvement without demonstrating that somebody else killed the Stacks."

"What's your point?" Shuzhen pushed up onto the ledge. Her suit was a dark blue one-piece. No straps. I examined the pattern of the tile until she'd wrapped herself in towels.

"Maybe we're looking at this from the wrong end," I said. "Instead of removing your client from harm's way, maybe we should see what we can do about the harm."

"Don't follow, Dave."

"We—I—could go see him. Ask if he'd lay off till after the trial. At least buy her that long."

"Ask who?"

"The Exiles. Terry Rhodes." Putting the notion into words made it sound all the more foolish.

Shuzhen reacted to the name with the trepidation it was due. Lawyers in Prohibition-era Chicago probably thought of Al Capone the same way. Fear and disgust at the folk-hero image constructed around a wealthy man who killed at discount and in volume.

"Didn't you get hurt last time?" she asked.

I couldn't deny it. Once I'd asked Rhodes about a missing woman he'd been photographed with. His response had been swift and emphatic: between him and his enforcers I'd been threatened, thrashed, pissed on and promised far worse if I asked again. That had been the least frightening of our encounters.

Terry Rhodes was the exception to the outlaw/businessman divide. He had money and was circumspect in his business affairs. Rhodes owned several legitimate companies, and his real estate holdings were probably worth a high eight figures. He was volatile and brutal, enjoyed hurting people, adored being feared. Rhodes derived endless amusement from imposing his will.

You could beg someone like that for a favour, and they might grant it on a whim. They might just as likely cut you horizontally across the belly, to give their dogs easier access to your vitals.

The shortest distance between Maggie Zito and safety was through Rhodes. Maybe I'd find him in a giving mood.

"It never hurts to ask," I said, wishing I could watch the person who coined that lie pose a question or two to the Exiles.

Shuzhen wrapped wet arms around my neck. "Just be careful, Dave."

The elevator smelled of chlorine, and she tracked water down the carpeted hallway. I heard her shower through the wall as I climbed beneath her roommate's comforter. George Eliot settled down into her basket on the floor. I fell asleep thinking of the view from the Stacks' float home, those large gleaming windows reflecting the sun, night falling as a boat stole through the water toward them.

EIGHT

I was up early. Judging from the bare cupboards in Shuzhen's apartment, breakfast was a forage-for-yourself affair. I made a saucepan's worth of black tea and paired that with a piece of leftover deep-fried yam. George Eliot nudged my shin and mewled. I dumped a cup of dry food into her dish. The little gourmet sniffed it, curled her nose and sauntered off.

Terry Rhodes was my first priority. How to get a direct line to him. What to say if I did. How to survive the process. Maggie Zito's sister was also someone I needed to speak with. She'd be number two. Number three on the list was the witness. Finding their identity would be difficult and legally dicey.

Having Jeff's help would have been useful. My partner could usually spot flaws in my approach that would save me time and stitches. Finding out what happened to him would be number four.

Shuzhen awoke around eight, heading straight for the coffee maker. A Bialetti, probably the most expensive thing in the apartment. While it percolated, she sat at her small kitchen table and riffled through the heap of documents for something. I noticed a tray of parched bunny ears and golden barrels on the windowsill. It takes studied neglect to kill a cactus.

Finally she found the paper she wanted and handed it over. A boilerplate Wakeland & Chen contract. Already filled in, dated for yesterday, and awaiting my signature.

"Sleep okay?" she asked.

I nodded. "You're making decent money now, right? You could afford a bigger place."

"You sound like my mom."

"No roommate, a bit more space. Maybe even a maid."

"I'd never find a spot this close to court." She added some wet salmon from the fridge to George Eliot's bowl. The cat deemed it worthy and began chowing down. "What's your place in Montreal like?" she asked.

"Near the market. Older, but nice."

"Do you think of it like home? Or do you miss it here?"

I poured the last of my tea and thought about how to answer that. My old East Van apartment had been my home for more than a decade. Shuzhen's place reminded me of it. A crowded waystation. Barely home-sweet-home.

Folding my arms in front of me, I said, "There's a Portuguese chicken place near Mount Royal, within walking distance of my flat. You line up like you've been conscripted. At the counter you call your order. A man with what looks like a battle-axe chops up a chicken thigh and slides it into a Portuguese bun. It's a perfect experience. The best sandwich I've ever had. If you can make a life with one or two perfect experiences in it, what do you need with a home?"

Shuzhen poured her coffee and sipped it and smiled.

"Yeah, you miss it here," she said.

I still had the card of Nina Rydell, vice president of Pronto Rides. I called her, said I was the handsome bookish gent from seat 3G, and did she happen to have a nondescript car I could rent for the next little while? Nothing with decals or a GPS. I'd need the use of it exclusively.

"In other words," Nina in 3F said, "you want a carshare where you don't have to share."

"I'm easing myself into the idea."

"You could just rent one."

"No GPS," I reiterated. "I can't have someone tracing where I've been."

"A real man of mystery."

"With a credit card. What have you got?"

She hit computer keys, dragged the mouse. "There are a few vehicles we've taken out of the pool for maintenance reasons. Older models. You okay with a vehicle that's five or six years old?"

"As long as it runs and I can pick it up now."

"Come down to the office and I'll get the paperwork ready. I can let you have the Beast."

I was expecting something in the nature of a Honda Accord. Instead the loaner was a Kia minivan done in matte purple. 300,000 klicks on the odometer, put there by indiscriminate drivers. The fuel door was bent and wouldn't close, the sliding door failed to slide, and there was something off about the wheel alignment. In the overcast morning light, she looked like a prune-coloured garbage scow slapped onto a trailer bed. The Beast handled about as well.

But she ran. In fifteen minutes, we had fought rush-hour traffic, making it to Maggie Zito's house in Hastings-Sunrise. Close to the racetrack and fairgrounds on the northeastern edge of the city, Hastings-Sunrise was a neighbourhood of mixed ethnicities, historically working-class. The streets were shady and the houses in good repair. Maggie's was no exception. The exterior was painted burgundy, even the front stairs. Moss clung stubbornly to the steep roof, and the eaves collected sheddings from a Japanese maple on the corner. Maggie's sister Briony had moved in for the time being to care for the kids.

As I knocked, a woman turned the corner at Kaslo, approaching the house. She saw me and slowed. I shuffled down a few steps.

"Ms. Zito?"

She held up her phone. "I'll call the residents association if you don't get off my property."

I wasn't sure who she thought I represented, but I complied.

"My name is Wakeland," I said. "I'm a private investigator hired by your sister's counsel. Could we talk?"

"Identification first."

I showed her my security professional's card. Briony Zito squinted at it. She was slimmer and taller than her sister, with an aquiline nose and fair hair. Dressed in a woven sweater in harvest orange, large brown buttons down the front. A black knee-length skirt and suede boots completed the ensemble. Her handbag was knit and bulky enough to conceal any manner of weaponry.

"Your licence is expired," Briony said.

"I've been out of town. Call Shuzhen Chen and ask her about me, if you want."

"Think I got her number inside. I was just walking the kids to school. Wait on the sidewalk, will you?"

I watched her unlock the door and step inside, heard the latch slide home behind her.

Waiting gave me time to consider my list. I'd skipped over Rhodes and gone straight to number two. Partly that was because I knew where to find Briony Zito, while I'd have to get a line on the Exiles president. It made sense to do the simplest thing first, get it out of the way. Also it was early yet, and Rhodes was a creature of the night.

Good reasons. Solid reasons. No need to even mention fear.

But I did fear Terry Rhodes. I wanted to be surefooted and prepared when I ran into him. Rhodes was mayhem in boots and padded leather. And I'd been away too long to jump straight into a confrontation.

I'd been waiting three minutes when I heard the engines. Big V-twins with the mufflers removed. The windowpanes shook. Three motorcycles turned onto Triumph Street, a trio of shovelheads riding single file. They slowed as they reached Maggie Zito's house. No vests or Exiles insignia. I recognized the one riding point from court, the older one with the beard. His stocky accomplice rode behind him. The third had a visored helmet. Average height, no distinguishing marks. The bikes passed the house, turned around at the intersection, and repeated their crawl.

Briony Zito stepped out onto the porch, clutching her bag with both hands.

The bikes swept by the house once more, engines snarling. The riders didn't acknowledge the woman on the porch. Maggie's sister didn't budge or look away. The leader shouted something I couldn't hear over the engines. I doubted it was polite.

As clandestinely as I could, I snapped photos of the licence plates. The riders peeled off at the roundabout, two heading right, the other straight through. Briony Zito may as well have been granite. She didn't move until they were all out of sight. The rumble faded to a distant purr.

Even in the silence, the noise seemed to linger for a long while.

NINE

We sat on the back porch, drinking tea in the shade. Briony Zito had put out a plate of Oreos and biscotti. Up close I saw that the plane of one cheek curved outward more prominently than the other. A very old injury. Nothing ever knits quite perfectly.

"That business with the bikers," I said. "They've done that before?"

"Pretty regular, every couple days."

"You call the police?"

"To do what? Complain about the noise?"

"It's a threat," I said. "At the very least harassment."

"Sure. Ever try proving harassment to a cop? And what's the best they could do? Park a patrol car 'cross the street. Now I got two groups to watch out for."

"If you're worried about security."

Briony shook her head. "They haven't tried anything. Just putting a scare into the neighbourhood."

That could change, but I didn't say so. Maggie Zito's backyard was a tangle of vines and tomato stakes, plump yellow and green zucchini. On the bottom stairs, a pile of red garlic dried in the sun.

"I should be starting work about now." Briony made no move to end our conversation. She pried open an Oreo and ate the half with more centre.

"Kind of work do you do?" I asked.

"Digital archivist. I have special dispensation to work from home. Well, from Maggie's home."

"Have you told your sister about the bikers?"

"Think she's got enough on her plate, don't you?"

The fence at the back had warped around the root system of a large maple. A squirrel darted along the roof of the standalone garage. The murder weapons had been found there. The padlock latch was secured with what looked like an old shoelace.

Even in disarray there was something neat and familiar about the property. Something essentially Vancouver. Before the yoga-wear moguls and e-commerce czars, this had been an immigrant city. Plum trees, homemade wine, gardens and low fences. The Zitos were of that place. Crude, fatalistic, not the least bit noble. I liked them and the way they lived.

"Cops yanked everything out onto the lawn," Briony said. "Once they'd done their tests they just heaped it all inside. Hard to find anything. Maggie always kept her shit tidy."

"Do you think it's possible she committed these crimes?"

Briony scowled. "Whose side are you working for?"

"Hers, but I get the sense she's no stranger to violence. Is she?"

Maggie's sister sipped her tea and deconstructed another Oreo. She spoke while chewing. "One time, Maggie and me were tossing rocks at cars. Dumbass kid stuff, y'know? Our dad comes home, sees what we're up to. He belts me across the face. My dad had a right hand like the shovel on an excavator. How come my cheek's like this. Second he did that, Maggie let loose. Rock in her fist, fired point-blank at his skull. Gave him a concussion."

"Protecting you," I said.

"More like retaliation. Someone hits her loved ones, she strikes back without thinking. Like with the cop. You hear about that?"

I nodded.

"I was there," Briony said. "He didn't even cuff her son, either. Just grabbed Dominick's collar like for emphasis. Maggie plows into him, takes him off his feet and dumps the sonofabitch through the window of that meat shop at 20th and Main. Cop's laying there amid rump roasts. More shocked and embarrassed than hurt. Was pretty funny, to be honest."

"Did she ever talk about getting revenge for your brother?" I asked.

"She spoke of it, sure."

"Can you tell me what happened to him?"

Briony stood and moved to the edge of the porch. She brushed the garlic aside and sat on the top step and yanked a weed out of the broken concrete.

"Beau was the middle kid," Briony said. "He was the first to leave home. Always liked doing his own thing. Used to work as a fruit picker, travelling around the Interior. Coming home at the end of the season, his little VW Rabbit loaded up with flats of peaches, bags of corn between the seats. Just a lovely guy."

"Were there witnesses to what happened to him?" I asked.

"Sure, dozens. Many as they needed. You know Hope?"

I nodded. A small town in the foothills near the mountain highway leading to the Interior. Gas stations, a pleasant main thoroughfare, a few homes.

"There was a rally that summer in the Okanagan. Bikers from all across the country, some coming up from the States. Beau was doing some picking over in Chilliwack. Just happened to be in the bar when a group of 'em stopped in."

The telling was difficult for her. Briony paused, stared at the torn-out weed in her hand. She chewed the stalk absently.

"He was drunk, they said—a bald-faced lie 'cause Beau didn't drink, hated what the stuff did to our dad. And anyway Beau was a pot sorta guy. Only reason he was in the bar, most likely, was to eat, 'cause where else can you get a meal if you're dressed in dirty overalls? They said he attacked them. They removed him from the bar with a warning."

"'They' being the Exiles."

Briony nodded. "Next thing they know he's being dragged by a truck, and they get on their bikes to save the day. Calvary charging to the rescue, according to their telling."

"The truck was never found?"

"Outside of the Lower Mainland, everyone and their dog's got at least one rusty-ass pickup."

"Did Maggie hold Budd Stack responsible? Him specifically?"

"Never heard the name till Maggie got arrested. They're all the same, though. If it wasn't him, it was a friend of his." Briony stood. "I imagine you want to look at the shed."

We took the walkway through rows of runner beans and pumpkins grown to late August proportions. The garage had a window, too grimy to see inside. Between that and the double sliding doors that faced the lane, it wouldn't be hard to get into the shed without tampering with the lock. Briony unwound the shoelace from the latch.

The floor of the garage bore muddy prints from multiple sets of police-issue footwear. Tools on the ground, a jumble of pitchforks, rakes, full-size axes. A blue snow shovel with a crack in the handle. A sledgehammer, various wedges and old pieces of rebar. Where the wall met the floor, curls of old leaves had gathered. I saw what looked like small brown dabs of blood.

"Maggie loved her garden," Briony said. "Her happy place, she called it. I try to keep it up, but between the kids and work, it's a struggle."

"Your sister ever lend tools to people?" I asked.

"All the damn time."

"So the neighbours knew she had an axe, a machete. Common knowledge."

"Sure, I suppose."

"Did they know she had a temper?"

"Most found out sooner or later," Briony said. "Ask any of them, though, did Maggie do this, bet they'd say the same thing. No way in hell."

Briony walked me out. The street was quiet other than the machine gun squawk of Steller's jays from the roof of a neighbouring house. I gave her my card. She tucked it into her skirt without examining it.

"You think I'm defending Maggie on account of she's my sister," Briony said.

I began to say, "In your place I'm sure I'd do the same," but stopped myself, thinking of Kay. In Briony Zito's place I didn't know what decision I'd make.

"The cops and prosecution think they have a solid case," I said. "To be honest, so do I. Not airtight, by any means, but solid. I don't need certainty to do my job, but so far nothing's convinced me she's not capable of murder."

"You don't have kids, do you?" Briony said. "Maggie gets fighting mad, and she might kill someone if she had a mind to. But she'd *never* leave her kids alone at night. Not for anything. That's how come I'm certain."

Her index finger stabbed my chest, driving home her point.

"My big sis may be a bastard, but she's a mother first."

TEN

Two o'clock found me sitting in a wine bar on Seymour called Uva. Natalie Holinshed had agreed to meet me. The crime beat reporter was running late. In the meantime I sopped up Buffalo Trace and water, trying to wrap my head around the loss.

For hours I'd steered the Beast through East Van and Burnaby, looking for the Exiles. Places I knew they owned or hung out. All gone. The Mounties had seized their clubhouse. The building was now up for auction, pending appeal. The Mountain Shadow Pub had become a row of ugly duplexes. One of their strip clubs was now a Test Prep Center that offered classes in English and Korean.

Living in Vancouver, you ingest small doses of loss every day. A fifty-year-old Chinese market, a café with a good six-dollar breakfast. What replaces them usually doesn't last. Eventually the smell of sawdust fades and you forget what you were mourning.

Now I was absorbing a year and a half of gentrification in one go. Sitting in a back booth with an eye on the door. The bar's sound system played piano jazz, "Stardust," "Paranoid Android," "All the Things You Are." Time was collapsing in on itself.

I saw Natalie Holinshed cross the street, sparing a grimace for the Beast. The dented purple barge looked out of place between the BMWs and luxury electric SUVs. I watched her spot me, check her watch, and jog the last few feet to make amends. She ordered a dirty martini and a club sandwich on multigrain, no mayo.

"A newshound meeting a source for a drink in the middle of the day," Holinshed said. "Very *His Girl Friday*. Did Maggie Zito convince you of her innocence yet?"

"I don't know," I said honestly. "Maybe it doesn't matter."

"Sure it doesn't." Her drink arrived. She extracted the olives and took a sip. "Tell me about Montreal."

"More mobsters than bikers, though not by many. You can tell where they live by which neighbourhoods get plowed first when it snows. Better nightlife than here. Worse weather. They've got the landlords under control, but that's changing."

"One East Coast winter was enough for me," Holinshed said. For a warm afternoon she was dressed in layers, Burberry jacket over cardigan over blouse. The cuff of the blouse bore a blue ink stain. She noticed and tugged down the arm of the jacket to conceal it. "What are we meeting for, Wakeland?"

"I need info on the Exiles," I said.

"Oh, good. Every time I run a story on them, I get a dozen new death threats. Misspelled horribly, of course. Apparently I'm a 'dumb count' who needs to 'mine her own busyness.'"

We had our section of the bar to ourselves. Across the room, a pair of well-dressed women, one of whom I recognized as a judge, guffawed in that three-martini way.

"It's important I sit down with Terry Rhodes," I said.

"To you, maybe. Not important to him." Holinshed dug into her sandwich, chewing with vigour. "An audience with the pope would be easier to get. A lot less chance of getting killed."

"That depends on the pope."

She opened her club, pulled back the lettuce. "Told them no mayo." Scraping the toast with her knife, she said, "I can't help you with Rhodes. Too fond of drawing breath. Anything else?"

"Tell me about the two men in court yesterday."

Holinshed slapped her sandwich together. "Really out to get your head kicked in, huh? I only know the big one, Charles Corso. Charlie the Priest is his *nom de guerre*. He's the sergeant-at-arms of the East Van chapter."

"Close to Rhodes, then?"

"As close as anyone gets. Bikers at that level, the ones still alive and out of jail, are sophisticated as hell. And more legitimate all the time. The risks are taken by the young guys, the prospects and support clubs. The Priest or Rigger Devlin, the top guys, they don't stick their neck out too much."

"Who's the other name?" I asked.

"Roger Devlin, known as Rigger. He runs Devlin Auto Body on Main and Terminal. Actually Rigger's wife Darlene runs it. Her name's on the property, she handles the day-to-day."

"Could I get a message to Rhodes through Devlin?"

"I suppose, if you want a .44-calibre rejoinder. Why do you want to see Rhodes so badly, Dave?"

Oscar Peterson came on the stereo. "Night Train." I drank some bourbon.

"I want to ask him to leave Maggie Zito alone."

"And why would he do that for you, seeing as how she killed his friend?"

"Fit of pique, maybe," I said. "What can you tell me about Budd Stack?"

"Probably nothing you don't know. A very bad man who retired and lived a nice comfortable life, at least till someone situated an axe in the middle of his chest."

"And his wife?"

"Jan wasn't your typical biker's old lady," Holinshed said. "More like the wife of a hockey star. Raised upper middle class, or what passes for upper middle class in Campbell River. Donated a lot of money, ran several of the fronts where Budd and the others washed their cash. I used to browse her dress shop before she sold it. Good selection."

"So who killed them?" I asked.

"Maggie Zito and an accomplice."

"No one else wanted them dead? A rival gang?"

Holinshed quaffed her martini and signalled the bartender for a refill. "A gang hit would be two in the chest while Budd was standing in his driveway. Maybe they'd hit the wife, too, if she was a witness. But there's no profit to killing Budd and Jan. For one thing you'd have Terry Rhodes to answer to. For another, they were retired."

The music changed. I didn't recognize the tune. Something with a lot of diminished chords.

"I don't think you ever retire from that life," I said. "Even if you mean to. There's always somebody you owe."

The journalist tore into the second triangle of her sandwich. "Still talking about them?" she asked. "Or yourself?"

ELEVEN

Devlin Auto Body was a wood-framed garage and muffler shop on the last remaining rough patch of Main. From the broken asphalt of the parking lot, you could fire a cannon and hit Science World, assuming your shot could maneuver through the forest of new apartment towers.

Neither of the Devlins were working this afternoon. I loomed over the service counter and fixed the young clerk with a dull hostile squint. Just another bruiser with a message for her boss.

"I got a delivery for Rigger," I said. "What's his address again?"

The Devlin house was on King Ed, a well-maintained Craftsman that had been extended along the corner of the property, giving the structure a Quasimodo look. A pair of Street Glides were parked out front. I looked at the photo I'd taken that morning of the bikes passing Maggie Zito's house. The plates matched.

The Devlins' fence was seven feet of dark-stained wood cut with a wave pattern along the top of the staves. A pair of signs hung on the gate: FUCK THE DOG, BEWARE OF OWNER and WE DON'T CALL 911.

Around back the fence was simple chain-link, reinforced with a freshly planted privacy hedge. The arborvitae shrubs weren't yet tall enough to block the view of the second-storey deck. A hot tub on it, two figures inside.

I unlatched the gate and took the steps briskly, hands up to show I came in peace. "Mr. and Mrs. Devlin?"

"Who in the blue fuck are you?"

The woman was blond, skin flushed from the heat, nipples the colour of spun copper. Holding an empty bottle of Mike's Hard Lemonade, she seemed neither self-conscious nor curious. The man had shaved his head but not recently; a horseshoe of stubble connected to a chinstrap beard. The third rider, I guessed, judging from his build. He tugged his wife's arm so her breasts submerged in the water.

"The hell outta here right goddamn now," he said. "I'll call the police."

"Your sign says you won't. I have a quick piece of business to discuss."

Rigger Devlin glanced at the open sliding door, at his pants and boxer briefs draped over a deck chair. The Devlins were about fifty, I guessed. His left arm sported the Exiles wing tattoo, while her shoulder had been decorated with a swan in mid-flight. They looked like a husband-and-wife team of restauranteurs, the kind that cheat their wait staff out of tips.

"I am not doing any more business today," Darlene Devlin said. "Worked eight damn days in a row plus this morning. Pass me another Mike's, will you stranger?"

The case of empties sat on the deck near the legs of the chair. "You're out," I said.

"Send Felix for another case," she told her husband.

"Fine. Later."

"If he gets 'em later I can't drink 'em now, can I?"

"What do you want?" Rigger Devlin asked me.

"To talk to your boss," I said.

"I'm my own boss."

The woman snorted.

THE LAST EXILE · 57

"Your higher authority, then," I said, climbing the last few steps. "Terry Rhodes."

Rigger re-evaluated me. Not just an annoyance but a crazy person, probably suicidal. "Never heard of anyone by that name."

"I'm the soul of discretion," I said. "Rhodes and I have spoken before."

"And you're still here." He nodded to himself, impressed.

"I have a favour to ask him."

Devlin nodded again. "I'll pass it along."

"I'd rather ask in person."

He seemed to give my request consideration. More than I would in his place. I turned a second too late and saw why. The blinds on the sliding door were slapped out of the way by the prospect I'd seen in court with Charlie the Priest. At my moment of recognition his fist came in low, aiming at my solar plexus. I stepped back too late. The impact knocked the breath out of me and triggered a coughing fit.

"You gonna go nicely?" Rigger Devlin asked me.

It took a moment before I could respond. "Not till you agree to tell Rhodes I need to see him."

"You're on my property. Felix here will stomp a hole through your face, I tell him to. You want that?"

The prospect was younger than me by a decade at least, short and compact, his features delicate and at odds with his vest and jeans. In a fair fight it would be close. I had no interest in close.

The bottles were at my feet. I could grab one if the prospect moved on me. He was waiting for the order but circling, trying to better his position. That told me he had a measure of self-discipline. More dangerous than I'd reckoned.

"Christ, you men are *sooooo* fucking boring." Darlene Devlin stood and chopped the water, splashing the three of us. "My one day off. Go away, stranger. Felix, please grab us another case of Mike's. Orange flavour if they have it."

Her husband was already salmon-coloured from the heat but looked like he was blushing. "I married a real sport," he said.

"I sure as shit didn't." Darlene laughed at her own joke. "Send these kids away, Rog, or you can forget about that blowjob."

Felix followed me down the stairs, closing the back gate behind us. He kept pace with me down the alley.

"Good shot," I said.

"Kept your feet."

"We're a real pair of dangerous guys." I inclined my head toward the house. "Been with them long?"

"Long enough."

"Is it everything you hoped?"

The prospect halted. "What do you care?"

"I don't," I said. "My name is Dave Wakeland. In addition to not caring, I'm also a PI. Or was before I retired."

He nodded, unable to figure me. "Felix Ramos."

"They give you a handle yet?"

"The Chop." He said this with some pride. "My family ran the Portuguese Chop House on the Drive."

"Yeah?"

"I used to work there after school. Till I ended up in Willingdon."

"That's where they struck you?"

He shook his head. "I put a guy in a wheelchair. When I got out, I paid the guy another visit. They put me in big boy prison for that. Not much of a choice in there."

"You have one now," I said. "I'll be at Tinseltown tonight, if Rhodes wants to find me."

Felix Ramos didn't reply. He regarded me for another moment, then turned toward Main Street. Maybe he was thinking the same thing I was. Yes, it would be too damn close.

THE LAST EXILE · 59

TWELVE

Four o'clock, and the mass exodus from downtown had begun. A two-hour commute each way wasn't uncommon: houses were almost affordable deep in the Fraser Valley, or halfway up the North Shore mountains. I'd always valued time over space, experience more than ownership. A house in the sticks meant little to me. But to people with different priorities it meant normalcy and a place to fight for. It meant home.

They were welcome to it.

Marie Chen was on the phone when I entered the Wakeland & Chen office. She cupped her hand over the headset mic and whispered "Jeff's still not in, Dave."

I had no real business here, but my partner's absence nagged at me. Eighteen months ago I'd left, believing that was best for everyone. Jeff had bet me I couldn't, but he'd never asked me to stay. Had he thought that I was leaving him holding the bag, sole proprietor of a fragile and damaged company? Were things wrong even then?

Marie said a professional goodbye and moved the mic away from her face. The desk was strewn with takeout cups and Tupperware. She closed her eyes for a moment, then remembered I was there.

"I told you Jeff's not around," Marie said. "He didn't come home. Just said he was working late."

"Any chance that's true?"

Marie sighed, a plaintive noise filling the silent office. "I haven't the foggiest anymore."

Their marriage had been both loving and empowering. I'd envied them. There had been cracks, disagreements, and I knew a couple of things about my partner Marie likely didn't. But they functioned as a unit, the Chens, Marie and Jeff, good parents and solid members of the community. Better together than apart.

"Shuzhen spoke to Jeff last night," I said. "He was in a casino. Any idea which one he frequents?"

"No. But I can check his bank accounts." Marie cleared a path through the clutter to her keyboard and typed. "He bought a meal at the River Rock steakhouse yesterday."

"I'll go see him," I said.

"Dave." Marie usually spoke my name with a certain abrasiveness. Her voice sounded too tired for that. "You don't owe him. Or me."

"Of course I do," I said.

Land is at the heart of every mystery. A finite commodity with infinite uses and therefore infinite value. Hunting grounds or farms, canneries or condos, neighbourhoods or viaducts, take your pick. In Vancouver every evil leads back to real estate. The Musqueam, Tsleil-Waututh and Squamish people could attest to that.

I had no proof that anything evil had transpired with the building of Bridgeport Station. Not even a whiff of impropriety. It may have been coincidence that a major commuter hub connecting Vancouver to Richmond and Surrey, to the airport and ferry terminals, happened to share space with a casino and resort hotel. That may indeed have been Just One of Those Random Things.

But it was damn curious.

I walked past the water feature in the River Rock's foyer. Under the watchful eye of the pit bosses and security, I walked the gaming floor, passing grottoes of slots and table games. No trace of Jeff Chen.

The casino knew their clientele. The machines featured dragons and pandas, or bearded gold miners with Disney eyes. Pai Gow Poker, Blackjack and Big Two. There were private rooms as well, for the whales. I could only hope Jeff wasn't in one of those.

Years ago we'd interviewed a blackjack dealer with a connection to a local mobster. The dealer was from Hong Kong, and Jeff had steered the interview between English and Cantonese. The surroundings hadn't impacted his work, I thought. But for a moment, my partner had seemed to feel a tug from the casino. I'd sensed a conscious effort to focus. Shutting out the neon call.

Bells went off close to me. A winner. That same sound Shuzhen described, slightly metallic, bells that jangled like coins. The woman who struck it rich was already stabbing the button to roll again. Nearby, a lounge act in a blue sequined gown vamped over the Doobie Brothers. How we doin' tonight, everybody? We feelin' the love?

If Jeff had been playing for a while, the casino had likely comped his room. I asked at the front desk if my partner had checked in yet, making up an excuse about a convention lanyard left in my booth. The receptionist looked him up, told me room 403 had a DO NOT DISTURB, but could she take a message?

I grinned wide and said I was sure to catch him later on.

Another quick tour of the slots, then back to the hotel and into the elevator. Just another guest going up to his room. Crammed in the elevator car with me was a family, parents and kids and a sour-looking grandpa clutching a barcoded winnings slip. I was first out.

Seventeen knocks on the door of 403, loud, followed by seventeen more. When I heard stumbling and bedsprings I pulled the DO NOT DISTURB card off the doorknob and held it to block the peephole. The lock disengaged.

The woman who opened the door had a pale pink streak through her hair. High-calved pants in black PVC, silvery halter that showed the dark outline of lingerie. A calfskin handbag hung off her wrist. She was barefoot, carrying her heels.

She smiled and tried to slip past, and when I didn't move, worked to squeeze by. From the door I could only see a corner of the bed, a naked foot. I heard snoring.

"Where is it?" I asked, keeping my voice friendly and low.

"I actually have another—could you move, please? I have to go."

I put thumb and forefinger on the purse. "The money stays here," I said.

"No law against accepting gifts."

My hand unsnapped the clasp. She turned to free the purse, felt the straps strain. I tilted it and the contents fell on the carpet. Cellphone, key ring, condoms, jelly, dental dams, mace and a wad of fifty-dollar bills. My foot swept it all farther into the suite. She backed up and I closed the door behind us. Or tried to. Before it shut she tossed a gold shoe against the jamb to keep it open.

"I'll scream."

"I'm not after what you earned by Christian toil," I said. "Just what you stole while he was out."

"I didn't steal shit."

When she crouched to refill her purse, I did the same, maintaining eye contact. The woman didn't know if I was hotel security, law enforcement or some shadowy associate of the trick. After a minute, she shrugged and unlocked her phone.

"Just a couple photos." She showed me. Scans of the front and back of Jun Fei Chen's driver's licence, his personal and company credit cards. "Look, I'll delete them, okay?"

She did, into the phone's trash bin and emptied. I helped her collect the rest of her belongings. Jeff turned on the bed but didn't wake. His clothing was heaped on the entertainment centre.

THE LAST EXILE · 63

"You dose him?" I asked.

"Nuh-uh. Just up all night and most of the afternoon." She lingered. "Do you work for him or the hotel?"

"Him."

A nod. I didn't present an ongoing problem. "I won't recover the photos. I mean, they're deleted, but you know phones, nothing's ever really gone. Anyway, I won't recover them."

"I trust you," I said. And did.

"Weird fucking night."

She left. I closed the door and saw to my partner.

Raising the blinds and throwing open the window caused the lump on the bed to stir. Jeff had looked better. A sauna, close shave, and a meal cooked at home would probably restore him. I called down to the front desk for the next best thing, aspirin and orange juice.

Jeff wiped his eyes, blinking at the rhombus of sunlight thrown across the bed. "Time is it?"

"Six o'clock. That's p.m."

He threw down three aspirin and quaffed the juice. "No coffee?"

"Figured you need motivation to get out of here."

Jeff rolled over so his feet were on the floor, staggered and walked naked to the washroom. He didn't shut the door. "Marie send you?" he said over the sound of pissing. "Or my cousin?"

"Here of my own volition," I said.

The flushing toilet and the patter of a shower sounded simultaneously. "When I bought you out, you signed a non-compete clause. Remember, Dave? Are you even still licensed?"

Our conversation continued once he'd dried and dressed and began the hunt for watch and socks.

"Card counting?" I asked.

"I can hold the numbers in my head, but they play with multiple decks. Shift things around to make it difficult."

"Think they call that 'gambling,'" I said.

"You wouldn't understand."

"Probably not. I don't have a wife and kids, a business and a mortgage. You do, though. Right now Marie's at the office trying to keep things afloat."

"Don't mention Marie again."

"She mentioned a couple things to me," I said. "A seven-figure debt to a company called Stoddard."

"Company finances are strictly confidential. Corporate officers only."

"Behind the trash," I said.

"What? Oh." Jeff stooped and retrieved an argyle sock from behind the wastebin.

"Can't you take them to court?" I asked.

"'Course I could. And Bill Stoddard can counter-sue. And we can spend a year seeing who's got more cash to hand over to their lawyers."

"What about an appeal to his sense of fair play?"

"Forgot how funny you are, Dave. When you're not being a prick. You see a set of car keys around here, little green fob?"

"By the clicker." The fob was a medallion that said BEST DAD EVER. "What if I talk to this Stoddard and maybe ask him to settle?"

"As a personal favour? White guy to white guy?"

"Yeah, I'll flash him the secret Caucasian handshake."

Jeff stepped into his shoes. Dressed, he looked more comfortable with himself. My partner had always been something of a clotheshorse. We cut an odd pair that way. The thousand-dollar suits and straight razor shaves weren't just luxury to him. They were camouflage. Jeff moved in a world that was white collar and often just plain white. His appearance was crafted to show he belonged in the boardroom as much as anyone.

Now, under the energy efficient lighting of the hotel suite, in three-day stubble and clothes he'd retrieved from the floor, Jeff

Chen looked tired and bled out. He avoided looking at the mirror. Or at me.

"Last I remember, Dave, you drove off. So what are you doing here? Feeling guilty?"

"More like pity," I said.

He slapped me. The open hand caught me flush on the cheekbone hard enough to rattle my bridgework.

"Don't need your pity and don't want help. Get gone, Dave. Tell Marie you couldn't find me. Or tell her nothing, I don't care. Go do whatever you're in town for. Get fucking gone."

I got gone.

THIRTEEN

On East Broadway I stopped at a military surplus. Ignoring the airsoft and paintball displays, I browsed the protective gloves, police batons, knives and other difference-makers. The proprietor was a bald white man in a Ministry T-shirt. In my experience with military surplus stores, there's always a bald white man in a Ministry T-shirt. He paused the conspiracy podcast he was listening to as I approached the counter.

"I'm looking for something in the way of brass knuckles," I said.

"Those are illegal, sir."

"In the way of."

Squinting to show he was giving the matter some thought, he gestured to the wares behind the counter. "Well, your best bet for defence is a pair of weighted gloves, with powdered lead sewn into the fist. Now that fall's almost here, wearing gloves won't look too suspicious."

"Something smaller," I said. "More authoritative."

"Sure, sure. We don't carry the brass variety, but carbon fibre knucks, we have a few of those. Your classic rounded edge or the spiked variety. Spikes add visual flair, plus they can punch holes in a dude's face, make him real ugly in a hurry. On the other hand, a rounded knuckle is a more impact-driven experience."

I looked at the variety of colours and shapes. "You test all these yourself?"

"Just read a lot. Keep up on the latest products, you know? We also carry plastic knucks. Plastic *will* break after one or two shots, but that might be all you need. And that way, you just toss 'em and no evidence. Single serving, you know?"

I tried a pair of each, found the finger holes tight on my often-broken knuckles. I walked to the climbing display, pulled down three large carabiners and a length of paracord. Holding the clips together, I wound the cord to connect them. The result was small, innocuous and easy to take apart. Impressed, the proprietor offered to neaten up the cord. I watched him burn the ends with a lighter.

"A suggestion I read about on a thread," he said as he rang me up. "Tape a bandage to the back of your hand. It provides a little cushioning—especially if you think these'll get much use."

"Always hope I won't have to use them at all," I said.

The proprietor smirked as if he didn't quite believe me.

I met Shuzhen for dinner at a Japanese grill behind the courthouse. Parking the Beast on the other side of Burrard, I took my new purchase with me, getting used to the feel of the carabiners in my pocket. I felt no safer. Still woefully unprepared for what might happen.

And what was that, exactly? I'd reached out to the president of the Exiles, hoping Terry Rhodes would agree to leave Maggie Zito alone. No telling how he'd react to my request. Scorn or derision, or agreement only to move on her anyway. Asking Rhodes for anything was audacious. I hoped audacity counted for something.

And then what? The favour granted, could I leave? What about Jeff and Marie and our failing company? *Their* company now. Did I feel responsible just because my name was still on the business? I had gone. I was still gone. Why didn't I feel gone?

Shuzhen was already at a table, turning over ribbons of marinated beef. Drinking an Asahi from a chilled pint glass. I ordered one as I sat down.

My partner's cousin was an attractive woman. Shuzhen was elegant and she moved with purpose, *had* purpose here in the legal heart of the city. I felt a longing for her, as well as a pang of regret. Under better circumstances we could be two old friends playing catch-up, redefining each other, with no one's fate hanging in the balance.

"Sorry for ordering without you but I haven't eaten all day." She divvied up the seared meat onto bowls of steamed rice. "Busy afternoon?"

"Somewhat," I said. "You?"

"Way busy. Crown is still holding back the name of the witness. Nimisha says it's probably because they're an informant on some other case. We'll get the name eventually. But all the while, Maggie stays in pretrial. The longer she's there, the more a plea would make sense. Nimisha thinks that's the Crown's strategy."

"Have you talked to Maggie today?" I asked.

"On the phone for a minute." Shuzhen spoke between mouthfuls of food, without slowing down either activity. "A new woman was transferred into pretrial yesterday, up from FVI. Maggie says she's the sister of some biker, not an Exile but one of their, what do you call them? Support clubs."

I nodded, taking a sip of beer. "She'll probably mind her manners till after her appeal."

"Unless the Exiles paid her."

A grim possibility. I didn't have a response. We ate in silence for a while.

"FVI is where Kay is," Shuzhen said.

"I'm aware." I had an address for my sister, courtesy of the Fraser Valley Institution for Women, but no idea what to say to her. Shuzhen let the matter drop.

I told her about my talk with Briony Zito and the bikers riding past Maggie's house. Skipping over my run-in with Rigger Devlin and Felix Ramos, I told her I might have an audience with Rhodes tonight. Maybe it was possible to guarantee Maggie's safety.

"If money were a factor," I said, "could Maggie raise some?"

"You mean buy herself protection?" Shuzhen hadn't considered it. "How much?"

"I don't know if Rhodes would even entertain an offer. But say he would. Ten, twenty thousand? I could offer that much?"

"If Maggie can't come up with it, I'll raise it," Shuzhen said. "If it means she'll be safe."

A simple decision, made without deliberation. Shuzhen Chen believed in her client wholeheartedly, in the righteousness of her cause. I remembered that feeling.

"You know generally in business, the clients are supposed to pay you," I said.

She picked up the tongs and laid more of the beef on the grill. "I'm still pretty new to the job," she said.

FOURTEEN

When it comes to the least efficient use of space in the city, Tinseltown would rank close to the top. Occupying a prime block of real estate between the hockey arena and Chinatown, International Village, as it's officially called, is a four-storey mall with free underground parking, a food court and cat café and a cinema. The bathrooms are frequently used for drug consumption, half of the shops seem perpetually closed, and the other half offer such a bizarre collection of wares, it's difficult to comprehend the business model that sustains them. An escape room, a shiatsu clinic and a cryptocurrency exchange. Tinseltown is gloriously non-viable. I was glad to find it still here.

I bought a bubble tea, just to have something in front of me, and sat in the middle of the low-lit food court. An escalator with a roller coaster's incline rose out of the court, carrying moviegoers over an abyss to the top-floor cinema. I had a view of both stairways leading down.

Would Terry Rhodes come himself? Sit down across from me by the Taco Time? Doubtful. If anyone came, it would be Felix Ramos, probably to scare me off. I had my improvised knucks in the pocket of my jeans. Plus a peach-flavoured bubble tea. What was there to be scared of?

At ten to nine a table of Indigenous women headed up for their film. Cleaners threaded across the floor, wiping tables. A security guard checked her watch.

There was Felix, hiking up the stairs two steps at a time. Dressed in dungarees and a leather jacket that swished as he walked. He motioned me to stand and follow him.

"Your boss say yes?" I asked.

No reply. Just as swiftly, Felix was down to the ground floor of the mall, already taking the curved staircase to the parking lot. I pursued.

In the near-empty lot, he mimed holding his arms out. "Gonna frisk you," he said.

"I'm unarmed, but go ahead."

Felix hadn't been trained on pat-down technique but knew what to look for. I'd looped the carabiners around my keychain, so what came out of my pocket was a jumble of metal and cord. Harmless and unwieldy, I hoped. He inspected it, weighed it in his palm, and handed it back. He kept my cellphone.

"As stated, no weapons," I said.

"I was 'sposed to trust you?"

"No."

"Take off your shoes."

I did, my lack of hesitation proof enough for him. Felix pointed to his bike, an older Gold Wing, the helmet hanging off.

"You want me to ride double?" I asked.

"Just keep up."

Out of the lot, slipping into the flow of nighttime traffic on Pender Street. More cars headed out of the city than in. People crouched in doorways, paraded shirtless, slalomed shopping carts down the sidewalk. Urban blight and urban renewal hand in hand as always. We left downtown. Felix drove fast but had no luck with the lights. I had little trouble keeping the bike in view.

The Gold Wing turned down Clark, passing breweries, a cab stand. Close to the port, in an area where factories and warehouses intermingled with low-rise apartments. The bike maneuvered through the open gate of a processing plant, the building painted the colour of buttermilk. The yard was full of refrigerated trailers and half-tons, SACKETT POULTRY printed on their sides.

A trailer had been parked flush to the fence, shielding part of the yard from street view. Behind this, a crescent of 4 x 4s, flat-bed pickups and Harleys. Young white men in Exiles support gear, hoodies and snapbacks, sat on crates by the side door. They bolted to attention as Felix deployed his kickstand. One knocked on the door, a patter of long-short-short-long, and as it opened, the other held it for us. From inside, the snarl of heavy machinery, a vapour carrying chemical and animal scents.

"He's inside?" I asked, meaning Rhodes.

Felix didn't nod or shake his head. "Fight night," he said.

The plant was in full production. Carousels loaded with freshly plucked chickens carried the carcasses through the stations of washing, beheading, snaking out the guts. Workers in white body suits, helmets and masks further processed and harvested the fowls. The floors were damp. We walked through, taking no safety precautions.

Another large high-ceilinged room, the killing floor. Crates of live birds were loaded on conveyor belts, carried through the machine, made dead, and hung on the prongs of the carousel to be fed through an opening in the wall. I was struck by the relative quiet of the room. Maybe I'd been deafened by the machines.

Felix knew where we were going. Down a corridor with a break room and offices, into a large tiled communal shower. Voices in English, French and Tagalog reverberated. Folding chairs set up around a ring the size of a hot tub with a green carpet and waist-high fencing. Coops stacked in corners, behind the crowd. A cockpit.

Two young releasers stood in the ring, with an elderly man I took for the referee. In each of the releasers' hands was a bird. Their combs had been removed, artificial spurs attached where their real ones had been cut down.

The referee made a noise and the two men thrust their birds at each other in a choreographed pattern, three times without letting go, the birds getting a sense of each other. The releasers withdrew to the sides of the small pit and placed the birds on a chalked line, and at the signal, let them fight.

At first nothing. Anticlimax. Then the one with red plumage flew at and above the other, a swift dart with the beak, the legs raised to follow with those terrible spurs. The other rooster, coloured black and gold, struck at the breast of the red bird. They circled away from each other.

Felix and I stood near the wall. I watched the crowd. Two dozen, most with the intense look of spectators with money riding on the outcome. Terry Rhodes was not among them.

End of round. The trainer of the black and gold bird made desperate ministrations, blowing air down the mouth of the injured rooster. The referee kicked feathers aside.

A world I didn't know and didn't much want to. Felix regarded the action with a similar disinterest. The birds were pitted again, and the spurs and bills became entangled. The red rooster was bleeding now. On the next release he ran to the edge of the pit, where the black and gold bird pursued.

A strike of gleaming spurs and it was over. The victor was given an injection, dressed and placed lovingly back in his coop. The loser throttled, tossed in a barrel with the others. Money changed hands in the crowd. A young woman at a folding table oversaw electronic transactions and the live feed of the bout. The referee employed a dust buster to clear the pit of feathers and debris. Another round of combatants was made ready.

Felix struck me on the arm and pointed. At the mouth of the back hallway stood Terry Rhodes.

FIFTEEN

The president of the Exiles glared at me, his grin laced with condescension. My blood iced over. Terry Rhodes was not especially tall. He was older now, his hair the colour of oxidized silver. The planes of his hatchet face were lined and clean-shaven. Eyes merry. He wore denim, flared jeans with a Western design embroidered down the legs, a denim jacket open to a bare chest.

I took steadying breaths and told myself this was an optimal place to meet him. Witnesses all around. He wouldn't want to disrupt the betting. I didn't convince myself—Terry Rhodes killed people in crowds. Who among the trainers and gamblers surrounding me would dare to pick him out of a lineup? Would I?

I circled the pit toward him, noting Felix Ramos trailing a few paces behind. Before I could speak, Rhodes shushed me. The referee was about to signal for the next match. Rhodes looked at the woman with the laptop, who nodded and flashed him five fingers. She did this three times. Fifteen grand, I reckoned. Rhodes nodded.

As the birds were pitted, I felt Felix's hand on my shoulder, steering me away from the arena. Ahead of us, Terry Rhodes was disappearing down the hall.

We caught up to him in a room piled with empty crates. With alarming dexterity he leapt up and spun, sitting on a crate, legs dangling over like a mountain climber perched atop a cliff. Everything below was what he'd conquered.

"Dave Wakeland," he said. "Son of Matt Wakeland the cop. You a birder, Dave, come to place a bet?"

"To ask a favour."

Rhodes rested his fists on his lap, leaning forward, mocking me with exaggerated interest. Being in his presence was disorienting, like trying to jump out of a spiralling plane. The ground kept slipping by. Behind me, Felix was pacing.

"I'm here about Maggie Zito," I said. "That's the woman—"

"I know. What about that pig interests you?"

A scrape of boots. Felix moved behind my left shoulder. A distant noise of bloody approval from the crowd. I squared up and came out with it.

"I was in court yesterday. I get the feeling something bad is going to befall Maggie while she's in custody."

"Oh reeeally?" Nodding his head, like this was the most curious thought ever given voice.

"I'd like you to protect her," I said.

"Sure, I'll protect the hell out of her. The ever-lovin' shit. Believe me."

"She's a mother, and—"

"You asking protection for the kids now, too? What's that worth, Dave?"

"She can afford to pay," I said.

"To you," Rhodes said. "What is it worth to *you*?"

Thrown by the question, I couldn't respond. Through Terry Rhodes I glimpsed a small and meaningless death, a windswept grave, a nothing legacy. Life to him was so much piss.

Unsure what he wanted to hear, I said, "I'd appreciate it very much."

"Would you ask me?"

"I'm asking now."

"Would you ask on your knees?"

"You mean beg?"

Rhodes inclined his head. "Yeah. I think a little begging is in order."

Felix's boot clipped the back of my knee before I could make the decision on my own. I dropped. The jolt numbed my shins and I skinned my palms. I began to right myself and felt Felix grip the back of my shirt, holding me in place.

"Please," I said.

"Please what."

"Don't hurt her. Please."

"What about somebody else?"

"Please don't let anyone hurt her or her kids."

Terry Rhodes gave a shrug and looked to Felix. "What do you think?" I couldn't see Felix's expression. The prospect didn't volunteer an opinion.

"I'm inclined to say yes," Rhodes said. "I like you, Wakeland. Not sure why. Maybe 'cause you're dumb enough to come in here and think I'll deal with you. Not dumb, but what's the word—brazen. Yeah. For a brazen sonofabitch, you grovel damn well. Yeah, I'm seriously inclined."

With his hands he pushed off the crate, hurtling toward me. Something metal gripped between the knuckles of his left fist. I squirmed and flinched but Felix snagged me around the throat.

Rhodes's fist pushed into my face, slowly and with force. Not a punch so much as a shove with a clenched hand. As he withdrew his fist, I felt a warm river of blood fill the pocket of my cheek. Between the knuckles of his hand he gripped one of the cockfighting spurs.

"Goddamn you are a pathetic fucking sight," he said. "I missed you, Wakeland."

Felix let me go. My hand felt the new puncture in my face. I swallowed blood. My fingers were stained with it. Rhodes wiped the blade on the knee of his jeans, crowing at top volume.

"The thing about hurting old Maggie, kid, is that I really, really want to. Budd Stack was my *companero*. When I came out from back East, he was a friend to me, as well as a boss. And when I sort of pushed him aside, Budd was real good about it. Not that he had a choice."

With the spur under his thumb, Rhodes shook his hand at me for emphasis.

"Budd was as old school as they come. His old lady, Jan, was loyal and a genuine piece of ass in her time. You don't get to touch my people like that. And you don't carve 'em up in the sanctity of their home."

He placed the spur up to my left eye. Tapped it on the brow thoughtfully.

"Not only am I going to unfortunate-accident that pig, I'll find whoever helped her, too. As the big dick around these parts, it's my duty. And you may find that highly objectionable, like those animal-rights shitstains that think cockfighting's a barbaric sport. *Nature* is a barbaric fucking sport. The birds are gonna fight anyway, it's what they're meant for, bred into them for millions of years. Those people in there are betting money on what nature decides."

He kicked me. I went back on my ass and tried to slide away but Felix struck my shoulder, knocking me flat, and the boot of Terry Rhodes sank down onto my chest. I was pummelled. My brain cast about for whatever I could say to stop the onslaught. That poor agitated sponge settled on a cold hard pebble that it hadn't realized was there, a fact I believed despite what I'd been telling myself.

"You kill her, you're a fucking idiot," I sputtered at Terry Rhodes through a mouthful of blood. "She didn't kill your friend. Someone's playing you like a bitch."

SIXTEEN

Felix Ramos herded me down the hallway to a walk-in refrigerator. He unlatched the door.

"Wait here."

"For how long?"

"Think he tells me?"

The prospect's jaw was clenched, his gaze on the move and avoiding mine. The good soldier, silent, obedient and not too curious.

The chilled air felt good on my cheek. Chicken parts in labelled white boxes were stored here. I walked in, sat on a pallet of drumettes and heard the door shut behind me.

One of two ways, I thought. Odds better than fifty-fifty. Far from a sure thing. With Terry Rhodes there were no sure things. I had intrigued him for the moment, staved off destruction for a while.

The door unlatched. Rhodes entered, carrying a bottle of Rémy Martin. He took a long pull while staring at me, capped the bottle of the cognac, threw it to me.

"For your cheek," he said.

I cleaned my mouth out and dabbed the infected area. The bottle was gold-capped, labelled XO and COGNAC FINE CHAMPAGNE. Rhodes leaned against the door.

"I'm a little fucking stymied," he said. "Either you said that shit to save your ass, or it's true. Which?"

"Both."

"Don't get fucking cute." He stepped toward me and took the bottle. Drank and wiped his chin. Up close he smelled of wood smoke and spirits and fine cologne.

"Cops found the murder weapons at her place," Rhodes said. "They got a witness saw her leaving. And this pig's got a hard-on for Exiles."

"The perfect frame job is someone you don't believe when they say they didn't do it."

"True, far as it goes." He shoved the bottle back into my hands. I drank for warmth this time. Our breath curled from our mouths, mingling in the cold room. "Prove to me right now she didn't kill Budd and Jan."

The request came all of a sudden, but I'd been anticipating it.

"The axe and machete were found in Maggie Zito's garage. No other blood found on her property. Murderers make dumb mistakes, little mistakes. But they don't clean everything spotless and then overlook the weapons."

"Maybe she was on the firewater. Or gakked out of her tits."

"She has kids and a full-time job. And Maggie's gotten into a few fights before, but she never pulled a double homicide. To use a great man's expression, it's not in her nature."

Rhodes grunted in amusement. "Hear they have a witness," he said. "Explain that."

"I can't just yet. I don't know who they are. But there's a number of reasons they'd lie."

"So what do you want?"

"Time," I said. "Enough time to figure out who killed the Stacks and framed my client. I can't do that effectively if I'm worried she'll catch the wrong end of a knife in the commissary, or hang herself in her cell."

"But what do you want?"

"I just said—"

Rhodes launched the bottle at the wall. The glass shattered. Aged cognac rained down on a skid of chicken thighs.

"I'm asking what's your angle," he said. "What do you get out of this? Old Maggie can't be paying you all that much. You trying to fuck her?"

"No."

"Fuck someone close to her, then? The sister? Her mouthpiece?"

Before I could answer, he was driving a fist into my shoulder, with affection but hard enough to sting.

"Think you're so fucking high-minded, don't you? Like you don't got the same inclinations as everyone else. Money. Pussy. Power. Respect. Slap whatever coat of paint you want, comes down to the same things."

I was in no position to argue. The heat of the liquor had evaporated. The frozen air burned my lungs. Rhodes stamped the floor, enjoying himself.

"What I heard, she's had a grudge against one percenters for twenty years. Her brother got hisself dragged by some fellas up in Hope."

"And she just happened to pick a retired biker and his wife for revenge?"

"Money, pussy, power, respect," Rhodes repeated. "Family."

I shook my head. "If she was going to blame someone for her brother's death, one face to represent all bikers, then wouldn't that face be yours?"

The changes were small but sudden and murderous. A dilation of the pupil. A grinding of the jaw, as if the feeling wasn't something he could work out of his teeth. The cords on his neck tightened.

Terry Rhodes lunged and put his boot through a box close to where I'd been sitting. As he struck, I shrank back against the wall. He kicked through boxes, staving them in, rustling the plastic lining and sending yellow-white shrapnel from broken breasts in all directions.

As quickly as it came over him he stopped. Rhodes sighed in contentment like a yoga mom after a particularly good workout. His expression turned avuncular.

"You bring up a fair fuckin' point," he said. "I don't know a hundred percent it's her. Puts me in a bind, 'cause people *think* it was. I let that go, they're liable to think less of me. Other hand, if it's a put-up job, the whole point is to get me to jump the gun. Save the taxpayers the cost of the trial. So I'm pretty much fucked whichever way I jump, aren't I?"

I nodded. Terry Rhodes's brain didn't work like other people's. From blind savage uncomprehending rage to a tidy summation of the problem within a minute. A pragmatist could be dealt with, a monster avoided, but someone who alternated between the two was hard to fathom.

"If you promise she stays alive, I'll find the truth," I said.

"Fuck the truth. I want who did this. Both of 'em, or however many they are."

"Their names?"

"Their hides," he said. "A six-figure bounty. On each."

"I'm not a killer."

"Well, not yet." Rhodes grinned. "Tell you what, Dave. Just bring 'em to me. Keep your hands ivory white and leave vengeance to the almighty."

Meaning him, of course. "I'll need to talk to people in Budd's world," I said. "Your world. That might not go over too well with Charlie the Priest and Rigger Devlin."

Rhodes mulled it over. "Then consider yourself deputized," he said. "Sign up Felix as one of your clients. Anything else you need, let him know. You got a week. After that, I got to assert myself. The dominant ape, you understand."

I nodded and moved to the door of the refrigerator. Opened it with his permission. As I stepped out into the relative warmth of the poultry plant, Rhodes called from behind me. "Wakeland?"

I turned and saw Terry Rhodes leaning against the doorway, looking oddly triumphant.

"Always knew I kept you around for a reason," he said. "You work for me now, Dave. Sooner or later everybody does."

SEVENTEEN

The closest hospital was in Burnaby, but I'd been sewn up enough over the years to have preferences and superstitions. A beat cop once told me, "If you get stabbed on the doorstep of any other hospital, you flag down a cab for St. Paul's and hope there's no traffic." Their ER was the busiest in the city and therefore the most effective. I headed there. The puncture had stopped bleeding, and I could stand the wait.

Half an hour later I was out, the recipient of three dissolving stitches inside the mouth, a tetanus shot and a piece of gauze taped to my cheek. I parked the Beast beneath Shuzhen's building and dry swallowed an anti-inflammatory pill. No painkillers. The ache would remind me of my bargain with Rhodes.

Shuzhen was in her familiar spot on the couch, Thai takeaway this time. I showered and changed, wolfed down a plate of cold pad see ew and scoured her cupboards for something alcoholic. A dusty bottle of Yellow Crane Tower behind the coffee grinder. With a water glass full of baijiu, I sat next to her and let George Eliot maul my hand. One more injury wouldn't matter.

Shuzhen caught a glimpse of my left profile. "Shit, what happened to your face?"

"Bad genes and too many unslipped overhand rights," I said. "I spoke with Terry Rhodes. He'll hold off on Maggie for a week, provided we find the real perpetrators."

"And what if we can't?"

The liquor stung my cheek and left a chalky, medicinal taste. My tongue prodded the stitches out of reflex. I tried to make my face reflect confidence.

"We have to find them, so we will. The motive for killing the Stacks, the identity of the witness, the reason to frame Maggie. One of those will lead to who did this."

"And then what?"

"Hopefully your client goes free."

"And someone else gets killed."

"The gristle and guts of miracles," I said. "If we can prevent that, we will."

Shuzhen nodded. Setting her laptop down, she moved to her knees on the couch. The robe slid up and up.

"How much does it hurt?" she asked.

"Not bad. I got off easy."

"Do you regret coming back?"

Before I could answer she embraced me, kissed the part of my mouth that was intact. I felt bare skin smelling faintly of chlorine. My hand moved the glass to the floor, came up to smooth her fine hair from her face.

"You remember?" she asked.

"Of course."

"Remember this?"

"We shouldn't."

"We want to. Don't we?"

"That's true."

"*This* sure wants to."

"Yes."

"Remember this?"

I remembered Grouse Mountain.

The first and only Wakeland & Chen company retreat—or "Skill Supplemental Weekend," as Jeff called it. Us and a dozen trainee security guards. A château with a conference room. The plan was to hike the Grouse Grind, all of us, using the uphill death march as a way to weed out the less committed. But it was raining that weekend and instead we took the gondola.

I spent the Saturday morning session showing recruits how to lock someone's wrist behind their back, how to pat someone down so you wouldn't get jabbed by a needle. Simple life-preserving tricks that got easier the more you did them. A few trainees took to the exercises naturally—my half-sister Kay for one. She'd been the most promising. My protege.

Near the end of the session, I noticed Shuzhen Chen at the back of the room. Dressed for the ski runs in a coat trimmed with faux fox fur, black leggings, blue mittens and a blue band in her hair. I hadn't seen much of her since law school, had never looked at her like this.

My partner's cousin, a former employee. Now closer to thirty than twenty and about to start articling. While Jeff took the recruits through the Chen System for Interviewing Witnesses, Shuzhen and I snowshoed a bit, had cocoa, caught up.

She had a place picked out in the Interior to live, between the judge's home in Vernon and the courts. There was a guy up there she'd been seeing off and on. Nothing serious. Her life was more or less on hold.

I remembered her vulnerability, my easy expertise, neither totally genuine. The Interior was hot and dry, physically beautiful, wealthy, white, rural, and a playground for rich Albertans in the summer. Good luck finding soup dumplings or a Fellini retrospective. But she seemed excited about her life, eager for something different. I envied her enthusiasm.

"How about we swap places," I said, mostly in jest. "You teach wristlocks and I'll go work for a judge."

"How 'bout you come with me?"

She said it with the same unserious tone, but her expression demanded a real answer.

"I don't think your cousin would appreciate it if I ditch class," I said.

Her hand left her mug, reached over, fingers resting atop mine. "Jeff's not king."

"Not yet, anyway."

"He's married. Got kids."

"So?"

"You're not," she said.

True. There was nothing holding me in place, other than history and inertia.

I gave her hand a squeeze and watched my thumb stroke her knuckles. "Maybe I'll come visit you."

An empty offer. We both knew it. Shuzhen's hand retreated from mine. Her expression became warmer but less tender.

"Don't worry about it," she said.

I remembered our little group dining together in the backroom of a steakhouse near the château. Shuzhen sat near the head of the table, close to her cousin, engaging the others in conversation. She didn't look at me, not once.

After the meal I put my boots on and trudged around the village for an hour, thinking of all the reasons this was a good idea. Consenting adults, each their own person, compatible as friends. I liked her sense of humour, her style, the way Shuzhen saw Vancouver as a place to explore, rather than, as I did, a constellation of voids.

Once I'd convinced myself that knocking on her door was a good idea, maybe the best idea I'd ever had, my conscience let slip with an absolute kicker: *and Jeff doesn't even have to know.*

She was having a nightcap with a few others in the lounge. I tiptoed up to bed, the plaster saint, holding tight to my celibacy and my blue balls and my ideals.

An hour later I wasn't any closer to asleep. A knock at the door. Shuzhen, the initiative hers. My ideals fell away along with striped thermal socks and a pair of black leggings and a pearlescent pair of V-waisted panties.

An all-night affair. We bruised each other. She imprinted herself on me, made noises I could still hear years later. We lay enfolded on the narrow bed, caressing each other, and later showered, and near dawn we recommenced.

Intimacy isn't casual for me. I sensed that about her as well. With a kiss she slipped out of the room, barefoot down the hallway, cradling most of her discarded clothes.

All Sunday I could sense we were teetering along the precipice, ready to tip into coupledom. A very easy woman to love, as easy as it would be impossible to delete from memory. The time apart was maddening. I ran my sessions distractedly, searched for her in the downtime to no avail. At the communal lunch, again she interacted only with the others, as if I was a ghost.

We skipped dinner.

Sunday was different, less exploratory, slower and more driven and more passionate. We knew each other physically and delighted in both the familiar and the surprising new angles to things, preferences, tastes. After, we lay across the covers and she traced a hand over my chest, from a bite mark she left to an old scar on the shoulder.

"What's that one from?" she asked.

"Who can remember at a time like this?"

Her hand pressed into the bruise, from prodding to cruelty. She kissed it. "I wish I could give you one of these. Not to hurt but to be permanent."

"I think you have."

Her lips teased up the shoulder blade, the chin, up to mine.

"Jeff probably shouldn't know about this," she said.

"I was thinking the same thing."

"Unless we wanted to tell him."

"Do you think we should?"

I read her face. Shuzhen was asking what we were going to be to each other Monday morning.

I wanted it both ways, all ways. Her forever, and the thrill of keeping it secret, at the same time openly declaring our love and to hell with everyone else. The superiority of the noble sacrifice, too. I couldn't see myself puttering around the Interior, or Shuzhen giving up her career to stay in town. Come Monday she'd be in training for the career she desired. Me, I'd still be waist-deep in the swamp, chasing down insurance scammers, alimony cheats. We would see each other on weekends and every other government holiday.

"What do you want to do?" I said. "I'll do whatever you want."

"Putty in my hands?"

"For another few minutes, at least."

She kissed me, fingers pressing once again into the dark indigo of the bruise she'd given me. "That's a lotta responsibility, Dave. I could maybe wreck your life."

"It could stand a little more wreckage like this."

"Mmm. But I'm not going to. After this let's just say 'to be continued.'" As she settled atop me, she closed her eyes. "You're gonna owe me for this. Big time."

I remembered too well.

I clutched Shuzhen tightly, pressing her to me, slowing both of us. I could feel her through the robe. After a moment our pulses normalized, her caress became a hand merely resting in a comfortable place. She pulled away, confused.

"Why not?" she said. "You got someone in Montreal?"

"Not anymore."

"I don't understand."

"I'm working for you," I said.

"So you think I'm taking advantage?"

She flung herself off me, back to her end of the couch, hurt. I knew she'd say something wounding next, and we'd be thrust into battles of ego and pride. I wasn't strong enough for that. I threw back the liquor.

"There's no one else," I said. "And I want you very much."

"So?"

"There are reasons why maybe we shouldn't just now, such as your client's life. Until we settle that, it's best we leave this where you put it."

"Where I put it?" Shuzhen said.

"To be continued."

She vacated the couch, angry but not angry and hurt. Me and my virtue, boon companions, washed the dishes and went to bed.

EIGHTEEN

I left early the next morning, in search of an omelette and grilled tomato, a proper cup of tea. Breakfast options around Shuzhen's building were slim. My orientation was off—too much new, a lack of the familiar.

The sheriff's run would be late today, some issue at pretrial. I'd meet Shuzhen there at eleven. That gave me time for breakfast and a small personal errand. I found a White Spot, ate, and read over the dossier the defence team had prepared on the Stacks.

Jan Stack had been born Janice McGuane in the mill town of Campbell River. Parents deceased. Jan had a younger brother, Gordon McGuane, Jr., a retired commercial pilot. Junior McGuane and his wife Lori lived in Deep Cove.

As a teen Jan had moved to Vancouver, where her world had collided with Budd's. They married soon after. She opened a dress shop, managing it herself. It probably started as a front for Budd's illicit streams of income, but Jan made it turn a profit. She opened a second location, then a third, buying the buildings rather than leasing. They bought a house, then another. No children. No domestic disputes or separations. The float home was in Jan's name. The Stacks had donated funds for a college's new library at the "Alice Munro Tier," twenty-five thousand dollars and up. Above the Atwood tier, below the Ondaatje.

Budd Stack was born in Barstow, California. Father unknown, mother an alcoholic and dead in an auto accident. After fifteen years of group homes, Budd emancipated himself and moved to Vancouver.

At eighteen he was working for a carnival company, Pacific Good Times. I remembered my father calling it "Pacific Good Crimes," since the workforce usually had outstanding warrants. The dossier didn't say much about Budd's early criminal years, how he'd earned his patch. Maybe he'd already become an Exile by the time he crossed the border. In any case, he became sergeant-at-arms of the East Van chapter, then president, then the top biker west of the Rockies.

And then came Terry Rhodes.

Faced with a more frightening and brutal choice for leadership, Budd didn't contest the matter. He moved into an advisory role. He and Jan sold their assets and retired early. By the time they made that donation to the college library, Budd Stack had been on the inactive list for a while.

On their last day, the Stacks had gone to dinner and a Whitecaps game. They'd had surf and turf at the Joe Fortes Chop House, then watched Vancouver lose to the Galaxy 4–1. Waiters and stadium staff had confirmed these details. No one dined with them. No altercations or incidents during the game. By all accounts, this was a night on the town and nothing more. Not the worst sendoff I could imagine.

And then they'd come home. Heard something upstairs. Budd had gone up with a pistol to deal with the intruder. He'd been stabbed instead, and Jan had run and been caught at the door by the second murderer.

Imagining Jan Stack's final moments depressed me. Her lifestyle had been built on other people's pain, and maybe she didn't deserve anything better. But Jan seemed to love her husband, and she'd lost him at the same time as her life. There was something tragic and poignant in that.

And what of Maggie Zito? If she was framed, then she was a third victim in this. That meant at least one of the killers had been familiar with both the Stacks and Maggie. More than that, they'd have to know their way around the justice system to set her up.

That left the mystery witness. Why would someone testify that Maggie was one of the killers? Part of the frame, or mistaken identity? Maggie was hard to confuse with someone else. Coarse and large, a walking embodiment of that sawdust smell from a vanishing Vancouver. Despite her temper she'd endeared herself to a lot of people. Her file was stuffed with letters from friends attesting to her good heart and character.

I had been so mired in my own feelings about returning to the city, I hadn't realized that I believed her. It had taken a strike from Terry Rhodes to make that clear. Maggie Zito belonged here, had worked out a way to live, and deserved to have that back.

I paid my bill and left. It was nine o'clock and I still had an errand to run.

Bill Stoddard was late arriving to his office, situated on Homer between a megachurch and the central library. I was early. When he asked for the day's appointments, his office manager pointed at me. Stoddard was a thin man with thinning blond hair, pale eyes, wearing a polo shirt with his last name stitched on the breast. Free advertising and a memory aid all in one. He said he'd see me just as soon as he was caffeinated.

As far as I could tell, Stoddard's business was renting office space to other companies, ranging from hourly use of a desk to leases of commercial property. There was an app involved, which somehow made the company "revolutionary" and "a game-changer hacking the very future of work." Their revolutionary status was attested to by framed business awards, a photo of Stoddard and the mayor playing softball.

A company with that many properties would have security as a line-item expense. Maybe Stoddard was overextended. Maybe there was some arrangement to be made.

Stoddard welcomed me into his private office, told me to call him Bill, insisted I accept an espresso. His office was heavily windowed. He leaned his chair back against the glass.

"I recognize your name," he said. "The Wakeland in Wakeland & Chen. Who, from what I hear, no longer works for his own company."

"I consult here and there," I said, wondering if he'd read up on me while I waited.

"So what can I do for you, Dave?"

"Paying us what you owe would be nice."

Stoddard nodded earnestly. He felt big here, could afford to be indulgent. His expression remained pleasant, but he picked a sleep grain off his eyelash and flicked it at the floor.

"Not going to happen, I'm afraid. Anything else?"

"There an issue with your finances?"

He shook his head. "It's been a good few years. Your finances, however."

"They're the reason I'm here," I said. "My hope is we can work something out."

A look of pity from the executive. "I don't mean to insult your business acumen."

"No, please, insult away."

"Okay," he said. "Your company's in the shit. You've taken on an unsustainable amount of corporate debt. Often happens when a company expands too fast and there's a market contraction."

"In my limited understanding," I said, "that debt could be recovered if you paid us what you owe."

"Payment would allow Wakeland & Chen to limp along a while longer, yes."

I set my coffee cup on the edge of his desk and folded my hands. There it was.

"My guess is you'll go into receivership within the year," Stoddard said. "At which point your debts will be settled for pennies on the dollar. So from my perspective, why pay now, when I can hold off and settle for a percentage at some later point?"

"A gentleman honours his debts," I said.

Stoddard laughed.

"You wrote to Jeff several times over the past year, asking for patience with his invoices. All the while he kept staffing your little empire."

"He did. That was nice of him, though a tad naive."

"I was hoping we wouldn't have to get lawyers involved," I said.

"That's entirely your call," Stoddard said. "I have a firm on retainer."

"Whose invoices you no doubt pay on time."

Stoddard showed me his teeth, even and white. I wondered how many I could extract before the screams alerted the office manager.

"The major leagues aren't for everyone," he said. "That man-of-integrity bullshit doesn't fly. You're strictly operations, Dave, not management. You got your company a few high-profile wins and some good press. You were also forced to resign from the police. Smarter than you let on, yet eager for a fistfight. Honestly, I figured the way you conduct business would end in a lawsuit long before now."

"So you bet on us to fail," I said.

"Most businesses fail. It's not a personal judgment."

"So how do you get another security contract when you're known in the industry as a welch?"

Stoddard had an answer for that, too. "It's cash and carry for now. But security is a competitive market. We had five bidders last time."

"I appreciate your candour," I told him. "It's a relief. I was worried this was Jeff's fault. Now I understand it's just you being a short-sighted fool."

Stoddard chuckled, nonplussed. It would be very satisfying to plus him. To reach across that desk and see how much force the wall-to-ceiling glass could withstand. Satisfying, but destructive to my purpose.

"From the start you knew you were never going to pay up," I said. "And I suppose if we won in court you'd just fold the company into some other corporate entity. Which means the only option left is to make myself a million dollars' worth of headache for you."

"Even then you wouldn't see that money, Dave."

"Guess we'll find out."

"A quick story before you go," Stoddard said. "I was part of a sales force at Overman Motors. A manager above us, very unpopular guy, quit his job. After a few months, he came back to work. Only they didn't give him back his seniority, so most of us were now above him. At lunch one day I heard two salesmen discussing him. One says, 'He'd fuck us, so why don't let's fuck him.' And I'll never forget, the other one shakes his head and gives a real knowing smile. He says, 'No, let's starve him, *then* let's fuck him.' They gave their former boss nothing, cut into his sales, put his paperwork at the very bottom, till finally he got cut. Guy never knew why."

I wasn't sure what message to take from that. My cheek hurt. I asked Bill Stoddard for some ibuprofen, swallowed them with my espresso and left. At least it was good espresso.

I expected Shuzhen to act cool toward me, given last night. But there was no change in her demeanour when I joined her at the courthouse. We took the elevator up to the conference room. She smiled and squeezed my hand.

"Productive morning?" she asked.

"Wakeland & Chen's major debtor didn't respond to my appeal for decency."

"Did you expect them to?"

"I don't know what I'd expected. But a cheque would have been nice."

Nimisha Nair was already in the room, her laptop and document cases taking up the table. The lead counsel's face was solemn.

"The run is just getting in now," she said. "There are going to be additional charges."

Shuzhen's expression turned puzzled. "What for?"

"There was a fight last night in pretrial. Maggie broke another woman's arm."

NINETEEN

Someone had blackened Maggie Zito's left eye. The iris was flooded with pink, and the tissue around the socket had bruised the colour of eggplant. Her lip had been split, and the infirmary nurse had reconnected it with black thread and decent stitch-work. Her knuckles were scraped, her left index finger in a splint.

"Don't we make quite the pair," Maggie said, nodding at my bandaged cheek.

Her injuries were a good sign, I thought. The fallout from a brawl. When they come to kill you in prison, they don't use fists.

"The corrections officer's report says you got into a fight with another detainee," Nimisha Nair said. "It says she antagonized you, but your response was out of proportion."

"Guess he would know better than me what's in or out of proportion," Maggie said.

"You attacked this person?"

"If that's what it says in the report."

Nimisha tapped her pen against her teeth, too seasoned an advocate to make a show of her frustration. "We need to answer these charges, Maggie. If we don't have your side of things, that makes my job a lot tougher."

A course of anger bolted through the prisoner. Flaring of the nostrils, hunching her shoulders. Her posture became stiffer and more square. Like with Terry Rhodes, an immediate change.

"And what about *my* job?" Maggie said. "Thirty steady clients plus a city contract. Think after this any of 'em will let me do their lawns? What about the half-dozen people who work for me? Your job any easier than theirs?"

"Maggie—"

"I don't got any more to say."

Nimisha began filling her bags with files. Shuzhen and I remained seated. When the lawyer was gone, I brought my chair closer to the table.

"Mind if we talk for a minute?" I said.

"Where the fuck do I gotta go?"

"The woman who attacked you. Do you think she was hired?"

Maggie's good hand rubbed the knuckles of the other. "This stays between us, right? You won't repeat it?"

"I promise."

"She was gadflying around, picking on me, trying to impress the others. You know the type? Figures out who the cool kids don't like. I can tell when someone's talking shit just to talk shit, and when it's for the benefit of a third party."

"You broke her arm?" I asked.

"Seemed a smart move at the time, and sure stopped her from hitting me with it." Maggie took an ice chip from the Styrofoam cup in front of her and slipped it into her mouth. "She threw down first, and got a couple good haymakers in before I took her."

"What was her excuse?"

"Apparently I took too long at the vending machine."

"So why not tell Nimisha?" Shuzhen said. "She can tell the judge. I don't get it."

"I know you don't," Maggie said.

"The co's report is one-sided because the other person talked," I told Shuzhen. "If Maggie does the same, word will get around."

Shuzhen shook her head at the unfairness.

To Maggie, I said, "The person I spoke to yesterday gave us a week's reprieve."

"If your cheek's any indication, I wouldn't put much stock in that."

"Whoever set you up knew the contents of your toolshed. They knew you had a grudge against the Exiles. They knew enough about your habits and your living situation to know you'd be home asleep. The number of people with that much info about you has to be finite."

"Almost sounds like you believe me," Maggie said.

"Have you ever had a serious fight with your sister?"

"Never."

"Inheritance, you date a guy she liked?"

"Briony's my blood," Maggie said. Finality in the words.

"All right. What about the father of your kids?"

"He's a good man. Health stuff keeps him near his folks, and his eye for redheads meant it was never gonna work out between us. But he wouldn't separate me from our babies."

"Neighbours? People you work with?"

"Known most of 'em forever. They like me."

"And the rest?"

"Afraid of me." She smiled.

"Ex-boyfriends, then?" I was nearing the end of my list.

"Well, there's Murray, but I don't see him…" Maggie didn't finish the thought.

"What about this Murray?" I prompted.

"Nothing about him. Murray Fong's a decent guy. Only I can't vouch for him a hundred percent."

"What do you mean?"

She rattled the ice in her cup. "Say you held a knife on my sister, told her to rat on me. Briony would tell you to eat shit and be smiling when she said it. Same as I'd do for her. That's how I know it couldn't be her. Not on purpose. Not accidental. Not on pain of death."

"And Murray Fong?"

"We were close once, and I like him. But he's not blood." She crunched another ice chip. "Maybe you wouldn't understand."

"Why wouldn't I?"

"On account you put your own sister in jail."

"That's not exactly how it happened," Shuzhen said.

"Kay made her own decisions," I said. "To cover for her would have landed me and my partner in jail and wrecked the company we built. The consequences were hers."

"You're big on consequences," Maggie said.

"When it comes to taking a life."

She nodded, and the intact portion of her mouth curled into a smirk. "Kay said as much. I wrote her the other day, when Shuzhen mentioned bringing you in. See what kind of guy you are."

The move surprised me. "And what kind am I?"

"According to your sister, there's no one better to have on my side. Says you're trustworthy, that you don't take shit. When you believe in something, you go at it with vicious intensity. Her words. But that belief takes a lot out of you."

I recognized something of myself in my sister's words. Kay was perceptive, smart, as strong of character as anyone. That made it harder to accept what she'd done. And I had mentored her. Kay saw how the job wore on me, heard my frustrations about the city. In a warped way, what she'd done had been for my benefit, my approval. I didn't know if I could accept that.

"My sister say anything else?" I asked.

"Why not ask her yourself?" Maggie said. "Kay told me she'll talk to you. When you're ready to hear it."

TWENTY

Johnny Rivers flowed through the tinny speakers of the Beast. "Mountain of Love." The weather had turned overcast, storm clouds building above the North Shore. A smell in the air of brushfire. Today was the final day of August.

Maggie Zito's ex-boyfriend lived above a ceramics shop on Carrall Street. Murray Fong worked as a digital-animation designer. He'd posted his resumé online, complete with a phone number, which he didn't answer. After enough rings, he spoke his name before a digital voice instructed me to leave a message. Answering machines had once been a space for bored creativity. Voicemail didn't lend itself to that.

Good luck finding street parking on Carrall. I left the Beast in the seven-storey parkade next to Chinatown Plaza and hiked back. Murray Fong's front door was at the top of a locked staircase.

I buzzed. I knocked. No answer. The shop owner didn't have a way to reach the upstairs tenant. The mail slot was jammed with flyers.

Strike one. Back to the Beast, down to West Hastings. Next stop: the Wakeland & Chen office. Jeff wasn't there, and I wasn't surprised. Marie was still behind the reception desk, staring at an aerial photograph of Burrard Inlet on the wall of the waiting area. She spoke into the headset, gripping a stress ball.

"Yes, still accepting new clients...uh-huh, yes, that's terrific... starting tomorrow, gotcha...That address again?"

The call ended and she typed something before allowing herself to focus on me. "Twenty-four-hour perimeter guards, two of them. That's three eight-hour shifts times two. Won't save the business, but it's something."

"You have the personnel?"

"I'll work it out." She placed a hand on her belly. "If necessary I can do it myself and bill for two."

I told Marie about my run-in with Jeff, omitting the casino and the call girl who'd tried to steal his identity. I also told her about my meeting with Bill Stoddard.

"He's an honest-to-God prick, isn't he?" Meaning Stoddard, I guessed, but the comment could have been meant for her husband. Marie peeled the foil from a cup of probiotic yogurt and unstrapped the headset.

"Speaking of round-the-clock shifts," Marie said. "I should rescue my mom from babysitting detail. Thanks for trying."

"What about Jeff?" I asked.

Her face turned back to the photo on the wall. The sun glinting off the towers. "I know you're covering for him, Dave. That look on your face, that's how Jeff always looked when I asked him if *you* were in trouble."

"What did he used to answer?"

"The truth. Always the truth." She stared at her hand, still poised on the life inside her. "It would be so easy to just feel one thing for a person. Love, hate. Simple, you know?"

I did.

There was a parking ticket tucked under the wiper blade of the Beast's windshield. The back wheel was within two metres of a hydrant. Strike two. I put the van in gear and merged back into traffic. The stereo burped out *The Incredible Jazz Guitar of Wes Montgomery*.

I was flailing. Without a solid lead, all I could do was pinball from one person of interest to the next. If Maggie's ex-boyfriend wasn't answering, I could try for an audience with Junior McGuane. Jan Stack's brother and his wife Lori lived across the bridge in Deep Cove. If and when the McGuanes told me to piss up a rope, I'd find somebody else to pester. There's always somebody else.

This was the essential confusion of the job. I understood it, even found it comforting. Everything beyond the job was what bothered me. Worry for my partner and re-emerging feelings for my partner's cousin. Fear for our client and fear of the people who wanted our client dead. Behind it all, the feeling I was travelling down a too-familiar route.

Getting to Deep Cove meant heading east through gridlock over the Second Narrows Bridge. Murderously slow during rush hour. The sight of the water exerted a calming influence, at least on me. I opened the windows and saw bumpers knit together all the way across into North Van.

Tailing someone during rush hour would be slow-moving insanity. You'd be stuck behind your mark, giving them plenty of time to scan around and make you. If there was a break in traffic, a well-timed light or turn signal, you could lose them with no means of following. It would be amateur hour. Foolhardy.

And yet.

When I changed lanes to turn onto McGill Street, so did a black Hyundai. When I zipper-merged, the Hyundai jumped the queue to keep the Beast company. And when I kept right onto the Mount Seymour Parkway, the Hyundai crept along behind.

Tailing is a tricky business, a balance between remaining invisible and keeping the target in sight. All the while reminding yourself the point isn't to watch them, but watch where they go.

This tail wasn't professional, but the driver clung tenaciously. In a race, the Hyundai would win. I loped down a side street, away from my destination. Suddenly free from the camouflage of rush-hour traffic, the Hyundai was following too close, and knew it, and backed off. That was my shot. I made a sharp left, and when the Hyundai was out of sight, I banged out another, left and then left again, gunning the Beast, weaving around the residential block.

The houses here were large and tidy, the front yards mostly gravel. I sped to the parking lot of a supermarket a short distance away, threaded the van between a pair of larger SUVs. I shut off the engine and watched for the black Hyundai.

Where had they picked me up? In front of the office was the most likely place. The Beast wasn't exactly nondescript. I hadn't caught a glimpse of the driver. Didn't know if they were working for the police or Terry Rhodes or whoever had framed Maggie Zito. I felt defenceless, surrounded by shadows. I was a target now.

TWENTY-ONE

My first impression of Junior McGuane: a lifelong square who'd discovered his freak streak late in life. The McGuane house was a clean Cape Cod with a tidy front lawn, befitting a pensioned pilot. The backyard was a strew of patio lanterns, tiki kitsch, plastic flamingoes and a bong. The desperate assembly of the company man determined to Really Live.

McGuane was narrow-shouldered and had a pot-belly and a shaggy beard. His haircut was one step wilder than a military high-and-tight. The effect was of a castaway in a made-for-TV movie where the star doesn't really commit. Robinson Cru-somewhat. Crocs and Bermuda shorts and a tan vinyl apron that said MAKE ROOM FOR A FOOTLONG.

He shook hands with me, asked what I was doing in Deep Cove. Not many people approached his house on foot.

"I don't want to intrude on your grief," I said. "I need to ask about your sister and her husband."

"Not a reporter, are you?"

"Investigator."

"Oh, for insurance." He scratched between his shoulder blades with a pair of barbecue tongs. "We're just about to sit down to a late lunch. Why don't you fix a plate and we can parlay a little?"

I took a seat at the picnic table. Lori McGuane was a tall woman with a deep tan and peroxide bangs. Braless in a denim jumper, she filled me a mug of what looked like cloudy lemonade.

"This is a salty dog household," Lori said. "Have you ever been to a salty dog household, Mr. Wakeland?"

"I haven't, Mrs. McGuane, but I'm driving."

"Lori to my friends. Cops'll let you have one without blowing too close to the limit."

The mug was large, rimmed with chili and kosher salt. The drink an almost even mix of Grey Goose, squeezed grapefruit and ice. She mixed another pitcher in front of me, refilled her own glass and banged it against the side of mine. "*Cin cin.*"

Her husband whistled as he manned the grill. I would have expected Jimmy Buffett or AC/DC, maybe Heart, but his music taste ran to classical. Junior swept the air with his free hand to the swell of strings.

"*Firebird Suite?*" I asked.

"Very good!" Lori beamed. "This is a Stravinsky household. And a salty dog household. Right, Junior?"

"Hmm?" Her husband was using the tongs to conduct.

"I said, 'This is a Stravinsky household and a salty dog household.' Isn't that right?"

"Hundred and ten percent, my love." He brought over the platter. "Lori is always right."

Salmon steaks, a foil-wrapped pouch of lobster meat poached in butter. The tongs and a salad bowl made the rounds.

"So you want to talk about Budd and Jan, huh? Such a terrible thing."

The fish was excellent, the bun stale, the salad from a bag. I was hungry enough, and polite. "When did you see them last?"

Junior pondered the question, a squeeze bottle of ranch dressing poised over his salad. "Happened about a month ago, so I guess…"

"The July long weekend," Lori said.

"Was it?"

"Canada Day weekend for sure. I remember 'cause we went to Mexico first week of June, and that was the first time we saw them since we got back. We had a cookout here."

Junior nodded. "Like I said, Lori's always right."

"Either of the Stacks mention anything amiss?"

"Only with the state of the world," Junior said. "China pushing us around. That clown in the White House. The usual."

"How retired was Budd Stack?"

"As retired as he wanted to be." A chuckle. "My sister and him did pretty darn all right for themselves."

"I told you we should've bought into that dress shop," Lori said.

"We're not hurting, are we?" He pointed at the feast in front of them.

"Junior put our retirement money in the hands of a friend of his," Lori explained to me. "That friend had a quote-unquote sure thing. How sure was it, Junior?"

"So I lost a little scratch," he said, a ribbon of lettuce hanging out of his mouth. "We're not on the street."

"A quarter interest in Jan's shop, coulda been ours for ten grand. Would have been worth how much when she sold?"

"Hey, enough," Junior said.

Lori topped up our drinks and piled food on our plates. Half moons of citrus floated in my mug. After a few sips her irritation was gone. "Anyway, Jan and Budd are in a better place."

"How much contact did Budd still have with the Exiles?" I asked.

Naming the group caused Junior to pause mid-chew, and Lori to futz with the table's umbrella.

"Who is it you're working for?" Lori asked.

My card simply says WAKELAND & CHEN. I had three left, shoved in my wallet between Montreal bar bills and scraps of paper with phone numbers and addresses. "We often get hired by property managers to assess security measures, offer recommendations." A true statement. It seemed to mollify her.

The couple spoke at the same time, Lori saying "The Exiles aren't what you think," while her husband said, "Budd wasn't a member." The overlap startled them both. Lori went ahead.

"They're just gents who like motorbikes," she said. "They have a few brews like anybody else, get rowdy and blow off steam. Like being in an Elks lodge, or what are those fellows called with the hats? Shriners?"

"Budd was chapter president at one point," I said.

"A jillion years ago," Lori said. "Honestly, I don't think Budd set foot in a clubhouse since retirement."

"Can you tell me about the trip to Mexico?"

"Acapulco. You should go sometime."

"June is the rainy season, isn't it?"

"So? They rent a villa. When it rains we use the indoor pool."

"Strictly a vacation?"

"What else?" Lori made another pitcher, squeezing the citrus with irritation.

"Did the Stacks make any other recent trips?"

Junior winced, removing a salmon bone from his mouth. "Not really."

"Kind of a sore spot with Junior," Lori said. "We have this gorgeous old Piper Cherokee, a four-seater with brand new floats. At our cookout, Budd asked if Junior would take him around the Gulf Islands the next week. Short notice, but he's my brother."

"Wasn't that big a deal," Junior said.

"It was. You had to go pick it up and put the floats on and buy fuel and file a flight plan, the whole big sloppy enchilada. And then Budd never showed. Something else came up, is what Jan said."

"He paid me for the gas."

"Sure, but that's—it's the principle. Right?" Asking me to back her up.

Never offer an opinion to a bickering married couple. I nodded noncommittally. "Where was it Budd wanted to go?"

"Oh, a little island-hopping," Junior said. "Up the Strait, maybe over to Vancouver Island. I think he got a new camera lens he wanted to try."

"He was an amateur photographer?" I thought of the framed photos on the walls of the float home. Some had shown smart composition, an eye for light and angles.

"Everyone's an amateur photographer," Lori said. "Budd just had money for the good gear. Everyone who retires early ends up looking for something to occupy their time."

I couldn't argue with that.

By the time I'd hiked back to the supermarket, the parking lot had thinned out considerably. The Beast stood alone in its spot. Doors still locked. Nothing placed under the front or back fender. No bundle of dynamite jammed beneath the hood.

I told myself this was the bulk of the job. Find people, ask them questions. Sift and repeat as necessary. But I felt frustrated after all that running around in traffic. What I had to show for it: a well-grilled salmon steak, a salty dog mixed stronger than riot punch, and a plane trip that never happened.

The McGuanes hadn't seemed too bereaved. True, the murders had been a month ago. There were also no rules for grieving. But these were close relatives who vacationed together, a couple with similarities to the McGuanes themselves. The reaper's bony hand had swiped through their family, and instead of grief they seemed a little buzzed, a little mellow. And maybe a little afraid of uncorking the wrath of Budd's former associates. The wrath of the Exiles was rightly to be feared.

Then there was the black Hyundai, waiting somewhere in the darkening afternoon. I didn't miss this part of the business, the danger paired so often with bewilderment. The testing of patience and nerves. Not knowing from which direction the next swipe was coming. Or when. Only that its arrival was certain.

TWENTY-TWO

Rush-hour traffic would have been awful even if the streets weren't being ripped apart. Three lanes on Hastings converged glacially to one, which ran through a pylon maze a block and a half long. The Beast wheezed an unforgivable stream of benzene and carbon monoxide.

I turned left on Nanaimo Street, a double-laned thoroughfare on the Eastside, where a few small wood-framed houses made their last stand. Here every homeowner seemed to be in their eighties or older, mucking up the designs of the city planners by remaining alive. Doubtless their grown-up children would sell the moment they inherited. Ring up the Goodwill to come take Grandpa's handcrafted bed, order the landscapers to yank up the tomato vines the old man had brought with him from the old country. As I moved up the stairs of the house on the corner, I silently prayed that every one of the holdouts would live forever.

The Itami house was painted an Easter blue. A rancher that had been raised to two storeys, clapboard above brick. On this stretch of Nanaimo, the lawns were taller than the sidewalk, the front doors taller still. From the porch you could look down to the harbour, the paint strokes of cerulean and aquamarine. Why ever leave?

Joe Itami opened the door, an ice cream pail of plums in his hand. He wore sweats and an old white undershirt, the kind he would have slapped his son or me for calling a wifebeater. White mossy chest hair licked at his throat. My father's old partner grinned at me in recognition.

"Wakeland," he said. "Come on in, Matt."

"I'm Matt's son. David."

Joe nodded, feigning comprehension. He headed back inside, leaving me to follow.

My father and Joe Itami had been partnered together during the Bad Old Days. They'd cracked skulls and chased the youth gangs out of the East Van parks. Joe had gone the management route, while my father remained on the street till his demise. He and Joe had stayed friends, and I'd tagged along with Joe's son Katsumi as a kid. Katz was now an inspector in Property Crimes.

I didn't resemble my father other than in general height and build. He and his wife had adopted me from his wife's troubled sister, who couldn't deal with a child. But in Joe Itami's brain, the connection had been made. Something in the way of early Alzheimer's or dementia. Joe was here with me, and he was with my father in the past.

"How's Katz doing?" I asked.

"He rides his bike real good now."

Joe's live-in caretaker was puttering in the kitchen, making jam. A woman in her forties, humming in an Eastern European accent. She brought us tea at the small kitchen table. As Joe and I spoke, I could hear the tintinnabulation of Mason jars being washed.

"Do you remember Budd Stack?" I asked Joe.

"Tough bugger. He rides with the Exiles."

I nodded. "Does Budd have enemies?"

"That's like asking if bull crap has a smell. Ever hear of the Popeyes? They sure don't appreciate the Exiles moving onto their turf."

The Popeyes had been patched over thirty years ago.

"What about Budd personally?" I asked. "Anyone hate him?"

Joe looked at his cup. From the kitchen I heard singing in Polish, a pleasant aroma of boiling plums. Joe's hand gripped my forearm, fingers digging in with a power that belied his eight decades. His stare lanced my eyes.

"You stay clear of Budd Stack, David. That fellow is dangerous."

"Budd's dead, Pop."

Katz Itami crouched in the doorway, unlacing his shoes. He hung up his uniform jacket. We shook hands.

"How you doing, Dave? Been years."

"A couple."

Katz was older than me. He'd inherited his mother's temperament and intelligence, along with his father's ambition and easy way with people. His mother had been delicately beautiful, and Katz's face had some of that delicacy, along with his father's square jaw. As good a genetic hand as one could be dealt.

I waited as Katz led his father to the back bedroom. I heard water running. Katz returned alone a few minutes later, pausing in the kitchen to compliment the caretaker on the wonderful smell and kiss her on the chin. Katz led me out to the porch, carrying a small wooden box of cigars.

"I know you caught that kiss," he said once his cigar was drawing the way he wanted. "Not much gets by you, Dave."

"She seems nice."

"More than nice. Drusilla is a godsend with Pop. Without her he'd be in a home, and I'd be another divorced cop with a father going through his second childhood. Dru is kind and patient with both of us. And smoking hot. We'll make it official at some point."

"Happy for you, Katz."

The cigar was fine. The coolness of the porch, the smells wafting out from inside, were comforting. Before us stretched the bent orange necks of the payloaders at the port, the water and, beyond both, North Vancouver rolling up the side of the mountains. If I ever owned a house, this was what I'd shoot for—sitting on the steps with an old friend and a view.

"You're here for that favour, aren't you?" he said.

I nodded, blowing out a trail of smoke.

Before Joe Itami had been diagnosed and properly medicated, he'd taken his son's uniform and service weapon, mistaking them for his own. He'd set out after a criminal from his past. However fearsome the perp had been back then, he was frail now, shivering with fear. Katz and I had put a stop to the kidnapping, kept things from becoming official. I'd banked a very valuable owe-you-one.

"I need the name of the witness who identified Maggie Zito as one of the killers in the Stack homicides," I said.

"Christ, Dave. Why not ask for half my damn pension?"

"It's information the defence is entitled to. Having it now could save my client's life."

"Can't do it. Wouldn't, even if it was possible."

"Okay." I drew on the cigar, letting the smoke dissipate on its own.

"More than just unethical," Katz said.

"So don't do it."

"You shit."

We smoked in silence. A pair of crows took off from the monkey puzzle tree across the street, the jagged branches shuddering in the evening breeze. An ambulance siren screamed from blocks away.

"How's your mother doing?" he asked after a moment. "That thing with your sister must have been tough on her."

"She's a tough woman," I said. "Haven't seen her yet."

"And Kay?"

"The Wakeland family reunion comes later. The task at hand is keeping Maggie Zito free of the Exiles."

Katz knocked a band of ash into a lacquered ashtray embedded in the back of a porcelain lion. The lion's eyes were double-rimmed circles with green apostrophes at the centre. I'd always thought those eyes held a howling madness. We finished as much of our cigars as we wanted.

"I promise nothing," Katz said. "I'll see what I can do. You want to stay for dinner?"

"Another time. Thanks. And congrats."

He nodded. "It's good to see you, Dave. It's also a little terrifying to think you're back at work."

"I'm still retired." Amending that a little as I took in my circumstances. "Semi-retired, anyway."

TWENTY-THREE

As I drove to the River Rock, I kept watch for the black Hyundai. I changed lanes on the Oak Street Bridge. No one made the same adjustments. A good thing—the Beast tended to shudder when I pushed her above eighty.

The casino floor was busier at night. There was a sharpness to the play, an irritation at the drunks or loudmouths. An etiquette to losing well.

Jeff was at a blackjack table near the entrance to the smokers' patio. The dealer was a young woman in a vest and hoop earrings. She wore the face of a trainee undertaker. Behind her, a pudgy pit boss sauntered by.

I waited until the player next to Jeff scooped up her remaining chips and walked off. My partner didn't look over until I'd bellied up and placed a bet.

"The hell are you doing?" Jeff asked.

"We're a team, right?"

He ignored me. The dealer showed an eight. I stood on seventeen. Jeff drew fifteen, hit, drew a queen. The dealer went bust.

"Beginner's luck," I said.

We both beat the house on the next hand, then I drew twenty and lost to the dealer's blackjack. Jeff hit on eighteen and got his three. We lost the next two in a row.

"Your system isn't working," I said.

"Shut up."

"'Work the system and we'll win every time.' Your words, pal. That's what you told me at the last place we cleaned out."

"He's joking," Jeff told the dealer.

"What was the code for an ace again? B-something?"

"Jesus, Dave."

I spoke to the dealer in my friendliest tone, "Ma'am, would you please lift your hole card a little higher?"

That was enough for the pit boss to mutter into his mic and shut down our play. "Gentlemen, could I ask you to take a short time out over this way?"

"You asshole," Jeff said as we waited by the teller's cage. Inside, the pit boss and dealer were in conference. Footage was no doubt being studied.

"We'll break the bank next time," I said.

"I was up sixteen grand. If they don't give that back to me."

"Then you'd owe a million and sixteen thousand."

"Took ten grand out of my savings," he said. "Had it up to seventy at one point."

"Least you're still up."

"Sixteen isn't seventy."

"It's not a kick in the dick, either."

We were motioned to the window. The teller cashed our slips and asked us politely not to come back. Have a wonderful evening.

Outside in the night air, Jeff seemed more weary than upset. He yawned and worked the tension out of his shoulders.

"Thought I was clear, Dave, I don't want your help."

"You were quite emphatic on the subject."

"And here you are, big fuckin' hero ready to bail me out."

"Maybe I need your help," I said.

"Not interested."

"Let me drive you home."

He held out his arms, supplicating before the universe. "If I said I wanted to take the train, you'd just hop on with me, wouldn't you?"

We walked to the second floor of the parkade. Jeff regarded the Beast with distaste. "Hideous," he said. "What happened to your old Cadillac?"

"Broke down somewhere near Detroit."

"This heap looks like a St. Bernard left out in the rain. Then dyed purple."

"But wait'll you see how she handles."

On the highway heading north, Jeff said, "So let's hear it. What my cousin's big case is."

"A mother of two who's been framed for murder."

"You're sure she's been framed? Because you're not the best judge of character."

"I'm a flawless judge of character," I said.

Jeff grabbed the dashboard as we shimmied into the other lane. "This thing handles like shit."

I told him about my meeting with Bill Stoddard. As I spoke, Jeff cracked the passenger window and tilted his head toward the breeze.

"Bastard saw me coming miles away," he said. "We won't get a dime out of Stoddard."

"I can be a pretty big nuisance."

"No fucking kidding."

We crossed the Oak Street Bridge, into the city limits. The Chen family lived in a nice three-bedroom condo on Quilchena Crescent. I wondered when was the last time Jeff had been home. He looked like an untroubled sleep was something other people lied about.

Jeff had been there for me, even when I made things difficult. I owed him.

Putting the van in park, I said, "I'd like to propose an arrangement."

"This'll be good."

"You and Marie and the kids take off for a month. Spend part of that sixteen grand on a vacation. Fix what you have to fix, if you both want to."

"And do what with the business?"

I pointed my thumb at my chest.

The buildings here were drab and clean, liveliness supplied by the greenery. Shade trees along the street, pots of Japanese andromeda on either side of the front awning. On the top floor the curtains were drawn, lights on inside. A banner hung below the planter box, EVERY CHILD MATTERS.

"Nice idea in theory," Jeff said. "But it wouldn't help long-term. It's not sustainable. I come back, then what? You burn out and leave again? We just keep alternating till one of us drops? How's that good for either of us?"

"We both have an unhealthy relationship to work. Which I lay at the feet of late capitalism."

"Yeah, joke about it." Jeff opened the door and peered down to find the curb. "I'm fucking tired, Dave. We let it go and the pressure goes with it."

"Along with what we built."

He climbed out, stared up at the top floor, shaking his head. A man dying of thirst, glimpsing what could either be an oasis or a mirage.

"Run it by Marie," I said. "Why not let her decide?"

He nodded, noncommittal, started for the door and paused. "I don't think I slept with that call girl," he said. "Pretty sure I passed out first."

"You're a good man, Charlie Brown."

"Yeah." The word flung back over his shoulder as he disappeared into the foyer. I wondered if Jeff was serious about taking down the shingle for good. Maybe he really would be okay with that. I wondered why I wasn't.

TWENTY-FOUR

Felix Ramos lived in a century-old low-rise on East Seventh, brick with turreted balconies and a rusty fire escape. The apartment was rented in the name of Elodie Martel. Felix stayed mostly offline, but his partner shared photos on her social media accounts, tagging him in one taken out front of their building. The fine art of deduction. I pressed the buzzer, feeling reasonably smug.

A moment later the side door of the building was kicked open. Felix appeared, in white track pants and the green and red jersey of Portugal's soccer team. The outline of a one percenters tattoo encircled his left arm. He carried a softball bat.

"Why're you here?" he said.

"Humankind has been asking that since the cave days."

"Fuck the cave days."

"Your boss told you to help me," I said. "Full cooperation, remember? Which right now means a cold beer and someone to bounce ideas off."

Felix dragged the tip of the bat along the pavement, leaving a grey mark like chalk. His head turned at the sound of a curtain in a first-floor balcony. A man holding a small child peered down at us.

"Inside," Felix said.

We took the stairs. The door of his third-floor flat was open. A woman in pyjamas was scooping leftover chili into Tupperware. I recognized Elodie Martel from her photos. Short hair dyed almost white, very pretty and very pale. Her pyjamas had Ewoks on them.

"Felix doesn't bring a lot of friends home," Elodie said. "You work at the port with him?"

"Around there," Felix said before I could answer. "This is Wakeland."

"Dave," I said.

The apartment was spacious, one large suite with a work table along the exterior wall. A Singer sewing machine, measuring mats and part of a costume laid out. Storage bins reaching to the ceiling. Designs taped to the brick.

"I'm a seamstress," Elodie said. "Actually I should get back to work, if that won't bother you?"

They kissed and do-si-do'd so she could get by. Headphones on, feeding material through the machine. Felix finished putting the dinner away and loaded the dishwasher.

"You have a nice place," I said. "Tough to make open concept work for two people, but it does."

He nodded. Proud of his home, comfortable here, yet on edge about his two worlds meeting. I wondered how much Elodie knew about the Exiles.

We sat on a pair of thrift store armchairs pulled close to the balcony. Felix brought over two bottles of Polish beer. He twisted the top off his. It wasn't a twist-top. I used the latch of one of the carabiners to open mine.

"How retired was Budd Stack?" I asked.

"Only met him one time. Barbecue at Rigger's place."

"But you've heard things. Could Budd have been working on something?"

Felix sipped his beer, the equivalent of a shrug.

"Say there's a beef between Rigger Devlin and Terry Rhodes."

"No one beefs with Rhodes," Felix said.

"Bad example. Between Rigger and Charlie the Priest. Is Budd someone who might be brought in to mediate? A known quantity, someone both parties trust?"

"Maybe. Probably, yeah."

"So he might have been doing that when he died. Might have come down on one side, earning the enmity of the other."

"Enmity?"

"Pissed one side off," I said.

A nod.

"Can you think of any recent trouble that might cause someone to get pissed off?"

Felix studied the beer label. Not a slow thinker, but someone who didn't volunteer his thoughts until he'd composed them to his satisfaction. I liked that about him.

"Everyone's always fucking each other over all the time. Rigger told me, when I started on the merch table, 'Try not to steal too much.' Just assumed I was gonna steal."

Selling one-percenter hats and hoodies was a cash business, the price whatever you could shake out of someone. I'd seen merch tables like that in Exiles-friendly bars. "And did you steal?"

"Not too much." Felix laughed. "I do what he says. Rigger is my sponsor."

I sensed that Felix Ramos hadn't talked about this since getting released from prison. He uncapped another beer and unburdened himself.

"Long as the guys at the top get paid, they don't give two shits about us. We get told our generation hasn't paid our dues. Dues to them means working for scraps."

"I've never seen a hierarchy that worked any different," I said.

"You asked about beefs. The Priest has a nephew my age, Lloyd Corso. Guy's treated like a fucking prince. Lloyd could fuck up a glass of milk. Crashed who the fuck knows how many cars. But his

THE LAST EXILE · 125

uncle's got his back, so Lloyd is unfuckingtouchable."

"What was the conflict?" I asked.

"Lloyd dicked Rigger Devlin out of seven grand for fixing Lloyd's Porsche. Tried to pay him in gak, which Rigger doesn't fucking touch. None of the top guys want shit to do with drugs, just the money someone else gets from slinging. Rigger says he'll hold onto the keys till Lloyd brings him hard fucking currency. So Lloyd smashes the window of the muffler shop, boosts his own fucking car. And because Lloyd Corso is the crown prince, he can't be taken out."

"So Budd Stack was called in to mediate between Lloyd and Rigger?"

"Between Rigger and the Priest. Lloyd got a talking to and Rigger had to eat the seven grand, plus the repairs to his shop."

"Was Rigger Devlin bitter?" I asked.

"You think he got stuck with that?" Felix tapped his chest. "Took me three months to make up the difference here and there."

"Is it possible he or the Priest held a grudge over that ruling?"

"Not to kill. Once you're with us, you're with us to the end. Another beer?"

"To be sociable," I said.

Elodie was humming to herself. The bones of her upper vertebrae stuck out from the loose collar of her pyjama top as she bent over the machine. Felix kissed her on his way back to the armchair. For a compact man he put away a healthy volume of beer.

"You know anyone who drives a black Hyundai?" I asked.

He shook his head. "Why, someone tailing you?"

"Could be. Tell me about Charlie the Priest."

"He's the number two. Says to do something, it happens."

"Like driving by Maggie Zito's house. Frightening her sister."

Felix nodded. "'Show of force,' he calls it."

"What about the wives?" I asked. "Any problems between Jan Stack and the others? Darlene Devlin, maybe?"

"Nah, they're all pretty close. Vacation together. Or did."

"And Lori and Junior McGuane? Budd's sister- and brother-in-law?"

"They were around sometimes. Not much."

Lloyd Corso seemed like someone I should talk to. Felix found an address for me. I said goodnight to Elodie, and Felix walked me down. In the foyer, he halted our progress.

"That kid I put in a wheelchair," he said.

I nodded. "What about him?"

"Killed my brother."

I waited for Felix to elaborate.

"Kid was League of Nations," Felix said. "The big bad dealer at our high school. Used to post up in the parking lot. My brother dealt a little, strictly to friends. No threat to the kid or his crew. After he shot my brother, I'd see the kid around school and he'd give me this little grin. Telling me so I knew. Police couldn't prove shit. Just another drive-by to them."

Felix stared at the rough line his bat had made on the walkway. He touched his stocking foot to it, seeing if it would fade.

"One day after school I see the kid with his pals hanging by the bike rack. Still grinning. He had a bike chain, red plastic on the outside. Started whipping it around. I walked up to him, right through the circle he was making with the chain. Put his head into the metal bar on the bike rack till his buddies pulled me off. That's how I ended up in Willingdon."

"And when you got out?"

"Found the kid, walked up and did the same thing."

"Regret?" I asked.

"No. I dunno."

"I'm sorry about your brother."

Felix nodded. "Guess I'm telling you so you don't think I'm some psycho. Undependable or whatever. Since you're with us now."

"With you?" I was startled by the phrase.

"Yeah," Felix said, pointing at me. "Like I told you, once you're with us, you're with us to the end."

TWENTY-FIVE

A late night spent looking for Lloyd Corso. I didn't find him, but in haunting the places he haunted, talking to those he knew, I was forming an impression of Lloyd. Not a favourable one.

The Cobalt, the Cambie, the Princeton Pub & Grill. No one had seen Lloyd in weeks. Ancient history in the nocturnal world of clubs and bars. Problem drunks and big spenders are the most easily remembered customers. A bartender will recall the aristocrat who leaves a four-digit tip for a perfectly shaken sloe gin fizz, or the loud-mouth who has to be ejected from the club and gives the bouncer bed bugs. Lloyd had a foot in each camp. He blew big money when he had it to blow. When he didn't, Lloyd cadged drinks from the regulars. Paying for things didn't seem important to him either way.

Dirty Lloyd, as he was known, was loud and calamitous, always coming in after the best score, the hottest chick, the most reckless cab driver ever. Being the nephew of the Exiles' sergeant-at-arms wasn't something he threw around often. Instead he liked to assume that power came from himself. Dirty Lloyd wasn't someone you fucked with.

He didn't hang around with his uncle's crew. Lloyd's companions were lower down the rungs. Baseheads, tweakers, slingers of expired prescription pills. They drank to socialize and to wash down whatever else they did. Lloyd liked playing pool. At one time he carried around a felt-lined case with a custom cue. The bartender at the English pub on Main told me how Lloyd had lost it.

"So Dirty's in here warmin' up, when dude comes in with his girlfriend. Think he was a paramedic. He and his girl start playing at the other table. They order a pitcher, they're havin' a good time. Dirty asks does the dude want to play him, maybe for the next round? Dude says no. Dirty keeps on him, one little game, we'll put a few bucks on it. Offers odds. Cajoles the shit out of the guy and will not let up. One game of nine-ball, my five hundo against your one. Finally dude's girlfriend says, will you play *me* for the same amount? Soon as Dirty agrees, they break and this chick runs the damn table. Sinks the nine, cool as can be, folds up his money and they leave laughing. Dirty Lloyd follows 'em out, and I didn't see exactly what happened, but he cracked that two-piece pool cue into three. Dude's lying there with a busted skull, she's wailing on the curb next to him. Ambulance arrives. Didn't see much of Dirty Lloyd after that."

I heard similar tales from others. Dirty Lloyd's car wrecks were part of the lore. *While his licence was suspended. Only two days after the Carerra was out of the shop. Flipped the damn thing right over and walked away, while the woman in the other car punctured a lung.* Lloyd's disappearance seemed to be a boon for other drivers and pedestrians.

After the bars closed I ended the night in a warehouse on Commercial Street. An underground punk-jazz show with cash bar, the music dissonant and searching, the small crowd made up of friends of the band, young professionals up past their bedtime. The makeshift bar sold cans of Pabst, loose cigarettes and whippets.

The kind of show Montreal does so much more easily, and means so much less because of it. Vancouver with its noise ordinances, its unofficial curfews, the gentrification that strips out old bars and warehouses—you have to work to be an artist here. A show like this took sacrifice. It cost.

But everything cost. Maybe that was why I was reluctant to let Jeff close up shop.

We'd started out as junior investigators at an information factory, the kind of PI firm where everything was done from your desk. From our respective cubicles, we looked across the aisles and, without speaking, agreed that we could do things better. And we had. And it cost.

No one taught us how to run a business. As a result we made mistakes. Your failures are more instructive than somebody else's successes. Wakeland & Chen had grown. Security consultations, background checks, personnel. The money from Jeff's side of the business had subsidized my messy and protracted missing persons cases. Those rarely broke, but when they did, brought us acclaim and good press.

I assumed my work made no financial difference. I also assumed it made a moral difference, a small but real contribution. Finding people, finding answers. That mattered.

It bothered me that Jeff no longer saw that as worth preserving. But whose fault was that? I'd taken something away with me when I'd left. And I'd let him down.

So it was only right I fixed things.

Someone jostled me, a nine-to-fiver in a short-sleeved office shirt and tie. Sweat-drenched and clutching a can of Old Milwaukee. He wanted a fight. I wished him luck in finding a worthy one.

When I got back to Shuzhen's apartment, her bedroom door was closed. I washed up and silently tipped myself into her roommate's bed. George Eliot settled next to me and let me scratch her throat. I thought many wise and boozy thoughts about loneliness and the human condition and mercifully escaped them into slumber.

I woke late. The note I'd left for Shuzhen detailing my limited progress had been turned over and re-affixed to the fridge. On the back she'd written, *No luck on witness. Long day today. Dinner at Floata at 6:30. Will order with or without you.* A heart in place of a signature.

Shuzhen's music taste was dead split between classical and K-pop. I put on a Yuja Wang album and brewed a double-strength, stomach-settling pot of Earl Grey. On her spare computer I delved into news stories relating to the Exiles.

I was looking for—I wasn't sure what. Some news item that would suggest pressure points in the organization. Dissension in the ranks, legal problems stemming from carelessness or bad luck. Something grave enough to warrant Budd Stack's involvement.

A city in the Lower Mainland was cancelling their RCMP contract, starting their own municipal force. One of the members of the new police board was childhood friends with an Exile. *Once you're with us, you're with us to the end.* Fascinating how enmeshed the gang was in the upper echelons of civic power. Fascinating, but a cause for Budd to mediate? No.

A man gunned down a year ago on the morning his trial was scheduled to commence. A known associate of the Exiles, and likely executed by them. Two in the chest, dead on his lawn in court clothes.

A brawl in the alley behind the Railway Club. Three million in coke laced with fentanyl seized from a stash house in Burquitlam. Two bodies exhumed from a North Shore campsite, both thought to be hangarounds who'd double-crossed the Exiles. Charlie the Priest's assault charge thrown out on appeal. A money laundering scheme Rigger Devlin was tied to, dismissed when the judge said the source of the funds couldn't be determined. Terry Rhodes was never mentioned by name.

Rigger Devlin had his chop shops, was into laundering cash and various types of fraud. Allegedly, of course. Charlie the Priest was more of the strong-arm artist. Older than Rigger, his lifestyle more reckless. I could see conflict arising out of their differences.

The outlaw and the crooked businessman. Charlie the Priest had backed his nephew Lloyd, who'd ripped off Rigger, embarrassing him. But then Rigger had Felix Ramos in his corner. If I needed someone watching my proverbial six, I'd take Felix and his bat over Dirty Lloyd and his two-piece cue.

Why was that? I wondered. A sense of maturity at odds with his present circumstances. Felix saw the path he was on, knew where it led. He seemed salvageable. But if Rhodes ordered him to shoot me, I doubted Felix would hesitate.

My tea had gone cold. Shuzhen had a microwave, but there's a level of desperation I prefer not to sink below. As I waited for fresh water to boil, I tried to knit the facts together, to use what I knew to figure out what I didn't.

Say Budd Stack was brought in to mediate some issue, maybe between Charlie the Priest and Rigger Devlin. Say Budd took sides on the issue. And say the loser resented that. They kill Budd and Jan, frame Maggie Zito for the crimes. Did that hold?

Yes and no. Terry Rhodes would have to be in the dark about the issue, or the matter had to seem resolved. The killer would need to know enough about Maggie Zito to frame her. Then there was the witness, who would have to be coerced.

It was a lot of work to stitch up an innocent person. I reminded myself the killer's goal wasn't to convict Maggie in court, just in the eyes of Terry Rhodes and his associates. Revenge would take care of the rest. If the person responsible was someone next to Rhodes, near the top of the corporate pyramid, it would be difficult to prove. Difficult and probably deadly.

TWENTY-SIX

At noon the Beast was parked directly opposite Murray Fong's walk-up on Carrall Street. Its driver was sitting in the window of Fat Mao noodle shop up the block. The van's alarm went off abruptly. And was deafening.

Car alarms are useless. They stop a thief about as effectively as a sign saying PLEASE DON'T STEAL THIS CAR. But the whoop of the Beast's new alarm soared over the noonday clamour of Chinatown. The alarm cut through indifference. It annoyed everybody. I'd installed it this morning for that reason.

"Shut that fucking thing up" and its Cantonese equivalent were hurled from open windows. Lunch-counter diners and coffee-shop lurkers paused their intake in irritation. The owner of the ceramics shop came out to find the source of the racket. And in the window of the apartment above, the curtains parted briefly.

I shut off the alarm using the fob. Truly a horrible sound, and far too loud. But now I knew that Murray Fong was home. I banged on his door, called out that I wasn't the cops or the bikers, that we needed to talk. When that didn't work, I threatened to turn the alarm on again.

"That noise was you?" he said, unlatching the safety chain. The frame of the door had been reinforced with a solid brass plate. The paint on the frame was new. He let me inside.

Murray Fong was average height, hair blond, wearing dress pants and a powder-blue silk shirt open to a St. Christopher pendant. He smelled of aftershave. The apartment was outfitted with an elliptical trainer, entertainment centre and leather sectional, a computer workstation in the corner with three monitors and an ergonomic swivel chair. Bare walls.

"Getting ready to go out?" I asked.

"Why, the clothes?" He shook his head. "Something I learned during the pandemic. If you're kicking around the house and you don't dress correct, shave, take care of how you look, you get depressed. I do, anyway. Look how you wanna feel, know what I mean?"

We sat at a long kitchen table laden with cookie tins, flattened cardboard, neatly sorted recyclables in bins. "You always work from home?" I asked.

"I'm in and out of the office these days. Half the builds I can do here just as well. We have meetings every week, but those are mostly remote. Everybody's on summer break."

"Interesting work?"

Murray batted his hand toward me. "All superhero spaceman shit. Pays the rent. You see that last *Godzilla*, the Japanese one? Cost a tenth of what we'd charge and was, you know, actually good. I'd kill to work on something like that."

He busied himself making coffee, tamping grounds and frothing milk.

"I'm working for Maggie Zito," I said.

"Yeah, saw the news about the trial."

"She won't make it to trial."

Murray's hands paused mid-pour, causing a dollop of milk to hit the tile.

"I hate to hear that," he said. "We didn't date all that long, but I liked her a lot. Sexy as hell, and she's got a great laugh. And her

THE LAST EXILE · 135

kids are cool. It was just our schedules never really matched up." He placed the coffees on the table, sat, jumped up and returned with a tin of sugar. "Not sure how you take yours."

"Who came to see you about Maggie?" I asked.

"Nobody."

"You mean nobody you recognized?"

"No—yeah—I mean nobody showed up."

"Let's not draw this out," I said. "Someone came to see you, and from how you're acting they really put the fear of God into you."

"Don't know what you mean."

"I know that feeling, being terrified. Even worse when it's in your own home. But Murray?"

"What?"

"Imagine how Maggie Zito feels right now."

A deep ragged slurp of air. The shame of what he'd done was working on him. He'd wronged his ex-girlfriend. Helped frame a single mother. After a moment I walked to the sink and wet a clean-looking dish towel. Murray blew his nose and dabbed his eyes.

"They brought bolt cutters," he said.

"You didn't recognize them?"

"No."

He'd been in the shower. They'd pried open the front door, ambushed him as he grabbed for a towel. A white male and female, judging from their voices. A quick glance at the woman's face before her gun was pressed to his eye. Maybe twenty years old, wearing sunglasses. He never got a clear look at the man.

They ordered Murray to spread-eagle on the tile. Hands brought together behind his back. The teeth of the bolt cutters placed around one wrist.

"They asked me questions," Murray said. "About Maggie. Who she lived with. What her work schedule was like. Shit like that."

"Did they ask about the tools?"

"I—I guess I told them. They asked did she have a weapon in the house, gun or whatever. I said no, but she had a machete and axe in the shed."

"What were the man and woman wearing? Take a second and picture them."

"I dunno. Dark clothes, I guess. Nothing that really stood out."

"The woman's hair colour?"

"Dark."

"Black, dark brown?"

"I dunno, I'm sorry."

"You're doing fine," I said. "What else did you notice?"

"She wore boots. I saw those up close. Dark brown, combat style, kinda scuffed up."

Murray was reliving it now. Eyes closed, arms tight against himself. Feeling the bindings, the confusion as to what the assailants wanted.

"I was staring at a little spiderweb crack in the bathroom tile," he said. "The woman said she'd cut off my hand if I said anything. Few days later, I read what happened to that old couple." Murray fingered the St. Christopher. "Shoulda come forward, I guess. Too scared."

"Understandable," I said. "Maggie's defence lawyers need to know this."

"You tell them. Just don't use my name."

"You have the chance to help spring Maggie by swearing to this in court."

"And wreck my life instead of hers. No thanks."

"Sure you can live with that decision?"

Murray's face scrunched in agony as the consequences ran through his mind. Maggie in prison. Her chances of making it through. What the experience would do to her children.

"Comes down to I can't," Murray said. "I'm a small man. Maybe I'm a coward. But people who do shit like that don't get 'brought to justice.' They get away with it. They go on killing till someone kills them. Know who told me that?"

"Maggie Zito," I guessed.

"That's what happened to her brother, and no one did fuck-all about it. Dragged him to his death in front of a crowd. And I'm supposed to stand up and put a target on my chest? When Maggie's not even safe in the court? You fucking first, man. I'll pass."

I couldn't threaten him to say more. An unknown woman and man had done that far more effectively. I could circle back, maybe get him to agree to being deposed. But I doubted it. Murray Fong was right. Nobody could protect him for a certainty. I left Chinatown trying to think of another way forward through the mess.

Nimisha Nair's office was on Davie, two blocks past the courthouse. I made a right on Expo Boulevard, looping around the stadium. I was staring straight ahead, keeping watch for the black Hyundai. I didn't see the truck until it jumped the light.

TWENTY-SEVEN

The truck was a tan GMC with a chrome bull bar. The windshield was tinted. If we'd both been idle and the sun had been right, I could have seen through it to the driver. But the truck was roaring through the intersection, veering across lanes, aiming for a point of impact lining up with my chest. All I could manage was to spin the wheel right and accelerate, taking the swipe at an angle. The Beast rocked, bouncing into the side of the Merc in the next lane.

We shuddered, went up and banged down hard. The shoulder belt cut into my neck. Horns were barking behind me and the truck was making a two-point turn. I rolled through the intersection, the Beast handling like a three-wheeled shopping cart.

Distance. The tan GMC had course-corrected and was racing after me. I swung around a dawdling Tesla and followed the crescent of Expo Boulevard beneath the viaducts. A quick left onto Beatty, executing the turns to feed onto the Cambie Bridge. The GMC had boxed me, forcing the van right, grinding the grille into the rear fender. The Beast was an empty beer can being crushed by bored fingers. The brakes slowed the push but in a contest of horsepower there was no comparison. The GMC wanted me to move right. No choice but to comply.

I let them push us, slipping from brake to gas, accelerating in the direction they wanted but faster than they could expect. The van continued the turn in a one-eighty. No mean feat to spin the Beast, but I did, facing traffic now, swaying like a boozehound back onto Expo.

"Well, shit," I heard myself say.

Below the bridge. A ripple of black smoke was hissing out over the windshield. A high-density, high-pedestrian area with lots of shadowy underpasses—the worst place possible for a race against a better vehicle.

Ahead, the fork with Cambie, feeding onto Pacific Boulevard. Past the fork was Helmcken Park, a small oasis of greenery on the right. The park's walkway was flanked by large concrete planter boxes. No vehicles allowed. I headed for the park at top speed, angling a little to the left, hoping my pursuer was too focused on the van to notice.

The turn would have to be quick and sharp, two qualities the Beast had yet to exhibit. I swung wide and wrenched the wheel. The van turned all right, two-wheeling, collapsing on its side like a hippopotamus shot through the brainstem. I skidded and glass popped and the passenger side floor mat slapped down on my shoulder.

The impact of the truck made a concussive slap. The planter box exploded. Concrete debris rained down on the van's side.

Glass in my scalp and a cut bleeding into my eardrum. There was no windshield anymore. A toxic breeze filtered out of the dead engine.

"You okay, buddy?" someone asked.

The tongue of my seatbelt was stuck. I muscled it apart and crawled down the obstacle course of broken glass, out through the newly ventilated windshield.

Helpful bystanders filmed the scene from the curb. One spoke into his phone, holding it flat on his palm and using the speaker function. And in public. How rude. I rolled free of the wreck, found my equilibrium, tried to stand, then tried a little harder.

The GMC had struck the planter flush, the grille cracking in two, spraying rubble and soil. The truck had accordioned a little but the integrity of the cab held. Even the windshield was intact. Slumped forward against it, on the inside, with his neck at an unsustainable angle, was a young man with stringy black hair and the whisps of a moustache. Bloody foam at his mouth. Dirty Lloyd Corso had found me.

The fire crew disengaged Lloyd from the wreck with delicacy. His neck was set in a brace and he was gurneyed into an ambulance by paramedics. I stood back and watched as the ambulance disappeared, the red and blue lights dwindling to two flashing pixels in a wash of grey.

The crash had rung my bell. Aside from some abrasions and a pinching pain in my shoulder blade, I counted myself in the "fortunately unscathed" category. The last image I took from the scene, before being driven to the hospital, was a pair of city employees slipping a chain around the Beast.

I could have drawn reasonable conclusions about why Lloyd had barrelled into me. I also could have answered the police officer's questions in a thoughtful and deferential manner. But I couldn't do both at the same time.

"What does Mr. Corso have to do with you?" Detective Sodhi asked. The investigating officer was a thickset bearded man in a pressed uniform and blue turban. Behind him, leaning against the door of the interview room, Staff Sergeant Ray Dudgeon observed us with amusement.

"I don't know," I said. "Ask Mr. Corso and tell me what he says."

"I'll be sure to, when he's conscious. But right now I'm asking you." Sodhi took notes on what was either a small tablet or a very large phone. "You're working for Maggie Zito's defence team?"

"What if I am?"

"Do you believe this incident stems from, or is in some way tangentially related to, that case?"

"Maybe."

"Do you think there's a connection to the Exiles Motorcycle Club?"

"Could be the Catholic Women's League."

The look Sodhi shot Dudgeon wasn't difficult to read: *this fucking guy*. Dudgeon shrugged.

"What *do* you think it connects to?" Sodhi asked me.

"If I had to guess. And that's all this would be. Pure conjecture."

Sodhi nodded, tapping his screen.

"*Amour fou*," I said.

"Beg your pardon?"

"Unbridled sexual desire. I have that effect. It's a real cross to bear."

"He's fucking with you, detective," Dudgeon said.

"I get that, sir." Sodhi did some one-finger typing. "You would think someone who recklessly endangered the lives of several people would be eager to cooperate. Get his side of things on the record."

"This *is* cooperation for Dave."

"I don't know the reason," I said. "You can ask me variations of the same question if you want. I have a lively imagination, and my answers will be amusing to at least one person in this room. Or we can revisit the matter once I've rinsed the glass out of my hair."

Sodhi strung me along for another five minutes, just to prove he had the power. I invoked the possible guilt of Charles Bronson, Walt Disney, Ann-Margret, the Mad Trapper of Rat River, and the novelist Eden Robinson. Eventually he gave up.

As I waited for my cab, Dudgeon followed me out of the station to the curb. He held out a cigarette. "Peace offering," he said. "If anyone asks, I'm undercover as a smoker to get information."

"Subtle. I barely recognize you."

"Feel the same way, Dave."

Dudgeon blew smoke away from us, using the motion to scan the street. Normal traffic patterns, no suspicious vehicles parked up the block.

"What are you doing mixing with the damn bikers?" Disappointment and surprise in Dudgeon's voice.

"Trying to keep my client alive."

"You think you can make a deal with these people?" He shook his head disdainfully. "You forget I grew up in Montreal. I remember the biker wars. The bombings. Journalists getting cut down in the streets. You get between these sonsofbitches and what they want, Wakeland, they bring the curtain down. Or worse. They end up owning you."

The cigarette tasted like old brake fluid. Too similar to the exhaust from the wreck. Dudgeon was likely right, but it couldn't be helped. I was in this now. Worse. I had volunteered for it.

"You want something Detective Sodhi can put in his little screen," I said. "Fine. My guess, this wasn't an officially sanctioned attack. If the Exiles wanted me dead, they'd use a professional hitter, not somebody's fuck-up nephew. This was off the books."

"So Dirty Lloyd did this himself?" Dudgeon examined his cigarette butt. "Find that a little hard to believe."

"Yeah, me too."

My cab arrived. I let the smoke drop and gave the driver a cross street a short walk from Shuzhen's place. Dudgeon lingered on his curb, his expression troubled.

I told the driver to go slow and mind the stale yellows.

TWENTY-EIGHT

The smell of woodsmoke infused the air, lingering on the tongue. From the window of Shuzhen's apartment I could see a haze draped over the city. Four hundred kilometres north, homes were being evacuated in the Interior. Wildfires were burning. A hell of a finale to the summer.

I showered and smeared antiseptic on my cheek and the cut along my temple. My frame sported bruises on the hip and shoulder. Well, I'd bruised before. George Eliot made a figure eight around my ankles, but the cat turned up her nose at the smell of ointment.

With the lights off in midday, the apartment seemed especially cluttered. I changed the litter and replenished the cat's water, swept the floors and dusted the blinds. I bagged the takeout containers and took them to the recycling bin in the building's parking garage. A good houseguest does their share.

There was a supermarket on Burrard, near the YMCA. I bought groceries. Back in the kitchen I rinsed a head of romaine lettuce and made a dressing. Oil and vinegar, mustard and black pepper. A spritz of lemon juice and a dusting of parmesan cheese. I sat at the counter and ate it straight from the bowl.

Nearly being killed sometimes makes a person philosophical. I believe in being an adult. Owning your choices, paying your debts, asking for help when you need it. Avoiding cruelty when possible. Beyond that you were on your own. A great many people sleepwalk through the miracle.

Lloyd Corso had tried to broadside me. Either he'd made that decision on his own or he'd been ordered to. His uncle, Charlie the Priest, was the person Lloyd would most likely listen to. But I couldn't rule out Rigger Devlin or Terry Rhodes. Felix Ramos, either. Or for that matter, Junior and Lori McGuane. Any or all of them could want my investigation cut short.

A man and woman broke into Murray Fong's home and questioned him about Maggie Zito. Days later the Stacks were murdered, and Maggie taken into custody. Charlie the Priest, Felix and Rigger Devlin ride past the house of the accused as a show of force. Then Charlie's nephew Lloyd tries to pancake me into Expo Boulevard.

I finished my salad and washed out the bowl. No answers or grand revelations. You move through the world as best you can, avoiding death and compromise. For today, at least. That was something.

The floor of Nimisha Nair's office was laid with well-travelled carpet, red with gold laurels. Bankers boxes were piled at every junction, turning the reception area into an obstacle course or art installation. The walls were glass. No one with vertigo would have lasted more than a week.

In Nimisha's private nook, I explained to her and Shuzhen what I learned from Murray Fong.

"Excellent work," Nimisha said. "And he'll testify to this on record?"

"I don't think so. Not the way they frightened him."

"We'll keep working on him, then. Anything else?"

I summarized what I learned from the McGuanes about Budd and Jan. Dirty Lloyd and the demolition derby on Expo Boulevard served as the finale.

Shuzhen was subdued. I thought I detected concern in her gaze, but I might have been finding what I wanted to. She took notes, seated next to me, rarely glancing over.

"Lloyd Corso sounds like a viable alternate suspect," Nimisha said. "Any idea who the female perp could be? Someone Lloyd palled around with, maybe?"

"I'll check into it. Any luck with the witness?"

"I was going to ask you that," Nimisha said.

On the walls were photos from various fun runs and walk-a-thons. A certificate thanking Nimisha and her spouse. A silver medal.

"We should talk about the Exiles," Shuzhen said. "Dave met with the leader. He said we have a week."

Nimisha didn't need to ask until what. She leaned back in her chair and studied the tiles on the ceiling. "A number of folks have come through this office claiming to be biker affiliated. Most are full of shit, of course. Dumb as lumber, bragging about their crimes, upset when I can't make evidence go away. Half the time I never see payment. But the real ones, there's no fucking around with. They pay up front and they take their sentence with gratitude for whatever I can do. My bet is you're right. We'll have our week. Then things will get lethal very fast."

In the hallway outside, I waited for Shuzhen. She bypassed me, gave instructions to a weary-looking paralegal, and only then gave me her attention. Arms crossed, not upset but in no way interested in a prolonged dialogue.

"How are you?" I asked.

"Things are busy here. If you don't have a real question, Dave—"

"Are you upset at me?"

"Disappointed in you. A little."

"I'm disappointed in myself," I said. "Why not take advantage of everything offered? What a lack of gratitude from the help."

That earned a glimmer of a smile. "You're not the help."

"And I'm not uninterested." I brushed a thumb over her cheek. "There's no one else. No ulterior motive. Timing, that's all."

"If that's true," Shuzhen said, "till then I'll just have to make your life hell."

TWENTY-NINE

Nina Rydell's voice on the phone was congenial and warm, a salesperson entirely in her element. "Hiya, 3G. How's the Beast working out?"

I told her about the crash. To her credit, Nina in 3F made the proper noises of gratitude that no one was killed, before moving on to matters of business.

"I suppose you'll need another ride," she said.

"How soon could your garage have the Beast roadworthy?"

"We do have a few other vehicles. A fleet, in fact."

"I get attached easily."

"It'll be a week at least until we get around to looking at it," she said. "If the damage is extensive, we'll probably just scrap it."

"Would you tow it to a body shop of my choosing?"

"If you're happy renting to own, we'll tow it wherever you like," Nina in 3F said. "This is turning out to be the most expensive plane trip of your life."

Hospital staff weren't sharing information about the condition of Lloyd Corso. "Alive and in no shape to talk" was all I could glean. I'd have to wait for an audience with the injured man.

When all else fails, walk. My destination took me over the viaduct. A listless afternoon, the first day of September still feeling like late summer, the breeze carrying ash and particulate. Cars streaked by on my left, past the upper tiers of the stadium where the Canucks played. Below, in Concord Park, equipment trucks and trailers had formed a white village. Something heroic being filmed, four-quadrant entertainment, where the bad guys were computer-generated and the good guys always had the right ideas. The viaduct carried me over skate parks and tennis courts, into the sooty brick of Main Street. Tents were staked out on the hilly sides of the overpasses. Shopping cart fortresses in the parking lot of the Ivanhoe. A large billboard advertised tuna in resealable pouches. Canned fish was out this fall.

The manager of the body shop had been topless the last time I saw her. Today Darlene Devlin wore high-waisted jeans and a snug polo shirt done in orange and brown, the company colours. She didn't remember me.

"Yeah, that van just showed up," Darlene said. "Some pretty ugly dents in it."

"Dents add character," I said. "Can you get her back on the road?"

"Depends what's under the hood. We can bash the dings out, replace the glass and the lights. But it'll sure be ugly."

"Ugly I've learned to live with."

A look of reappraisal. Eventually it hit. "You came to our house the other day," Darlene said.

"When you ran out of hard lemonade."

Darlene Devlin had a nice bawdy laugh. She held up a Yeti water bottle in the same colour scheme as her shirt. "At work I gotta stick to H_2O. You got business with Rigger, you said? Or you just know him?"

"I know his boss."

She wasn't buying. "Lift up your shirt." When I hesitated, she said, "It's just you, me and the fencepost, handsome. The mechanics won't mind. I showed you mine. Up with it."

THE LAST EXILE · 149

I did.

"Well, you're not wearing the Exiles brand," she said. "Picked up a few dings yourself, though. Some women find that sexy."

"My experience, scars tend to be appreciated more in the abstract. Not something you want to wake up next to on a regular basis."

"Mmm, I don't know about that." A French-tip nail prodded the scar close to my ribs. "What's this one from?"

"Pickett's Charge. Our battalion took out a lot of Rebs that fateful day. Earned a commendation from General Grant himself."

"Fucking with me," Darlene said, withdrawing her hand. "Not too many people do that. I'll have my guys take a look at your wreck."

As her guys raised the carcass of the Beast and examined the extent of the damage, Darlene and I sat in her air-conditioned office. I had a cup of tea that was lukewarm when I got it and chilly by the time the inspection was done.

Darlene had taken bookkeeping classes and made a point of telling me the shop turned a healthy profit. Legally, I took as her meaning. Darlene and Rigger had the life they wanted. A teenage daughter in the honours program. Holidays every Christmas and summer break.

After closing her door, Darlene extracted a bottle of Black Bush from her desk. "Irish up your tea for you?"

I emptied the cup into the trash and held it out. "Must be a tough time," I said, "given what happened to Budd and Jan Stack."

Darlene tipped back her whiskey and refilled, shuddering. "So tragic. Jan showed me the ropes. How to run a business, but other things, too. Like being a boss to men without them resenting you. How to be in their world and make it ours. Jan was so clever at that."

"You must have known them pretty well."

"Sure. Our place in Acapulco is round the block from theirs. Me and Jan and Lori used to have our little get-togethers when the husbands were gone. Girls' nights in, we called them."

"Lori McGuane?"

Darlene nodded. "Hard to believe that's the last time the three of us'll ever hang out. Maybe that's why I'm drinking so much." She grinned. "Maybe I just like to drink."

"What about Charlie the Priest?" I asked. "He vacation with you, too?"

A fervent shake of the head. A refill. Darlene shook the last drops from the bottle. "Charlie doesn't vacation. Not married, either. Fact, I've never seen him with a woman, which is okay by me, no judgments here."

"Is he close with your husband?"

"Why're you asking about the Priest?"

"His nephew wrecked my van," I said.

Darlene rolled her eyes. "That little brat. Still owes me for the work I did."

"Your husband doesn't like the Corsos, does he?"

"Oh, I wouldn't say that. Hard to explain. Their world..." Darlene looked at me and frowned and took a long sip. "Your world, too, I guess. Men can be such great friends, and then so hurtful to each other."

"A pretty dumb species," I agreed.

"People should just get along. And drink more. That's what I believe, anyway. Fuck 'em all to hell."

Before I could redirect the conversation, the door opened. Rigger Devlin himself, in a long-sleeved version of Darlene's shirt. No nametag. He scowled at me, scowled harder at the bottle in front of his wife.

"Work hours and you're boozing," Rigger said. "We talked about this."

"You talked. I was just entertaining your friend."

"That what this shitstain called himself? My friend?"

"I brought you some business," I said.

THE LAST EXILE · 151

He nodded as if that, too, was its own separate headache. "From your little crash. Thanks so much for putting the focus on my place of fucking business."

"According to the internet, you have a very good reputation. Three and three-quarter stars."

"Fuck off, Wakeland."

"The guys are already on it, babe," his wife said. "Relax your sphincter a little. I'd say have a drink, but we seem to have killed the bottle."

She found this unbelievably funny. Rigger stared at her, hands on his hips, with the patient irritation of the embarrassed husband. Then he turned to me, pretended she wasn't in the room.

"So why are you actually here?" he asked.

"A legitimate repair job," I said. "Though a friendly discount would also be nice."

Rigger went along, seeing it as the quickest way to get rid of me. A moment later he took me over to the van, snatching the clipboard from one of the mechanics. "Engine needs a new belt and battery. Drive shaft is hooped."

"How soon?"

"My guy at the yard can get the parts this afternoon. Couple days?"

"Tomorrow night would be better."

Almost in spite of himself, Rigger nodded. "All right. She's leaking oil, but at her age that's pretty common. Worth keeping an eye on, though."

I thanked both the Devlins, started for the exit, turned back and gave Rigger my best Peter Falk. "Hey, any idea how I can reach Charlie the Priest?"

Rigger blanked, then his features contorted in displeasure. "That turd sandwich. Why?"

"I'd like to ask him if he killed the Stacks."

"Crazy enough to."

Rigger walked closer to me, out of earshot from his wife and the mechanics. Tapping the clipboard on his thigh.

"Terry told me to play nice, but I don't like cowboy shit. I don't like seeing my wife boozing at work. The last thing I need right now is to piss off the Priest."

"Shaky ground between you?"

"Ground's a fucking minefield."

I was taller than Rigger Devlin, younger and more fit. He didn't give off an aura of menace. Still, there was something unyielding in his expression. If backed into a corner, he'd claw and snap as ferociously as the others.

"Felix could help you get a line on the Priest," he said. "He's at the man's beck and call."

"But not yours?" I asked.

"Mine too. Felix is low muchacho on the totem pole."

"You know totem poles aren't vertical hierarchies," I said. But Rigger was already walking back into the well-lit mouth of the garage.

It was beginning to rain.

THIRTY

Floata was on the top floor of a shopping complex in Chinatown. The restaurant had an expansive dining area with red flying walls that could create private chambers for parties and the like. Shuzhen was sitting in one such enclosure, alone at a table for six.

A quick embrace and a peck on the cheek. I noticed a child's backpack hanging off one of the seats. Marie's purse rested on another. A moment after I'd poured the tea, the Chens made their way back from the washroom. Jeff carried the children.

My partner looked subdued but content. Fatherhood was a role he enjoyed. In a powder-blue dress shirt and a tie featuring the Tasmanian Devil, Jeff seemed like he'd got some of the neon out of his blood.

The kids favoured him, Jax almost six and Rena three. Marie looked less careworn away from the office, tired but content, easing herself into a chair.

"You remember Uncle Dave," Jeff said to the kids.

Jeff's life had evolved. Expanded. Unlike mine. For a moment I envied him. To put down roots and marry and have a family—there was something to be said for it. I was the same person as before, only older. A year and a half away hadn't changed that. Uncle Dave. Right.

"What happened to your face?" Jax said.

"Car crash. Always buckle your seatbelt."

His small finger reached up to poke my cheek.

"Don't do that," Marie chided.

There was no business talk. Soup and noodles made the rounds, long beans and gai lan and snow crab. Egg tarts and taro cake for dessert. Marie took charge of the conversation. With slightly forced good humour she asked Shuzhen about her apartment, recounted her own decorating woes, and questioned me about what I'd gotten up to in Montreal.

"What did you miss the most about Vancouver?" she asked.

"The weather."

"I thought you'd say the people."

"The people, too."

"He drives like he's from Montreal now," Jeff said. "That car wreck was on the news."

Marie retreated from the topic. "Has your love life suffered since you've been back?"

"It's never been anything but suffering."

Meant as a joke, but the Chens exchanged a look. Rena flattened a piece of taro with her fist. Marie wiped her daughter's hand.

"Now a good time, Jeff?" she said casually.

He nodded, pushing his plate away. Staring at me. "What we discussed. Marie would like to take you up on it. Me too. Please."

That please sounded like it hurt to say. Now wasn't the time to needle him about it. I made a silent promise to needle him sometime in the future.

"Okay," I said. "Take a month off and leave the business to me."

"What'll you do?"

"Vertical reintegration of our core business values. Reduction of negative synergies. Don't worry about it, Jeff."

In truth I had no idea. A seven-figure debt was more than I could comprehend. Maybe I'd get lucky and the business would run itself. In any case, I had a month to learn.

"Should we shake on it?" Jeff asked.

"Anything more vigorous and the ladies will get jealous."

We shook, and it was damned awkward. Neither of us was comfortable with overt demonstrations of gratitude. Jeff's need for help, my joy at paying him back for his—if we'd been alone, that would have been transacted with a manly nod.

But it was possible we'd ended up in this mess by being emotionally stifled. It was good to say, *thank you, you're welcome*. There is nothing more boring than holding to a pattern of behaviour that brings the same lacklustre results.

"This means a lot to us," Marie said.

The bill came, and they insisted. While we waited for the machine, Jeff said, "Why 'the ladies'?"

"Sorry?"

"You said, 'or the ladies will get jealous.' Why would my cousin be jealous for you?"

"Just a wisecrack," Marie said.

"Are you fucking her?"

His wife's hand on his arm. "Jeff, the kids."

Jax put his hand in his mouth. The only one of us moving.

"Are you?" Jeff repeated.

"Right now I'm sitting at a table," I said.

"Are you? Just say."

Shuzhen stood, ripping her purse from the back of the chair. "I guess I can fuck anyone I want." Swearing at her cousin, she shouldered past the waiter, who carried the portable debit machine and a tray of hard candies. If the waiter overheard us, he wasn't the sensitive type.

"A real bastard," Jeff said to me.

His family waited in the car on the top level of the parking lot. He took something from the back, a black nylon case, and thrust it at me. Slamming the tailgate harder than necessary.

"Shuzhen is right," I said. "Her choice."

"Still a bad choice."

"You don't think I'm good enough for your cousin?"

"No," he said, "you're a walking fucking disaster."

"I think I'm heroic and fun to be around."

The bag was heavy. Inside was my .357 revolver and a box of cartridges. Next to it, my father's old flashlight, a police-issue aluminum baton that happened to light up. An effective bludgeon at times.

"Thank you for trusting me with this," I said.

"You're an asshole." Jeff unpocketed his keys and took a step away. "Try not to get killed."

I walked the distance back to the apartment, cutting over and back on the chance I was being tailed. When I arrived at Shuzhen's building I saw her Mercedes idling across the street. She was behind the wheel, clear-eyed.

"Get in," she said.

We headed in silence over the Burrard Bridge, down to Vanier Park. My bag of weapons sat on the floor of the car. Shuzhen stopped in the parking lot near the Planetarium.

"The Radiohead laser show?" I asked.

"I come here to think sometimes. Or when I'm too pissed off to swim."

On foot, she led me along the water, past the boxy apartment tower overgrown with ivy. The building always reminded me of a green plastic toolchest my father had owned. Probably thrown out when my mother downsized.

A few joggers and nighttime couples passed us. A man sleeping lengthwise on a bench. Otherwise we had the greenway to ourselves.

"He can be so patriarchal sometimes," Shuzhen said.

"Probably comes from a place of caring."

"It comes from it's none of his fucking business."

"Very true."

"Don't agree with me."

"Okay."

To our left, the dark spread of English Bay, a few pleasure vessels cruising into False Creek. Safe harbour. The sun almost gone, the city not yet lit up. Shuzhen ran her arm around my elbow.

"I was worried," she said.

We walked for a while, past the Maritime Museum. Cargo ships and barges crowded the horizon. On the grass, gulls attacked a discarded sack of popcorn. Someone had left a sweater on a bench, the arms folded neatly into a square.

"So what are we going to do?" Shuzhen said.

"About Lloyd and the Exiles? I'm not sure. Common sense says they're involved, at least some of them. The evidence points a different way." I gestured at the water. "Using a boat, using an axe and machete. Those are very particular methods. A singular MO. Lloyd wouldn't have the patience, and Terry Rhodes wouldn't waste the time."

"Maybe it was pirates," Shuzhen said.

"Of one kind or another."

"What about the business?" She made a point of squeezing my hand. "No offence, and I know you mean well, but you don't know shit about running a company."

"Don't tell anyone," I said.

Bill Stoddard cheated Wakeland & Chen out of a fortune, and that rankled. Waging a campaign of terror against him would be satisfying, if unlikely to pay off. None of it was life and death. As we walked, I decided to focus on getting Maggie Zito out of pretrial. I'd figure out the money as I went.

Shuzhen halted. We were holding hands and I felt myself tugged back gently to stand with her.

"When I saw Maggie this morning, all beat up, I was worried," Shuzhen said. "Then I learned what she did, how she broke that woman's arm and treated it like nothing."

"She's in survival mode. It's a different mindset."

"I know, but for a moment I thought what a shitty thing I'd done. Dragging you back into this."

"Kicking and screaming," I said. "Without a say in the matter."

"Don't be glib. You were out, Dave."

"On hold," I said. "I don't think out exists for me."

She held me to her. My palm stroked the nape of her neck. Night had driven out the indigo and the vessels in the harbour were dark shadows beneath the stars. I should have offered reassurances but had none to spare.

THIRTY-ONE

September 2 lasted approximately fifty years. In that time, I ran down roughly a million leads, interviewed a third of the continent's population, consumed north of ten thousand cups of weak Earl Grey tea and racked up cab fares equal to the gross domestic product of Cameroon.

I tried running down the black Hyundai to no avail. The GMC that had rammed me had been stolen weeks ago from a parking lot in Richmond.

The male and female pair who attacked and interrogated Murray Fong had pulled no other robberies or home invasions. At least none where the victims had lived to describe them. No pattern of criminality to go on.

I tried the financial angle, running credit scores and looking up real estate. The Stacks and the Devlins had excellent credit. Charlie the Priest owned two homes and a cottage on Vancouver Island but had taken out a second mortgage. The McGuanes had paid off their home, and Junior had a good pension from the airline. Dirty Lloyd's credit was as bad as his driving.

Briony Zito owned a condo outright and had credit card debt. Nothing major. Maggie had borrowed against the house but had paid the loan off. Her business had significant debts, and Briony was keeping up the minimum payments.

I ran a check on Terry Rhodes and came up empty. A ghost, nothing to his name on paper.

No chance of speaking to Lloyd, who would be guarded in the post-op wing all day.

No word from Katz Itami about the witness.

A day spent striking out can sometimes still feel productive. If nothing else, you've eliminated several options that are *not* the lead you want. But September 2 felt endless, lugging my bruises and my reheated questions around the city, strikeouts piling up, each shrug or *I dunno* adding to the weight of the day.

I phoned Ray Dudgeon and asked if I could walk through the float home again.

"Why?" he asked. "To 'soak up the scene,' get in the headspace of the killer? That what TV detectives are doing these days?"

"Maybe I missed something," I said.

"You mean *we* missed something." Dudgeon was eating at his desk. I heard him pull the phone away as he chewed. Considerate of him. "I'll arrange for a constable to let you in. Remove nothing. Any money you find, I'm in for twenty percent."

In the late afternoon I stood on the small top deck outside the Stacks' bedroom, watching the water. I'd spent two hours going through every room on every floor. I'd examined the baseboards and flooring for secret holds, even running my hand around the ledge of the narrow gangplank along the side of the house. Nothing was secured in the water.

I tried to imagine the killers coming across False Creek at night. Lashing their boat to the cleat on the deck. Forcing the back door and waiting inside for Budd and Jan Stack to return home.

Very little had been left to chance. How had they known there was no alarm, that the place was guarded mostly by Budd's reputation? Had they been inside before?

I watched a party vessel careen below the Granville Bridge, canned music drifting over False Creek. The view and the roll of the current took some of the sting out of the day's frustrations.

After a while I took out my phone and called Felix Ramos. I told him I needed to speak with Charlie Corso. One on one, at the Priest's earliest convenience.

"Wouldn't advise it," Felix said. "The Priest is pissed at you. He was pissed even before this thing with his nephew."

"I made Lloyd try to flatten me into the viaduct?"

"The Priest doesn't think like everyone else."

For an Exiles prospect to say that was something. "Has he been in the Stacks' float home before?" I asked.

"What the hell's a float home? You mean the houseboat?"

"Whatever you call it—do you know for a certainty the Priest has been inside?"

"Think I drove him there a couple times," Felix said.

"And Rigger Devlin?"

"Dunno. Probably."

"What about Lloyd? Could his uncle have taken him along?"

"How'm I 'sposed to know everyone who's been through every fucking houseboat?"

"Float home," I said. "Get back to me about the meeting with the Priest."

Felix told me he'd try. I asked how Elodie was progressing on her costume.

"Don't try to be my friend," Felix said. "Got enough dead friends."

That made two of us.

Before I left the float home, I took a last look at the photos in the hallway. Budd Stack had taken them, according to the McGuanes. Otters at play. A seagull poised on a bench, blurry with motion as it flung off water. A sleek white yacht passing below the crest of the bridge, sunlight playing off the windows.

Some people collect paintings from convicted killers. Others use art as brownie points weighed up against the artist's misdeeds. A person's soul comes through their work, they say. I didn't know if I believed that. What if it's our own soul we're looking at, a mirror image? What if terrible people can have that ability? I admired Budd's photos and that fact made me uncomfortable.

The gull photo's frame was askew. Probably difficult to keep something level when the wall itself was sitting on water. The ident techs might have taken it down for examination.

Or they might not have.

I lifted the gull photo off the wall, turned it and examined the cardboard matte. No bubbles or seams. Nothing printed behind it. No Swiss bank numbers, microfilm or list of Soviet spies. I checked the other frames in turn. Zip. One last set of nothings to round out the day.

THIRTY-TWO

In the morning I borrowed Shuzhen's car and drove out of the city, east to Buntzen Lake. First through the gate when the park opened, I parked the Merc and walked the trail around the lake as the day warmed up. On the beach, I tossed my wallet and shirt on the sand, rolled up the cuffs of my pants and waded in. I thought of other times I'd come here. A case of Molson, someone's parents' station wagon.

Things were different now.

You're closing in on forty, Wakeland. You've been doing this work most of your life. Yet you're out of practice. Your partner is on leave. Your sister is in prison. Your business is a million dollars in the red. Your client is a violent offender who's also innocent, and you're dealing with a criminal organization that has killed people for shits and giggles. You also might be in love with your partner's cousin.

Where does that leave you?

The deep end, as always. I swam back in the direction of shore.

The parking lot was filling up now, camper vans and coolers. I draped a towel over the driver's seat before climbing in. A text had come in from a number I didn't recognize. *Noon. GameTown on Main.* Felix had set up the meeting with Charlie the Priest.

With two hours to kill, I left Shuzhen's Merc in the courthouse parking lot and walked down to the office. I let myself in, not bothering with the lights. In the closet, I found a dry cleaner's bag with an old blazer and dress pants. The outfit had been hanging there for over a year. I dressed, strapping on the shoulder holster, adjusting it so the revolver's bulk wouldn't be obvious. In the reflection of the office window I looked smartly dressed and reasonably competent. The wound on my cheek was no larger than a shaving cut.

I sat at Jeff's desk, opened the blinds, watched the dust spin in the morning light. Outside the window, a man kicked the side panel of a bus, storming off down Hastings. I sympathized.

Here's your chance. After years of second-guessing Jeff's business strategy, muttering under your breath how you'd do things differently, what's your first act going to be?

I had no idea how to drum up business. The white-collar world seemed full of Bill Stoddards, people with no values or vision, who were clearly profiting nonetheless. Add thirty-something years of East Van class resentment and you had an ape in a company blazer who felt more at home being punched than taking a meeting.

And what did that say about my idea of home?

"Mr. Wakeland, how are you on this beautiful morning?" Bill Stoddard was in a fine mood. He had me on speakerphone, judging from the connection. I imagined he was tipped back in his chair.

"I wanted to see if we could come to some sort of agreement," I said.

"As I told you, if you'd like to take this to court, by all means."

"I'm in court enough as it is." Stoddard's invoices were in front of me. "Last year you threw a birthday party for your daughter at Hatley Castle. You rented four security guards plus a metal detector."

"Yes, and she had a lovely sweet sixteen, thank you."

"You didn't pay us for that, either."

THE LAST EXILE · 165

"There's no point in you and I going over the same ground—"

"Different ground," I said. "Jeff billed you directly, to your home. Which I assume you wanted. Unless you were billing it on behalf of your company?"

A few seconds of silence. I enjoyed them.

"What's your point, Wakeland?"

"Call me Dave. I just wrecked your credit score, Bill. Your personal score. In the eyes of the banks, you're a bum."

"Over a few thousand dollars?"

"Gotta start somewhere. Do you use other company resources for personal use? I emailed your business partners to suggest they double-check."

"You're proving an irritation," Stoddard said.

"There's more coming. But don't let it ruin this beautiful day."

He told me to go to hell.

A real mature use of time and resources, I thought. Why not just put up a billboard across from his front door. YOU OWE ME MONEY, ASSHOLE.

Not such a bad idea.

GameTown had the look of a failing small business—the stencils on the windows of Mario and Solid Snake were sun faded and peeling. The sidewalk sign had been used to prop open the door. Lights off. Blinds drawn.

If it was a trap, there was nobody who'd come for me. And now that Jeff was on vacation, I had no one to call. I didn't want to involve the police until I'd found the answers I needed. For the same reason I couldn't call Shuzhen—as an officer of the court, she had less freedom to interpret things, and if I was being honest and a little chauvinistic, I didn't want her near the Exiles.

Kay would have been the one. By now my sister would have been well-trained, seasoned and as competent a security professional as could be. For the first time I understood what had really been taken from me—what I'd been robbed of, these last years. I could have done better for her. We could have helped each other.

No one else. So be it. I moved the sign and stepped into GameTown.

The cracked blinds let in a faint etchwork of grey light. Games and consoles from the last fifty years crammed the shelves. The display cases held more modern systems, as well as the valuable antiques. Posters on the walls for *Battletoads*, some variation of *Mortal Kombat*. Tabletop games and RPG guidebooks were stacked on the floor.

Next to the cash register was a chessboard under what looked like a glass pastry dome from an old diner. The beaded glass had a layer of fuzz on the top. Inside was perhaps the ugliest chess set I'd ever seen. Luigis and Yoshis instead of knights and rooks. Another display case held an old Nintendo gun next to a dead silverfish. I wondered how much money the business made or lost every year. A street-level space on Main Street would cost a steep rent. How much of Charlie the Priest's money was washed here through cash transactions?

No one was inside. I made my presence known by rummaging a pile of cartridges. I'd had *Punch-Out!!* back in the day. *Blades of Steel* and NBA *Jam*. A place like this, you could draw nostalgia deep into your lungs like opium smoke, hold it and never re-emerge.

The backroom had boxes of wires and power supplies. A disk-cleaning machine. A computer monitor displaying a bouncing deck of cards as its screensaver.

"I'm here," I called out. *Here*, I texted the number.

My skin felt dry and tacky from the dust. Flies buzzed. The office computer made that wheeze-tick that old computers do. I had to piss and wanted to wash my hands. A sign on the wall said

NO CUSTOMER WASHROOM but there was a door at the other end of the backroom.

The washroom door opened partway. Was stuck on something. I recognized that dead-weight feeling. Putting a shoulder against the door caved in the hollow plywood. Whatever was behind the door slumped and was shoved away. I reached in for the light. No switch. A bare bulb, a chain hanging down from its socket.

From outside, a sound familiar to me from Maggie Zito's house. The unmuffled engine of a bike.

On the washroom floor was a body. The face had been bloodied past recognition, the chest flattened by heavy boots. The buzzing was loud here, an uproar of flies, the smell of blood fetid and unmistakable. The dead man wore a blue silk shirt, now damp with fluid. Murray Fong had been wearing the same shirt.

Assaulted by the sight and gagging on the smell, I lurched out of the office and through the shop, catching my cuff on the corner of the display, as the window exploded in a bash of glass, the engine furious and right out front, the blinds swaying frantically. Through the slats a projectile, sailing toward me, shimmering with fire.

THIRTY-THREE

The bottle was made of thick green glass. If it had shattered on impact the spray of burning fluid would have engulfed me. Instead it whacked the display case, took a rightward bounce and exploded against the floor. The flames went up.

Trapped, the fire spreading between me and the door. The heat fierce. I retreated into the office. Trying to think of how deep the building was. Shared walls, or was there a back entrance? Where would that be?

I heard a second bottle crash. The front room was ablaze now, the punched-out window feeding oxygen to the growing conflagration. No secret escape hatch in the washroom. No windows. From the floor, what was left of Murray Fong grinned up at me.

Shoving against the shelves in the office, guessing whoever ran the shop was cramped for space. If there was a back door in here, it had likely been blocked by shelving. My hand felt behind the case— yes—the frame of a door, a stubby handle.

I knocked the buckets of cables down, the shelves, too, rocking the case away from the wall. The handle was now visible. The fire was creeping into the office, a loud chuckling sound as it consumed the shop. A stink of burnt plastic and circuitry. Smoke. I tucked my nose and mouth into my shirt. The case rocked back and forth and each time a millimetre farther away from the hidden door. I rocked it more vigorously. The case shuffled like a very tall and very awkward person dancing for the first time.

A manual fell off the top, pages spraying across my head. No matter. The case was far enough away now to reveal the door. No hinges, which meant it opened out. I hit the door where it had been papered over with posters. No movement. Again, still nothing. Like striking brick. The door was boarded up from the outside.

Now the fire was feeding off the shelves of books and cardboard, devouring it all, toeing over into the office. My eyes watered.

I could run through. Accept that I'd be burned. Maybe the Priest wasn't waiting outside to finish me. On the computer desk, there was a mug full of screwdrivers. I took hold of the largest one, a flathead, thinking it was better to rush for safety, to go out swinging for their eyes, rather than being pressed farther back by the onrush of flames. Like a trapped rat—no, bad comparison. Rats could chew their way through walls. I'd be trapped like that dead silverfish in the display.

Into the washroom. Up onto the toilet seat. I couldn't chew but I could dig. Balancing, I pried out the fan and tossed it, ripped down a handful of wiring, prodded at the ceiling material with the flathead. I was rewarded with a face full of rubble. I kept digging, jabbing, working out chunks of drywall with my free hand, knees braced against the tank, now standing on the tank, my head up to the hole and then through, followed by a shoulder, wishing I was a narrower man, hitting wood and digging around it. A joist.

Up into the ceiling. Braced against the rafters. Bashing through a stained and water-weakened subfloor to claw foam, to slice linoleum. Pulling myself up into another washroom and leaving the fire below me. Gnawing right out of the hellmouth.

A second-floor apartment with a back staircase. A dead sprinkler system on the ceiling, the nozzle painted over. I tumbled down the staircase to the alley, leaned against a bin for organic waste. Almost fitting.

Someone asked if I was okay. I wanted to tell them *yes, fine*, and *please leave me alone*. I had breathing to do, and that took concentration.

From out front I heard sirens and the cutting tenor of the fire truck. Music.

THIRTY-FOUR

I offered the cab driver double the meter for the mess I was making of his back seat. We looped around English Bay until I was sure we weren't being followed. I told him to drop me at the new Oakridge complex at the foothills of Little Mountain. My mother's address.

Hanging around to tell the police about the body would have been sensible, as would getting checked out at the hospital. I was too filthy, too pissed. Revenge was never something I wasted time on. The job entailed a certain amount of unrecoverable loss. An allotment of personal damage. Life worked pretty much the same. The successes meant nothing without the risk, and it all went by too quickly to keep score.

But this was murder, intimidation and torture all at once. It was also a violation of trust. I'd been out of my mind making a deal with the Exiles, but I'd held to my side of it, dammit.

Did Terry Rhodes sanction this? Did he know about it at all? I'd make sure to bring it up the next time we spoke.

My eyes stung from the smoke, and my face had that dried-tears feel to it. Still warm from the fire. At the back of my throat I could still taste drywall dust.

The Priest on his own, or with Rhodes's blessing. Or maybe there had been no meeting at all, and this was Felix Ramos's work. The prospect proving his value to the Exiles.

My revolver was still in its shoulder rig beneath the ruined blazer. It hadn't made much of a difference.

My mother's decision to sell her house had been motivated by finance, a way to clear her debts using the equity. The home she'd lived in for forty-odd years now sat empty, waiting for her neighbour to die and the neighbour's kids to sell to a land assembly. Then that block of Laurel Street would be made into something charmless and high-density. Like her new home. The Oakridge neighbourhood, which had boasted a dowdy mall and a good library when I was a kid, was now a vibrant mixed-income community in the heart of the city. Residential towers and parking complexes, a shopping centre larger than a Gulf island. My mother buzzed me in and told me which elevator would convey me to the seventh floor.

A stiff, informal but awkward hug, trying not to get crud from the fire on her shift, tracking plenty of it onto her welcome mat.

"What are you doing here, David?" she said.

Ours was not a warm relationship, but neither was it contentious. Knowing she was my adoptive mother, biologically an aunt, made this easier. Agnes Wakeland was tough, a police widow, and had disdain for dangerous professions and reckless people.

"In town for a few days," I said. "I was hoping you might have a spare change of clothes."

"All your junk you either took or I threw out."

"Maybe a gentleman caller left something?"

Shaking her head, my mother said, "Strip, and I'll throw these in, if it's not too much of a madhouse in the laundry room."

The blazer went straight into the trash. She scowled at the pistol but didn't comment.

The shower felt good. I stayed under until the smell of the fire had rinsed out of my skin. Some lilac-scented conditioner just in case. I sat wrapped in a towel, in my mother's second favourite easy chair, as she watched a Jays game on cable. When the game was finished, 4-3 over the Phillies, she shut off the set.

"So what trouble were you in this time?" she said. Not accusatory. My son, this is what he does.

"Fire. Long story."

She nodded. "And who are you staying with?"

"Jeff's cousin."

"Is she Asian, too?"

"Of course. Why would you even—"

"Well, these days, I don't like to assume." The racist's pre-empt: you young people and your world of surprises.

"Shuzhen's a lawyer," I said. An equally dumb rejoinder.

"You must like her quite a bit."

I shrugged. "Why must I?"

"To come here to clean up instead of going straight to her."

"All right," I said, "I like her, and I'm using you. That's what family's for, isn't it?"

"You tell me."

My mother woke up her iPad and checked her mail. Nodding, she opened an old spiral notebook and wrote "+20" and the date. Recording her wager and the payoff. She'd had the same style of notebook for a decade. I could relate to that.

"Up or down for the week?" I asked.

"A few bucks up. I just play with pin money. So easy now, it's all online."

"Jeff gambles a bit. Blackjack."

She nodded as if unsurprised. "Well, those people..."

I held up my hand, waving off her treatise on the Oriental mindset. "Isn't there a *Law & Order* we can watch?"

"You say something. I respond. Then you get upset."

"Because your response is shit, Ma."

"Fine."

"I'm sorry." Apologizing for taking umbrage at bigotry—that was family in a nutshell. I cast about for a safe topic. "How do you like your new place? Neighbours nice?"

"They're all right," she said. "I'm doing a little gardening. Arvind, the man across the hall, he used to work at VanDusen Gardens."

"Great."

"He's from Trinidad. Well, his family is Indian, but he was born in Trinidad."

"Like V.S. Naipaul."

"Who?"

"An author. Never mind. That's great you get along with somebody."

"Actually," she said, grimacing with embarrassment, "Arvind is taking me to a restaurant tonight."

"A date? Damn."

"Just a little supper."

I suppressed the smile that I knew she'd find patronizing. "Happy for you, Ma." I was, and surprised, and curious.

"He's bald," she said after a good silence.

"Maybe it'll grow back."

We played bridge, and she skunked me, taking another ten dollars, which she entered into her notebook. I made tea while she rotated the laundry. Pouring her a cup and settling back into the chair, I watched her frown at my collection of scars.

"You know doctors can get rid of those with whatsitcalled, cosmetic surgery."

"They serve as a good reminder," I said.

"Of being careless?"

I let her have that one. Spending time in her world always felt claustrophobic. Narrow, insulated. The things I loved about the city she was happy to keep out. At the same time, though, she'd embraced the tide of development that had led to my leaving. When the time came, she'd adapted better than I had.

"Have you seen Kay yet?" my mother asked.

"Haven't, no."

"Written to her? I'm sure she'd like a letter."

"I'm not sure I'd like that," I said.

"What did you just say to me about family using one another? Where she's at just now, David, don't you think your sister could use you?"

I patted my chest, a direct hit. She had me.

When I was dressed I hugged her and wished her well on her date. My mother said she hoped whatever I was in town for would work out for the best. Two people who fundamentally misunderstand one another, uneasy at the bond that connected them. That was also family.

THIRTY-FIVE

In my scramble from the fire, I'd cracked the screen of my phone. It no longer lit up but rumbled with an incoming call. The speaker was broken as well: Katz Itami's voice was distorted and low, missing the tenor frequencies.

"The other day, what you asked me for," Katz said. "That picture of our dads from way back? Took a lot of searching, but I found it."

"That picture means a lot to me," I said.

"Pretty fragile, so I'd rather hand it over to you in person."

"Your place?"

"How about CRAB Park? Soon as you can."

Quarter to four now. I got up and dressed with the lights off. George Eliot triumphantly filled the warm vacancy in the bed. I had gone to the apartment planning to tell Shuzhen everything but had passed out before she got home. Later when I woke up I heard her in the shower, probably coming back from a swim. I'd slipped back into sleep.

She woke up as I was tying my shoes. "Something up?" she asked, standing in her bedroom doorway in her robe.

"Maybe a lead on the witness," I said.

"I'll drive. Ready in five minutes."

The streets were empty and she drove fast, cornering the way all owners of European luxury cars must want to. Breakneck down

Pender, turning over the connector to the meeting spot. CRAB Park, short for Create a Real Accessible Beach, had been reclaimed by the city from the dying cannery and logging trades. Wealthy young mothers and middle-aged professionals kept to the beach and jogging trails, walking carefully bred dogs or pushing carefully bred children in strollers. The poor and homeless held to the grass, some pitching tents. Every so often the city would issue a compassionate-sounding press release and sweep the tents out of the park. Homeless problem solved.

At present it was raining, and the only person on the beach was Katz. He held a large grey umbrella and wore a camel hair trench coat that billowed with the early morning breeze. The image created was of a lone mourner at a rained-out funeral.

"Who's this?" he said. "Thought we'd be alone."

"Shuzhen Chen, Maggie Zito's lawyer."

"I shouldn't be telling you this shit, let alone somebody else."

"She's not somebody else," I said. "It's Shuzhen's case, and she can keep a secret."

"Glad one of you can."

"Dave only asked on my account," Shuzhen said. "Thank you for helping us."

Katz shook his head but raised the umbrella to offer a corner for our protection. He unfolded a page of yellow paper torn from a legal pad.

"They're playing this very close to the vest," he said. "Your guy is a key part of Eiger."

"What's Eiger?" I asked.

"Means 'ogre' in German. It's a mountain in the Swiss Alps, one of the most dangerous to climb. Operation Eiger is an inter-agency clusterfuck waiting to happen. The feds, the Mounties, and a dozen local PDs banding together to smash organized crime."

"Who's the target?"

Katz shook his head. "Not sure, only they're based here in BC. The Mounties like to get clever by starting their code names with the same letter as the region they take place. E as in Division E, meaning the West."

As in Exiles, I thought.

"What's Operation Whatever have to do with the witness?" Shuzhen asked.

"Their testimony is a big part of Eiger's first round of indictments," Katz said. "That's why the Crown is being so tight-lipped. They're probably being leaned on to keep the name out of court documents."

Katz consulted his sheet. I was half under the umbrella, one shirt sleeve soaked. My feet dug in wet sand.

"North Face is the code name they're using. Through family ties, the witness has connections to the upper echelons. What else, North Face is being paid for his testimony. Mid-six figures from the memo I saw."

"So Maggie's case is separate from Operation Eiger—nice name, by the way—but shares the same witness."

"Appears that way, yeah."

The rain had turned fierce. I stamped in the sand, trying to stay warm. "How does a guy with top connections somehow witness a double murder? Right place, right time? His whole testimony could be a yarn spun to save his own skin." A hardened criminal bargaining for their life would have no qualms throwing an innocent woman like Maggie Zito under the bus.

"I can't judge the veracity of his testimony," Katz said. "What I do know, Eiger is a top priority. Careers get made off cases like this."

"In other words, if North Face is full of shit, no one on your side wants to hear it."

THE LAST EXILE · 179

"Fuck you, Wakeland."

Shuzhen intervened. "We need North Face's name and tombstone details. Please."

Katz looked like he wanted to leave, even if it meant storming into the water and swimming away. But he held up the sheet and read off the name. "Corso, Lloyd. Know him?"

"He tried to run me over the other day," I said.

"Shame he isn't a better driver."

Dirty Lloyd Corso, the marquee witness in a major organized crime operation. It made a certain kind of sense. Lloyd knew the top players in the Exiles organization, courtesy of his uncle, yet wasn't a biker himself. I didn't know why he'd frame Maggie Zito. Proving Lloyd a liar would be difficult. Careers were riding on his testimony. Lives, too.

"I appreciate this," I told Katz.

He didn't answer. Shuzhen and I headed to the car as he walked to the waterline. At last glance, Katz Itami had twisted the yellow paper into a torch and was trying to set it on fire, turning the umbrella and his body to shelter the small blue flame. It seemed like a hopeless endeavour.

THIRTY-SIX

"My first-year torts prof used to give us these brain-busters." Shuzhen scraped cappuccino foam from the rim of her cup with a spoon. "Theseus buys a ship from the Acme Shipbuilding Company. He replaces each individual part of the ship. He then finds the hull has sprung a leak. For extra credit, write five hundred words on why Acme isn't liable. That kind of thing."

I nodded and continued playing with the string from my second pot of tea. We'd been in Dose Espresso Bar on West Broadway for some time, sitting under a painting of Bret "The Hitman" Hart. We had talked around Dirty Lloyd Corso, AKA North Face, the whys and hows and what-nexts. Nothing had been decided.

"My favourite brain-buster was about lying," Shuzhen said. "Your witness is a compulsive liar. He tells you he's lying. Is he telling the truth? What's the strategy for deposing someone like that?"

"What's the answer?"

"Isn't one," Shuzhen said. "Marks were assigned based on how well you argued either way."

"I was kind of hoping there'd be an answer."

Shuzhen pushed her cup away, suddenly restless. "If this guy's like you say he is, it wouldn't be hard getting Lloyd on the stand and pointing out he's full of shit. We might even get his criminal record admitted. And any promises the Crown made to him."

"A six-figure deal is a substantial promise."

She nodded. "But the Crown knows all this, too. Part of their deal would be for Lloyd to admit to everything he's ever done, get it all down, so that it can be presented as proof of his honesty. An inveterate liar telling the truth. See what I mean, Dave?"

Too clearly. What I couldn't see was a way to defuse that testimony in time to do Maggie Zito any good. Lloyd's criminality would be no surprise to anyone. Even if his deal caused a modicum of outrage, the prospect of netting top bikers would be an acceptable trade-off to most people. To me, under normal circumstances. Rolling up the lower rungs to grab the higher ones was standard practice.

There was a darker problem that I hesitated to mention to Shuzhen. Doubtless one of the targets of Operation Eiger would be Terry Rhodes. If the nephew of his sergeant-at-arms was planning betrayal, that information would be valuable to Rhodes. And dangerous to anyone who withheld it from him.

Chances to successfully prosecute someone like Rhodes were scant. Jeopardizing the operation could leave him on the street to inflict damage on new victims. On the other hand, if the investigation fell apart, which seemed very possible given their star witness, anyone who sided against Rhodes would be a target.

Lloyd was still in the hospital. Trying to speak with him unofficially might be possible, but that plan had drawbacks. Nothing would be on record, so it wouldn't directly help Maggie out of custody. It would tip our hand to anyone watching. And, of course, there was no reason to think Lloyd would tell us the truth.

I wondered how they'd spin their star witness trying to run me off the road. Honestly, my lord, they might tell the judge, who's to say which vehicle was chasing which?

Shuzhen had pulled a compact from her pocket. She stared at the mirror and grimaced. "I look like a cat's ass. Three hours' sleep and no makeup."

I watched as she cleared her side of the table, pulled her hair back and began pencilling and lipsticking. I liked watching the process.

"Are you going to tell Nimisha?" I asked.

"Not sure yet. I promised your friend Katz I wouldn't. But if it's in Maggie's best interest, how can I not, right?"

She softened the dark bands under her eyes. Checked the mirror and found the result acceptable. So did I.

"What's your next step?" she asked.

"Felix. He owes me an explanation."

"Does he, Dave? Seems you think he's on our side."

"Not quite." I struggled with how to express what I thought about the prospect.

"Pass me a napkin, will you?"

I did. Shuzhen wiped her mouth and began applying a shade of chrysanthemum red.

"If Felix was behind torching that shop I'd be surprised. Rhodes told him to assist me. I don't see a lowly prospect like Felix going against the boss of bosses."

"There's more to it, isn't there? You don't really think he'd go against you."

"We're cut from the same cloth."

"He's a fucking biker, Dave."

"Similar cloth, then. As a teen I boxed at the old Astoria gym. There was a group of us. Nobody had what you'd call a normal home life. That age, the wrong friend, the wrong pill, one too many slaps at home—your whole life gets determined."

"Bullshit," Shuzhen said. "You always get to choose."

"That's my point. Some of the kids everyone thought hopeless turned it around for themselves."

Pouting, Shuzhen retouched a corner of her mouth. "You think Felix is gonna change?"

"He doesn't think he has a choice. There was a time I felt that way, too."

"And how'd you fix it?"

"Still working on that."

She smiled and shut her compact. "How's this look?"

I leaned over and kissed her, hard enough and long enough to make a mess of her work.

After the family butcher shop went under, and he was struck by the Exiles, Felix Ramos found work at the port. He had his forklift ticket and his St. John Ambulance certification. He put in enough hours to justify his income tax records, paid his union dues regularly and ate his lunches alone.

At noon, two food trucks were set up for business along the fenced enclosure near the entrance to the port. Another was stationed in the shady beachfront parking lot of New Brighton Park. At 12:06 I watched Felix buy a katsu curry and take it to a secluded bench. One of his napkins blew away toward the water.

An hour earlier I'd picked up the van from Devlin Auto Body. Rigger wasn't in today, but Darlene Devlin took me through the refurbishments. I'd been lucky, the scrapyard had a few Kias from which to poach the parts. The passenger door was stiff, and the sliding door was now manual only. The upholstery on the middle bench didn't match. The dents had been knocked out with a mallet, and they'd given the Beast a new coat of matte black paint. Cheap and ugly, but it drove, and the sound system still worked.

I listened to *Let England Shake* and watched Felix fork brown curry into his mouth, alternating his attention between his phone and the view of the water. No one approached him. A few other workers congregated to smoke or eat tacos.

The bikers and the ports: a long association. The day job of many members also gave them control over the millions of shipping containers that came through each year. Since the port police had been disbanded, there was little supervision. An open secret who ran things now. Where was Marlon Brando when you needed him? Not on the East Van waterfront.

At 12:22 I left the van, walking behind the bench at a diagonal, with trees and a jungle gym hiding my approach. Felix didn't spot me until I was twenty feet from him. I wanted him to spot me there. His reaction went from annoyance to surprise. "The hell are you here for?"

"I'm a ghost," I said. "I burned up in a fire you set."

"I don't set fires, Wakeland."

"You set up that meeting."

Felix let the container fall to his feet. The gulls on the nearby trash bin took notice. I kept my hands in my pocket and drew closer. My shoulder rig was unsnapped, the pistol an easy reach beneath my flannel shirt.

"I just do what they tell me," he said.

"Must make for a shitty existence, having no free will. Not much fun, you ask me."

"Hey, you wanted that meeting. I was the one told you not to push it."

Not backing down, not fleeing, but not defensive, either. "You're saying I provoked you into burning me alive?"

"I don't know shit about that."

"Yes, you do."

"Calling me a liar now?"

Flexing his hands, tense. Injured pride could be a way to deny what you did, playing up how offended you were even to be suspected. Felix wasn't going that far. He lacked the dramatic urge. At his feet, one of the gulls darted in to peck rice.

"Had to know," I said.

"So now you know. All I did was pass on your message."

I held up my phone, the cracked screen showing the text I received. "Recognize this number?"

Felix shrugged, shook his head.

"I still need that meeting with the Priest."

He scraped the grass with his foot, causing the bird to flutter off a few feet. "Time for me to get back to work."

I shifted into his way.

"We gonna throw hands in front of everybody?" he asked.

"If that's what it takes. Since I've been back I've been slapped, stabbed, run over and set on fire. I'm an absurdly hard person to kill, Felix. You can't scare me off or bribe me. I can't take a hint, and I'm not amenable to reason."

"That's a very nice little speech."

"Till now I've been cutting you slack because I think there's something decent and salvageable about you. I'm prepared to be wrong. Now take out your other phone and make the call."

Felix looked around, at me, past me. People were starting to pay attention. He sighed, reached into his pocket, and brought out a second, smaller cell.

"How'd you know?" he asked.

"It's what I would do."

He dialed a preprogrammed number. "Put the man on," he said. "Right…Yes, sir. Wakeland…Well, I guess he *wasn't* inside since he's right here."

Felix's voice was becoming petulant. He forced himself to answer with respect.

"That's right, sir. A meeting…I finish at four…I can't leave now…no…all right." Stabbing the screen to end the conversation.

"We're meeting right away?" I asked.

Felix nodded. "Fast enough for you, asshole?"

THIRTY-SEVEN

The parking lot behind St. Paul's was moderately full. I parked the Beast in a corner with a view of the side entrance. The stereo played Nancy Wilson, *Yesterday's Love Songs/Today's Blues*. The best voice committed to two-inch tape, for my money. Next to me, Felix occupied himself with his phone.

After eleven minutes of waiting, the only people I'd seen were hospital staff, nurses in scrubs, a couple of harried-looking surgeons.

"Thought you said our meeting was right away?" I asked.

Felix didn't look up from his screen. "This is what it's like all the time. They make you wait. Sometimes just for the fuck of it."

"He's visiting his nephew?"

A nod. "We meet after."

If speaking with Lloyd Corso was out of the question, laying eyes on him might still be worthwhile. Opportunity presented itself. "Let's pay our respects," I said.

At a kiosk in the lobby I bought a Mylar balloon that said BEST WISHES ON YOUR SPECIAL DAY. We took it up to the post-op floor, smiled at the receptionist and headed toward Lloyd's private room. A uniformed constable was posted out front and scrutinized us as we approached.

"How's Lloyd holding up?" I asked him.

"One visitor at a time. Already someone inside."

Through the inset I saw the Carhartt-covered back of Charlie the Priest, blocking most of the bed. The blinds were open and sun bathed a spray of baby's breath and pink camellias in a grey vase. Cards galore. Everyone wanted Lloyd to get well soon.

The Priest patted the foot of the bed-bound figure and turned to the door. Saw me and did not shrink in fear or try to escape through the window. Charlie Corso opened the door when he was ready.

I presented him with the balloon. "For your nephew. How's he doing?"

Up close Charlie the Priest gave off a smell of stale coffee. Older than he looked at first glance, but with an athletic roll to his broad shoulders. The white wool trim of his jacket had faded orange. His beard was greying in patches, uneven and tangled.

The officer stood, ready to jump in. We both expected strong words and violence. But the Priest took the stem of the balloon, gave a curt nod of thanks and floated it into Lloyd's room. He pointed toward the exit and said he'd be right down.

As we waited for the elevator, I saw the Priest in conference with the police officer.

"Get to test out your theory," Felix said.

"What's that?"

"Whether or not you're hard to kill."

The parking lot was emptying. We watched an ambulance pull through the turnaround and disgorge a patient on a gurney. No siren or lights. I thought of a nurse I'd once dated, a widow. I wondered what happened to her.

The Priest stormed out, spotted us standing by the van. His stride closed the distance immediately.

"Juvenile fucking stunt. Fucking idiot." He was speaking to Felix. "You brought him here?"

"You told me—"

Before he could finish the sentence, the Priest swatted him across the skull, hard enough to knock the prospect's knees into the asphalt. Felix stayed down a second out of deference, spat and rose up.

"And you." The Priest turned his wrath in my direction. "You put my nephew in here. They're saying he's gotta get screws put in his spine."

I knew what was coming. The accusation would be followed by a blow. You'd be too busy protesting your innocence to ward it off. I'd just seen him do that to Felix. Discipline in the ranks, imposing his reality on the world.

When his hand wound back I lunged forward, my left fist gloved with metal. The knucks caught him on the ear. It was like striking a side of beef. The Priest took a step back. Shocked, maybe a little impressed.

"Mr. Tough," he said.

"Not tough, but curious why you tried to kill me."

"Did I?"

"GameTown. A Molotov cocktail. A dead man named Murray Fong."

"Don't know shit about that. You were in court, though. Working for that bitch that killed my friends."

"Someone framed her."

"Bullshit." Spittle had trickled into his beard. He slurped it back and wiped his chin. "Ask your questions or get out of here," he said.

"Before he died, what was Budd Stack working on?"

"His fucking tan. Came home from vacation, a few weeks later he's dead. And Jan, too. That pig in court's gonna pay, I don't give a fuck."

"Did Lloyd know the Stacks?"

"Course. His fuckin' godparents."

"I need to speak to Lloyd," I said.

"You leave him the fuck alone."

"Either I talk to Lloyd or Terry Rhodes. Ask your nephew which he prefers. Your boss might be interested in what Lloyd's been doing behind his back." Grinning, I added, "You too."

"Terry and me are tighter'n shit. Closest thing to brothers."

"That's who they always send for you."

For an instant all three of us seemed curious what the Priest would do. What he wanted to do was obvious. He scowled and snorted and heeled the dirt and somehow held his violent impulses in check.

"You'll get your meeting," he said. "Keep in mind, though, you got family, too."

"How'd you know?" Felix asked as I put the Beast in gear. We headed back toward the port.

"Know what?"

"That the Priest was thieving behind Terry Rhodes's back."

"You tell me," I said.

He thought about it as we trailed through traffic on Hastings. A brawl outside the gospel mission. A few blocks east, a film crew adjusting a light diffuser.

"You just guessed," Felix said.

"Not a guess. Everybody's stealing all the time. You told me that. And if they're not, it doesn't matter. The rumour's enough to get him killed."

"The Priest has been with Terry forever. He trusts him the most."

"That's why it's believable."

I let him off at the turn for New Brighton. Felix wasn't a dope, but he didn't grasp how much his world was ruled by power and paranoia. This wasn't a gang. This was palace intrigue, and trust wasn't possible. Every neck was only a whisper away from the block.

THIRTY-EIGHT

I spent an hour at the office working on matters unrelated to Lloyd Corso or his uncle Charlie the Priest. Mostly looking for money, which didn't want to be found. The firm's lawyer, Shauna Kensington, told me over the phone that suing Bill Stoddard wouldn't be financially sound. "Double or nothing territory," she called it.

Jeff hadn't restocked the office liquor cabinet. In fact there no longer was an office liquor cabinet. I slugged back tap water, trying to think of a solution that didn't exist.

"We could sue him personally," I suggested.

"Dave," Shauna said, in the tone she reserved for judges who were hard of hearing. "Even if you won, my fees would eat up a big chunk of that. Plus the time we'd both be spending."

"You could waive your fee," I said.

"And you could make another million. Guess which is more likely?"

"What about the principle?" I asked.

The lawyer laughed at me. "The principle, Dave, is you got into business with a skeeze, got overextended and now he's playing the odds you won't survive it. Now that isn't what you'd call gentlemanly conduct, but neither is it illegal."

"So I can't sue?"

"Of course you can. You just can't win. And I can't afford to work a losing case on the cuff."

I hung up and stared around the reception area, trying to convince myself Shauna's assessment was wrong. A losing case.

Well, defeat wasn't the end of things. Scuttle the company, declare bankruptcy, take the small payment Stoddard would pony up and go our separate ways. Jeff could find a job in the corporate sector easily. And I could slink back to Montreal.

Or not.

I thought about this as I locked up and went to meet Shuzhen. She'd texted me an address on Jervis Street, along with the word *Labyrinth*. The destination was a half-hour walk from the office, through Davie Village. A bar, I figured. As I got closer, I saw the severe angle of an Anglican steeple. The doors were open.

Inside, up a double staircase, was a large room with a blond wood floor. Painted on it was what looked like a maze. A sign said this was a painted replica of the labyrinth in Chartres. Shuzhen was among those walking it, barefoot. I slipped off my Red Wings and joined her.

"I thought Labyrinth was some cool lawyer bar," I whispered.

"There are no cool lawyer bars."

She carried her suit coat, a grey knit Ann Taylor, a white shirt and blue scarf around her neck. The ends of the scarf, I saw, covered a faint tea stain on the collar. She caught me looking and adjusted it.

"Want to walk with me?" she asked.

Unlike a maze there was only one path. The few people ahead of us moved through it silently, weaving concentrically toward the centre. I followed Shuzhen, stepping into the space she had occupied. The idea was to move through slowly, in contemplation. Sure I was missing something, I aped the others and tried to look deep in thought. All I thought about was the distance between myself and the woman in front of me, of closing that distance, circling her with my hands, kissing her ear and throat. Damning thoughts for a place of worship.

We walked out into the street noise without exchanging words. The foot traffic on Davie was heavy and swift. We merged into it and I took her hand.

"You do this often?" I asked.

"I like walking it. Clears my mind."

"It's quiet," I said. "There aren't many quiet places in the city anymore."

We crossed the street, moving single file as a gaggle of overdressed executives marched past, one of them walking in the street. The smell of cologne faded back into exhaust and fried food. Our hands were still joined.

"I go into things all the way," I said. "Half-ass nothing. Jeff is the same. It's been very effective, but there's been a cost, or at least diminishing returns."

"You both need a hobby," Shuzhen said.

"I need something. Especially looking at you, with swimming and labyrinths and career."

"Women have to work smarter."

I could feel her pulse, her tempo moving through my fingers. Through Nelson Park, the benches full of pigeon feeders and can collectors.

"What do you want?" she asked. "When this is all over."

"Nothing major. A million dollars and a home. World peace."

"Can't help you with any of that," Shuzhen said. "Would you like to go back to my place?"

"Even better."

THIRTY-NINE

Two objects can't occupy the same space and time—but we did our best.

This was and wasn't the first time. We were different people now, older, both tougher and more fragile. There was surprisingly little awkwardness, no tremor of guilt. This time we weren't getting away with something. A tenderness familiar and exciting.

"You know I still haven't seen your room," I said. We lay across her roommate's bed, Shuzhen curled into my side. Sharing the lone bottle of Tsingtao from the back of her fridge.

"And you never will. My room's a mess, and the mattress isn't as comfy." She rested the bottle on my chest for a moment as she shifted position.

After a while, I asked what she was thinking.

"That this is different but also not different. When I started work at the office, you were kind of intense. Not mean but, I dunno, standoffish."

"Glad I wasn't mean," I said, putting the bottle on the nightstand, resting my hand between us. "You were different, too."

"How?"

"I don't know the right word. Bubbly?"

"Fuck you, I was never 'bubbly.'"

"Excited at the world, I guess."

"I felt anxious," she said. "Before I moved here I didn't know Jeff all that well. I saw him at big family events in Guangzhou when we were kids, but not often. Talk about intense. Plus, back then I was homesick."

"What about now?" I asked.

"Homesick? Oh, sometimes. But this is home, too."

I put my hand to better use and kissed the corner of her mouth.

"Where's that hand going?" Shuzhen asked.

"Someplace smutty."

"Oh. Good."

Two people in a bed was one too many for George Eliot to make a comfortable nest. In the early morning, while Shuzhen slept, I got up to heat water for tea. The cat stared at me quizzically from atop a couch cushion.

"You'll have the place to yourself soon enough," I told her.

At seven the intercom rang. Shuzhen padded from the washroom to the wall and answered. I heard Ray Dudgeon's voice asking if Dave was there.

"Would you tell him to come down please?" Dudgeon's voice was exceedingly polite. A sign something was amiss.

"Tell him yourself," Shuzhen said.

"Dave, I've got a request to bring you in for a talk. I'm not here alone. Save us both a lot of hassle if you get dressed and come down."

No choice. Why now? I was achingly close to meeting with Lloyd Corso, finding out why he'd implicated Maggie Zito. Lloyd's uncle had promised me that meeting. It was in Charlie the Priest's interest to do that. Wasn't it?

Shuzhen in her bathrobe watched, arms crossed, as I gathered my clothes. My shirt had ended up beneath the bed. With a foot she dragged it out and flung it at me.

"You're just gonna do what they want?" she asked.

"Pretty much. A phrase like 'bring you in for a little talk' has an unspoken 'or else' attached to it."

"You have rights. I'm your counsel and I'm coming with."

"Not necessary," I said.

"Wasn't asking."

Dudgeon was waiting in the lobby with two burly constables in rain slickers. It was pouring outside. The staff sergeant looked away from Shuzhen, bashful.

If Shuzhen felt self-conscious standing in the lobby in her robe, interrogating three cops, she didn't show it. "Is my client under arrest?"

Dudgeon looked to me to explain, but I gave a hard luck shrug.

"The deputy chief constable would like a word with Dave."

"How long a word?"

"I'll have him back in an hour, hour and a half."

"I'll pick him up from the station in one hour from now exactly," Shuzhen said. "Future requests come through my office. No more unofficial chats."

"Dave and I are old friends," Dudgeon said.

She nodded her head at the others. "They're not."

Before we left, she took a photo of me and one of the three officers. Documenting my condition and the people responsible for me. As he led me out to the car, Dudgeon said, "Should've got in bed with a lawyer a long time ago."

The box smelled of bleach. No cuffs, just a table and chairs and bare brick walls. A camera up in the corner. 7:45 going on the end of the world.

When they banged you into the little room and left you to pore over all your misdeeds, they were allowing your own mind to do their work for them. Given enough time, an anxious brain plays out all the scenarios it's seen on TV. All the clever and brutal things that can be done.

My time on the police force had been brief but instructive. I'd watched suspects break down, minds stewing in paranoia. Knowing how it works doesn't mean it won't work on you.

Given enough time, they get everybody.

Just a friendly chat, I reminded myself. How exactly did Ray Dudgeon know where I was staying? Had he worked it out of my mother, or had she volunteered the information? Or was I under surveillance?

I waited, thinking of Shuzhen. Could still feel her teeth on my shoulder, the stubble spot she'd missed on her left calf. I no longer felt guilty and I wondered if that was progress, if that made me more or less mature. Before, I'd never envisioned a future between us. And now?

Uncertain. All I knew was that our time together was special. It made the world more wondrous and more frightening. It made being away from her hurt.

Time cabled out. Moments that could have been millennia. Continents split and swamplands dried up. Civilizations rose and fell. And long after God called the game, the door finally opened. My visions of apocalypse dispelled. Ferguson MacLeish walked in alone. The deputy chief constable of operations sat and made himself comfortable.

"You're really in the shit," he said.

FORTY

For whatever reason, it felt important that I not speak. Not immediately. I had to show MacLeish I wasn't shook. So I sat with arms crossed like a juvenile delinquent in an old movie. All I needed was a cigarette pack rolled up my sleeve.

Years ago MacLeish orchestrated an undercover operation that backfired tragically, ending in violence. I'd brought a small part of his failure into the open. An unforgivable offence. Since then, he made my work difficult. To thank him for this, I mailed the deputy chief a Christmas cake each year. *Best wishes for the season, compliments of Wakeland & Chen.*

"A lot of shit," MacLeish repeated. "You left town, David. All was right with the world. There's no future for you here. You know that, don't you?"

I didn't respond, unsure if I could deny it convincingly.

"So here you are, caught up in things you can't comprehend, trying to accomplish who the devil knows what." MacLeish laughed. "Not feeling too chatty, are we?"

He rotated his ankle. The joint creaked loudly in the small room. MacLeish adjusted his sock and set the foot down.

"The nature of civil service lies in subordinating one's preferences to the good of the community. To further the interests of justice. I tell myself, let Wakeland run on a little farther before he suffers the consequences. Everyone knows what those consequences are. I suspect no one knows better than him. What do you think, David?"

He waited, smug. The master of time, doling it out for my displeasure.

"Nobody likes a gloater," I said. "Charge or release."

MacLeish addressed an invisible audience. "Behold! The power of speech returns to him."

"What do you want?"

"Who told you where to find Lloyd Corso?"

"No one. He found me."

"Why are you going to such lengths to talk with him?"

"I fall in love too easy."

"What does the word *Eiger* mean to you?"

"Second tier Eastwood. Nice John Williams score."

MacLeish searched my face for what I knew. He nodded as if he'd found something there. Another old cop trick. I was getting sick of those.

"Understand something, David. If you jerk me around, I guarantee you'll suffer a wrong outcome. Your half-sister will be up for parole in the near future. And the lawyer who hired you, Susan Chen, will have her conduct scrutinized."

"Shuzhen," I said, instantly regretting the correction. It told him what mattered to me. MacLeish smiled in satisfaction.

"Tell me the truth and be convincing about it."

I gave him my reason for searching for Lloyd, leaving out what Katz had told me about Operation Eiger. Lloyd was my alternate suspect: dangerous, volatile and under the protection of his uncle Charlie the Priest.

MacLeish nodded. "I believe you."

"You should."

"What's the part you omitted?"

"Nothing," I said.

"We know each other too well, David."

I sighed, playing at being defeated. Not a great stretch of my acting ability. "I think Lloyd killed the Stacks on his uncle's orders. I can't prove it, but I believe the Priest was involved in something and Budd Stack found out about it."

"Are you working for Terry Rhodes? What's the nature of your relationship with him?"

"I'm steering a ship through pack ice," I said. "He's the ugly cliff on my portside. Guess who's looming starboard?"

MacLeish looked up at the camera and made a circling gesture with his finger.

"Do not contact Lloyd Corso. Steer clear of him."

"Even if he tries to run me over again?"

MacLeish smiled deathlessly. Meeting adjourned.

FORTY-ONE

"No strappado," I called to Shuzhen as I was led into the lobby of the station. "Minor instruments of torture only."

The officer behind the desk looked relieved. Having to spar with a pissed-off Shuzhen Chen was stressful work. As we cleared the doors of the station she said, "What was the point of that?"

She was dressed for rain, blue raincoat and duck boots. I hadn't brought a coat. Bracing myself, we made the walk to the side street where she'd parked.

Before we spoke I examined the inside of the Mercedes. The floor mats, visor, glovebox and charge port were all clean. Nothing to show the stereo had been disturbed. Even so, I streamed music, Oliver Gannon and Miles Black's *Broadway*, and kept my voice low.

"All they care about is Lloyd Corso," I said. "Katz was right, Lloyd is definitely part of something major. I've been warned to stay away from him."

"But he's our witness."

More than that, if my hunch was right.

"This would make a good puzzle for your torts prof," I said. "Lloyd's testimony could put Maggie Zito in prison for a crime Lloyd himself probably committed. If she lives that long."

Shuzhen shivered. "Don't say that."

"There were two killers at the Stack house. And Murray Fong told me a man and woman braced him about Maggie. Assuming these are the same two people, and that one of them is Lloyd, he has an accomplice who's likely female."

"But how do we find her if we can't go near Lloyd?"

I didn't know. Another question was bothering me as well. Operation Eiger could be the last real chance to put away Terry Rhodes and the upper management of the Exiles. If Lloyd was discredited, that would mean Rhodes would go free. What was more important—saving our client, or cutting off the head of local organized crime?

I didn't have an answer for that, either.

Felix was out on a beer run. Elodie buzzed me in. I waited in the living room portion of their open-concept apartment, watching her pin a pattern to fabric and glance up occasionally at *Forensic Files*.

"Background noise," she said of the TV. "When he's home I use my earbuds, but when I'm on my own I hate working in silence. Know what I mean?"

"Plus you get to learn all about ninhydrin."

Elodie smiled and adjusted one of the pins. "You don't seem like the guys Felix usually hangs out with."

"I'm pretty singular."

"What I mean is, they're tough—not that you're not—but tough is their thing. Their defining characteristic."

"Is it Felix's?"

"He can be sweet when he wants to."

Elodie clicked past an ad that popped up on the screen. The show resumed. I recognized one of the talking heads, a retired profiler. Serial predators, he was saying, are creatures of habit.

"How well do you know his friends?" I asked.

"We've been to Rigger and Darlene's place a few times. Parties, mostly. Rigger seems to really like Felix."

"What about Charlie the Priest?"

Elodie looked at her work table, smoothing the fabric. "I get the sense he's a big shot, and he and Rigger don't get along. I probably shouldn't say more."

Felix's boots on the landing ended our talk. He entered clutching a cloth bag shaped around a six-pack.

"What fucking now," he said, glaring at me. To Elodie: "Why'd you let him in?"

"He's your friend, isn't he?"

"No, just an asshole I work with."

Felix uncapped a beer. He moved to kiss her on the cheek but she didn't respond.

"You're being fucking rude," Elodie said.

"I just like to leave my work at work, that's all. It's fine." That wasn't sufficient. Felix sighed, and said to me, "Sorry. What do you need?"

"Info on Lloyd and his associates," I said. "Could Lloyd pilot a boat?"

"Dirty Lloyd couldn't drive a self-driving car. But maybe he's master of the high seas, all I fuckin' know."

"The associate I'm looking for is female," I said. "Violent. Not connected to the Exiles, at least not directly. And she probably knows her way around a boat."

"Sounds like a personal ad," Felix said. "Long walks on the beach. Must love boats and axes."

"Who does Lloyd know that fits that description?"

"Nobody that fits all of that."

"The first two then," I said. "A woman capable of real violence."

Felix settled onto the couch. He looked toward Elodie as if expecting her to return to her work. Instead she perched on the arm of the couch and took the bottle from him. He opened another. The TV remained paused in the middle of a re-enactment.

"Think I'd like to hear this," she said.

THE LAST EXILE · 203

Felix's expression told me I was responsible for any domestic misery that arose. Taking heavy pulls on the beer, he said he'd seen this one woman with Lloyd. The meeting had been memorable.

Felix had been on merch detail at the Mountain Shadow Pub. In walked Lloyd and a group of young women. *Very* young, high school seniors he'd guess. All of them waving new driver's licences, complete with holograms and barcodes. A burnout named the Rabbit sold fake IDs out of his parents' basement a few blocks away. Whatever his faults, the Rabbit did exceptional work.

The table of kids ordered round after round of Skittle Shots, Fireball whiskey with a candy dropped into the glass. Screaming and smashing the empties down, howls of laughter when one of them puked. A real mess, right at the table. Lloyd had simply walked over to Felix's merch station, grabbed a pile of ONE PERCENT PROUD T-shirts, and used them to mop up the sick. The remainder Lloyd handed out to anyone who'd soiled their clothes. No payment or thank you, no acknowledgment of Felix.

More shots. Customers left. When the Skittles ran out, they used cinnamon hearts. When the place ran out of Fireball, Lloyd insisted on single malt Scotch. The bar staff didn't want a problem with the nephew of Charlie the Priest, but neither did they want to go out of business.

Felix was used to raucous drunks, to nights deteriorating into unpleasant scenes. Lloyd had no official standing in the club, but as a lowly prospect, Felix wasn't going to cross the crown prince and risk pissing off the Exiles' sergeant-at-arms.

Last call. The group had thinned to Lloyd and three others. One was a woman in a black halter, the smallest and youngest-looking of the group, but the loudest. She seemed to be the one dictating how the night went. Combat boots with blocky heels up on the neighbouring stool. Smoking, and when the waiter asked could she please put that out, laughing and telling him, "Don't worry, sweetie, it's not tobacco."

Felix could recognize a problem waiting to happen. Usually by that time of night, he was packed up and gone. But intuition told him to stay. The woman was a danger, and Lloyd was weak. If anything happened in the Mountain Shadow, Felix would be accountable to the Priest. So he stayed.

The staff made all the passive-aggressive hints that it was closing time. The bill. The lights. Stools up on nearby tables. Felix had already stowed his unsold merchandise in the car. He sat with arms crossed, waiting.

Even sensing danger in the air, the violence was sudden and seemed to come from nowhere. The waiter was smiling, regretting that they needed to cash out the machines, so if you're paying with credit, and is this all on one bill? The bartender and other waiter had their jackets on, smokes and car keys out.

Lloyd began saying something about not having his wallet, and the waiter was nodding, just wanting the night to be over. If Lloyd wanted to rip off the bar, that meant nothing to the staff.

The glass straw knifed into the waiter's chest smoothly, puncturing him with a single blow. The tube clutched in the fist of the woman in the halter.

The table went over. Screams. One of the drinkers fell back, ending up on her ass, legs splayed out, laughing. The waiter fell into Lloyd, trying to scramble over him and away from his attacker. The straw protruded from just below his throat, like an intubation tube. Blood spurted from it.

Felix watched the waiter wriggle and flop to the floor. Lloyd pushed against the wall, away from the injured man.

"You *never* fucking disrespect my friends," the woman howled. Seeing the bar staff petrified, she hurled glasses at them.

That was the moment. Felix strode over to Lloyd and dragged him out into the night, away from the scene. No arguments. He placed Lloyd in the back seat of his car, next to the boxes of hats, and drove.

"Allie's fucking crazy," Lloyd was telling him. "Chick just goes zero to a hundred and fifty like that." Felix remembered Lloyd trying to snap his fingers, making several drunken attempts.

While he told the story, Elodie sat still, holding herself. She looked nauseous, angry and ashamed all at once. But not surprised.

"Did the waiter die?" she asked in an empty voice.

"Don't think so. Punctured lung, and some burn marks." Almost despite himself, Felix added, "After we left I heard Allie tried to set him on fire."

"Jesus Christ."

"Do you know Allie's full name?" I asked. "Where she lives? Anything that would help me locate her?"

"She must be in jail, right?" Elodie said. "I mean she didn't get away with that."

Felix shrugged. "Cops never really went to that bar."

"Because it was one of yours, right? Protected by your friends?"

She left the couch abruptly, galloping across the room and smashing the bedroom door closed.

"Ruining my home life telling you this," Felix said.

"She didn't know who you're mixed up with?"

"Does now, thanks to you." He sighed, tipping the last bottle up for the dregs. "Anyway, that's the only time I saw Allie. The pub's gone now. I wouldn't know how to find her."

"Where would you start looking?" I asked.

"Not my job."

"Let's say it is for today."

In the silence I watched Felix stare toward the bedroom, perhaps listening for evidence of how deeply he'd hurt his partner.

"If he made her an ID, I guess the Rabbit might know how to find Allie," he said.

"Then let's go ask the Rabbit."

FORTY-TWO

The Rabbit's proper name was James Morganstern. He lived in the basement suite of his parents' investment property in the Kensington neighbourhood of Burnaby. Not a glamorous or trendy suburb. Not much to recommend the architecture, which tended toward flat-roofed boxes in various shades of oatmeal. Kensington's virtue was its proximity to Hastings Street, which ran from the heart of Vancouver to the university atop Burnaby Mountain.

A parent's basement is shorthand for loserdom, but basements run from dirt-floor cellars to just-about-ground-level three-bedroom suites. The Morgansterns had set their son up in the latter. The house, a generous two-storey with its Christmas lights still up, had been partitioned. Ground floor, top floor and basement all had separate addresses, 101-A, B and C. The laneway house was 101-D.

Three market rentals plus whatever they charged their son. Not a bad racket. In Vancouver you were either a landlord or at the mercy of one.

We swept around the block. The Beast's headlights burned unevenly now, slightly cockeyed. The lights were on in the basement suite. Felix had the passenger window rolled all the way down.

"You wanna wait here," he said. "I'll go ask him about Allie."

I could imagine what that would entail. "How about we both go," I said. "I'll ask, you intimidate. Think you can pull off silent and menacing?"

That approach was fine with him.

The front door of 101-C was around the left side. The tenants hadn't done much to beautify the exterior. The pathways were gravel and the grass was patchy and trampled. Empty pots were lined up beneath the eaves. One served as a repository for cigarette butts and the wrapper from a Crunch bar. Music filtered out, New Order, "Age of Consent." We could see through the windows down into the dining room, a tiled space with no furniture.

A pair of waifs in fishnets sat cross-legged on the floor. A redhead, freckled breasts peeking over her vinyl bodice, packed a hash pipe. The other, bald and pale, stared into her compact while applying black lip pencil. The Rabbit was kneeling, genuflecting with the camera, snapping test shots.

Felix knocked twice and then kicked the door open.

The redhead dropped the pipe, spilling the contents of the bowl onto the tile. The other ignored us. James Morganstern stared open-mouthed as we pressed inside. I dropped the volume on the boom box.

"Hey buddy," Felix said.

"I paid this week already, dude. Kind of in the middle of a shoot."

"Short recess," I said, waving casually at the models. They glared back, testy.

"Could you come back in like a little while?" the Rabbit asked. "This is a paying gig."

We weren't going anywhere. He huffed a bit, showing the women how this clearly wasn't his fault, entirely out of his hands. "Five minutes, mmkay? Sorry about this."

"This doesn't count towards the hour we paid for," the redhead said.

"No, I know, it's cool."

Outside, in the yard, he lit a cigarette. The Rabbit hadn't gotten his nickname from any physical characteristic. No buck teeth, no Alice in Wonderland tattoo. An ordinary-looking white kid, peroxide blond above dark roots, the type you'd imagine went to a lot of warehouse raves. Back before warehouses became condos.

"A woman named Allie," I said. "Young, probably nineteen or twenty. You made her ID."

"I make skillions of IDs. Pays better than boudoir shoots. Photography business is in the toilet."

"I think you'd remember Allie."

Felix fed him the description. The forger shook his head as he listened, not wanting to recognize the person. Recognition dawned anyway.

"Hang here a sec." The Rabbit set his cigarette on the lip of the pot and slipped back into the house. I watched the filter accumulate ash, its balance becoming precarious. The man truly lived on the edge.

He re-emerged holding his laptop by the screen, typing with the other hand. A thumb drive inserted, its contents scrolled through. He clicked his tongue, no luck, switched out the drives. Doing this standing looked more trouble than it was worth.

There's nothing more boring than watching someone else use a computer. He was going to be a while, standing there with the laptop now balanced on his palm. Felix was texting Elodie, pausing thoughtfully as he composed.

"What's the photo shoot for?" I asked the models through the open door.

The one with the shaved head was trying on a silvery blue wig. "None of your fucking business."

THE LAST EXILE · 209

True enough.

"Boo fucking yah," the Rabbit said. "I knew I had her saved. She got her learner's at sixteen, so all I had to do was scan it and Photoshop the dates, then print out a new one."

"A fake, you mean."

He nodded as if the distinction was minimal, spun the computer screen toward us. "This the chick?"

Felix squinted at the screen and nodded, it was the chick. Allison Creel, twenty-one years old according to her licence, with an address in the West End.

"So this is what you do for a living," Felix said as we drove toward English Bay. "Shake people down for answers?"

"In a sense." I imagined he was thinking that it wasn't very different from his own occupation.

"And it pays?" he asked.

"Sometimes."

Felix slouched against the passenger door, staring at me. "How's someone get into this?"

"Different ways. My partner, Jeff, went to business school. Data management. Me, I quit the police force and needed gainful employment. Fit the skills."

"Didn't like being a cop?"

"Authority encouraged some bad habits," I said.

I offered to drop Felix at home on my way, but he declined. "I'll come with. Allie might try something. Then I'd get in shit for it."

He was enjoying this, I suspected. And what wasn't to enjoy? Racing across town on a calm September night, the city lit up and poised to offer us its secrets. That feeling we were on the verge of being welcomed into the hidden kingdom where things make sense, where random violence isn't random and coincidence never occurs.

The trip to the kingdom exacted a heavy toll, paid in ugly little instalments, due for the rest of your life. But in the hot moment when a case seemed ready to break, none of that mattered. Addicted, I thought. I hadn't been retired for the past year and a half. I'd been in withdrawal.

FORTY-THREE

The Creel family lived in one of the older art deco buildings along English Bay, a few blocks from the Stanley Park Seawall. Ask anyone from out of town where they'd most like to live and this would be the answer. All buildings should be as clean, all lawns as well trimmed and as generously sprinklered. In the space between the neighbouring towers, I could even see the beach.

"This place is pretty tits," Felix said.

The buzzer worked, but the intercom was shot. One of the Creels made a noise and the door clicked open.

Inside, the building had a feel of rundown gentility. Legacy tenants who'd bought long before the prices had hit seven figures. Real estate is always on my mind, is intrinsic to how I think about Vancouver. Since I'd been back, though, I hadn't spared much time to think of my own living situation. If I stayed, I'd have to find a place. And the money to afford it.

Mrs. Creel met us in the hall, waiting as the elevator doors opened. Allie's mother was forty going on seventy, swaddled in a thick robe the yellowish green of a dead Christmas tree. Bare feet on the faded red polypropylene. Her bottom lip had recently been stitched.

"He's sleeping," she whispered. "What's this about?"

"I'd like to talk to your daughter Allie," I said, producing my card. Mrs. Creel stared at it as if strangers had been handing her business cards all her life. Social workers and counsellors, debt specialists, officers of the court.

"Allie dudden really live here," Mrs. Creel said. "I mean, her mail comes sometimes, but we don't see too much of her."

"Where does she live?" I asked.

"Oh, she's got friends. Always new ones."

Mrs. Creel didn't want to know, and didn't mind admitting this. Her daughter's itinerancy was a fact, like the seasons.

"Allie know a Lloyd Corso?"

"I'm not familiar with her friends. Just that she got lots of 'em."

Felix crowded her. "So tell us about the ones you know."

Mrs. Creel said "Well," and scratched her back. From inside the apartment came a loud "Fucking *shit*." Bedsprings, some piece of furniture being bodied out of the way. The woman shuffled away from the door, upset at us.

"You woke him," she said.

He stormed out, a large man, broad across the chest, with a farmer's tan and heavy upper arms with enough fat on them to quiver. A tattoo of a lion on his left breast. Hair dirty blond, turning auburn at the sideburns.

"Fucking tryna sleep working fucking nights twelve on, five off, and this the fucking thanks." Elbowing his wife aside. "The fucking noise three hours I gotta be up what the *fuck* do you want."

Already swinging one of those big arms in my direction, aiming to catch me in mid-explanation. Cheap-shot artist, I thought. I backed off and saw Felix charge into the man, catching him off-balance. The two of them spilled through the open door.

The apartment was as rotten inside as the rest of the building was spotless. Curtains drawn, smoke heavy in the air along with the

THE LAST EXILE · 213

smell of chicken grease. They tumbled over umbrellas and galoshes, a pair of grimy steel-toe boots. Felix landed beneath him. His hand slapped the wall, sending a framed diploma down. Glass shattered. The man grunted, moving to his knees, and flung a paw at Felix's right ear.

I didn't pull the pistol until I was inside the apartment, pushing past Mrs. Creel, who was watching the struggle with fear and delight. *Look what my man can do.*

He had a bull neck with a stack of hot dogs along the back. Swift for his size, already moving to his feet. As he turned I drove the butt of the pistol into his temple, then struck him again on the way down.

The big man sputtered, made a lapping sound. I kept an eye on Mrs. Creel, the gun trained on her husband. Ask anyone who's responded to a domestic disturbance: the danger can come from the quiet sullen ones as easily as the loudmouths hurling furniture.

The corner of the diploma frame had caught Felix above the eye. He was bleeding but pulled himself upright. The power was out in the apartment, the microwave and oven clocks dark. Fruit flies flitted over glasses on the kitchen pass window.

A tyrant stepdad and a complacent mom, ruling over a sty. I felt sorry for Allie. Mrs. Creel moved closer to the knife rack.

"Stay put for a while," I told the man, turning to address his wife. "And you, please don't be dumb enough to pull a knife on me."

She moved away, licking her tongue along the corner of her mouth.

"Now please give me my card back. Paper is expensive, and I don't have many left."

Mrs. Creel pulled it from the pocket of her robe and set it on the counter.

"Why is the electricity off?" I asked.

She shrugged. "He dudden like noise while he sleeps. Won't let me watch TV."

"What a joy to be you. Where's your daughter?"

"Tolja I dunno."

I pointed to Felix. "Imagine this guy was going to stomp a deep hole in your husband and throw you down it, unless you got in touch with Allie. In those hypothetical circumstances, do you think you could?"

"Changes her number all the time, don't even ask anymore."

"Email?"

"Dudden reply."

Hitting the brute had released histamine and adrenalin. It was hard to stay calm. "Chat, then. ICQ. PGP. Whatever the hell."

She shook her head. "We don't do that. It's government poppa-ganda. They take your information, sell it to the Russians an' Chinese."

Felix let out frustrated laughter. He was holding what looked like a pizza flyer to his bleeding forehead.

"Let's kick the dogshit out of them," he said.

"Sorely tempting." I looked between the couple. "You better give him something. My friend's not fully domesticated and I don't know how long he'll stay in a pleasant mood."

From the ground came a mumble. "Tellum." He repeated the word, speaking to his wife.

Mrs. Creel looked away, drawing back into the persona of the meek and passive mom who didn't know what was going on. She used the cuff of her robe to clear dust off the microwave. "Really nothing to tell."

"Tell us anyway," I said.

"Tellum," the man on the ground said. "Go on and tellum 'bout the *Rap Rider*."

"Oh, they don't want to hear, I mean that's not…"

"What's the *Rap Rider*?" I asked.

"Boat," he managed to get out.

Mrs. Creel glared at her husband. "We came into some money a few years ago. Bought a little cabin cruiser. The *Rap Rider*. It got stole."

"By your daughter," the man on the ground said.

"Oh shush, she didn't—"

"Day after I cut her off—"

"One's got literally nothing to do with the other—"

"'Surance papers still sitting there, she won't fill 'em out—"

"I haven't got around to it, that's all—"

"Still making payments on a boat I don't got—"

"Quiet time," I said. "You have a boat, which was stolen, you haven't informed the authorities, and your daughter might have taken it. That's a fair summary?"

"I don't think it's fair to say she did," Mrs. Creel said. "Anyone coulda."

A croak of laughter from the ground. "Then where's the keys at? Lost 'em off my ring?"

"Is that impossible?"

"Look for 'em right now, whydoncha."

I nodded to Felix. We were done here.

Felix had the sun visor down and was staring at his smile in the vanity mirror. Prodding a molar with his finger. "One's loose," he said. "'Magine living like that, in a building that nice."

"Imagine being their neighbour."

He chuckled, wiping red spittle off his jaw. "Guy seemed long overdue for a shit-kicking, didn't he?"

"Puts him on a very long list."

"You don't think it's good for an asshole like that to get smacked once in a while?"

"I used to." I kept my eyes on the road. "Now I just think where it travels. We humiliate him, he takes it out on the wife. And who does she take it out on?"

"Who the fuck cares?" Felix said.

The day was settling into evening. I hadn't spoken to Shuzhen in hours. Hadn't eaten. I needed time to make sense of what I'd learned.

I wanted to say something true and profound about taking the long view, about treating all life as precious, even if it smelled like processed cheese and dirty underwear. About how so much evil was built upon people setting out to do harm in a righteous cause.

"I wish hitting people was a little less satisfying," I finally said.

Felix only nodded his head.

He had the van's door open already as I pulled to the curb in front of his place. He dropped down and raised a hand in goodbye without looking back. I wondered if he'd come clean with Elodie, if they could patch things up. Maybe Felix Ramos had begun to second-guess the road he was on. I hoped so.

At Shuzhen's apartment I found her snoring softly on the couch. Wordlessly I took the floor in front of her. My fingers covered hers and she responded.

"Tough day?" I asked.

"Not anymore."

From the couch to bed, still entwined.

In the morning I let her shave me, both of us perched on the edge of her tub as she tried to draw as little blood as possible. Scrapings of foam with red threads slid down the tub. She did even, meticulous work, and demanded her reward right there on the mat.

It was late morning before she checked her phone and saw the message from Briony Zito. The news was bad. Something had happened at pretrial.

FORTY-FOUR

The move came after breakfast, while the prisoners were waiting for the sheriff's van to take them to court. Always a holdup. If not the van then paperwork, or the prisoners themselves needing piss breaks or pussy plugs or some piece of vital correspondence they'd left in their cell. Meanwhile the others waited. You could make enemies by making people wait. But then Maggie Zito already had enemies.

Six women in the morning run. Maggie was always prompt. She *wanted* to get to the courthouse. Better food, better conversation. You caught the breeze of real life. More than that, court was where her future was being decided. Damn right she wanted to be there. Gearing up for the trial, strategizing, coming up with questions for her counsel. The sooner the court business was over, the sooner she'd be back with her kids, hearing about school and playdates and whatever they found in the park that afternoon. Back in the house she'd lived in her entire life. *Her entire life* was what Maggie was fighting for.

She knew the woman causing the holdup only as Mar. A new transfer, neither of them interested in the other's story. They weren't going to become friends. Mar seemed withdrawn, shaken by prison. Maggie had her own issues.

The other five waited. Jensen, O'Doul, Shuckey and Truong. The latter two whispered among themselves. O'Doul shuffled in place, restless. Jensen leaned against the wall, bored and sleepy but eyes open.

Maggie was cautious the moment the cell doors opened, doubly cautious in the showers. She stared at no one, moved efficiently, caused neither guard nor other inmate a disruption that could spin out. My deal with Terry Rhodes meant nothing. She didn't trust Rhodes or anyone else.

Jensen was the most like her. The woman made a point of being on time, not causing any problems. She seemed lost in the details of her case, the way Maggie imagined herself to look. Jensen was slim, in on some sort of extortion charge. Her trial had been going on for months. Long enough the guards called her Ash and were friendly to her.

When the lockdown siren went off, the COs made the prisoners prone themselves on the floor. Five starfishes, five downward-facing snow angels, waiting for the scuffle in B Pod to end. A throng of guards stomped past them.

Maggie was thinking about whether this would delay the run. She didn't see Jensen make a nose-blowing gesture that the guards overlooked. She didn't see the object that slipped from Jensen's sleeve into her palm. Pages torn from magazines, rolled tightly, soaked with saltwater, then baked until hardened into a dowel. Sharpened into a slender stabbing tool.

Lockdown ended. They were allowed to stand up. The guards concerned themselves with locating Mar. Jensen sprang up a little faster than usual, like someone executing a burpee.

The strike was aimed at the organs beneath the ribs but Maggie was in motion herself, standing up, and Jensen overcompensated, driving the tool into Maggie's right armpit. Her left hand sought purchase on Maggie's left hip. The tool drawn out and driven in again at a sharper angle, Maggie folding with the impact.

The weapon wasn't built for repeat use. By the time Jensen drove it in for a third time the tip had broken off. Maggie turned. She fought, unable to stop the shiv but redirecting it into her forearm. She rolled, dislodging Jensen, who disengaged. Surrendered. Her job done. A correctional officer pinned her. The room was flooded with reinforcements from the observation area.

Maggie struck out feebly at the guards who tried to examine her. Blood loss and adrenalin, ears full of the pounding in her skull. To their credit the guards recognized an injured animal caught in fight-or-flight. They were patient. They stopped her flailing and put pressure on the wounds. When she lost consciousness, they prepped her for the medical bay.

She was stabilized, the wounds closed, anaesthetic given. Maggie was transported to Surrey Memorial Hospital. During her first surgery, a segment of hardened, salted paper was removed from her right ventricle. The cardiac specialist who removed it proclaimed it was the damnedest papercut she'd ever seen. The trauma surgeon and the nurses, who had all seen worse, didn't laugh.

Ash Jensen was separated, new charges added to her case. Her statement was taken down. Maggie struck first. The weapon was Maggie's. Jensen merely defended herself. When it was pointed out the footage from the pretrial cameras didn't correspond to her version of events, Jensen's response was a shrug. She remembered it her way.

I found out all this later, after Jensen's trial. At the time I only knew that our client had been hurt. While Shuzhen and I were waiting for the outcome of Maggie's second surgery, a man walked into a consignment store in the Kitsilano neighbourhood. He asked for Brian Jensen. The seventeen-year-old hadn't visited his mother in over a year. Too busy trying to earn next year's tuition. Their last chat had been virtual, on Mother's Day.

Brian Jensen had no idea how the man knew his name, or why the man passed him a small paper bag. Inside were seventy soiled hundred-dollar bills.

FORTY-FIVE

The friends and family of Maggie Zito occupied a turquoise hallway in Surrey Memorial. Shuzhen was slumped in a bucket seat to my right. Across from us, Briony paced. Her niece and nephew sat with cereal bars and Nintendo Switches, listlessly waiting for news. They hadn't been told the details of the attack, but they grasped the raw wound at its centre. Mommy's been hurt.

I was an interloper here. Useless as a band-aid during a bridge collapse. I began taking orders for food when Nimisha Nair arrived toting boxes of donuts and samosas. Superfluous even for that.

Shuzhen would stay until there was news. I made my exit before guilt could start to outweigh concern. In the parking lot I called Felix and told him I needed to see Terry Rhodes right fucking now.

"I'm not his secretary," Felix said. "Yours either."

"Tell me where he is."

"I can get in real shit—life or death shit—"

"Want me to drive over and ask Elodie?"

A hesitation over the line. Felix exhaled into the receiver. "He golfs at Shaughnessy sometimes. You got a death wish, you can maybe find him there."

The Shaughnessy Golf and Country Club had been around since 1911, built by the railroad on Musqueam land to add prestige to their western terminus. The many-gabled clubhouse opened onto tennis courts and a long covered patio. A flag blew in the breeze off the Fraser River.

The overcast late morning was suitable weather for golf, and the course was busy. Members only, plus their guests. Collared shirts required.

The unsung virtue of a flannel shirt is that it has a collar. I buttoned up and tucked in, told the greeter I was a guest of Mr. Rhodes. He nodded as if that were any other name.

Rhodes was sitting in a private nook of the restaurant, its glass walls looking out onto the links. A fine afternoon for golf. He was dressed as I'd never seen him before, in earth tones and a bone-coloured cardigan. Harder than the people around him, which was noticeable even from a distance, but he didn't stick out. On the contrary. He belonged.

At his table were a trio of men with the air of wealth and good fortune. I recognized two of them from Jeff's business magazines, the other from the cockfight. Salads and club sandwiches and Bloody Marys and light beer. One of his companions was telling a long and bawdy joke. Rhodes spied me, but his expression didn't change from amusement poised for laughter.

"—just sucking and sucking for all she's worth. And then all of a sudden, the hooker stops. Backs away. Guy says, 'I wasn't finished.' Hooker says, 'You paid me for an Angry Penguin.' And the guy says, really upset about it, 'So why's it called an Angry Penguin?'"

The joke teller stood, waddling like a man with his pants around his ankles and a fading hard-on. The table howled. Rhodes's laughter was polite.

"Fitzhugh tells it a little different," one of the tablemates said.

Rhodes waved at the greeter as we approached, okaying my presence. "This is Dave Wakeland. I knew his father a bit. I'll sign him in later."

"Of course." An instant smile. Any friend of a member.

Rhodes adjusted his cardigan and excused himself from the table. We walked outside, past the pro shop, entering an overhang thick with golf carts. The breeze was picking up, and in the shade my skin was clammy.

"Maggie Zito was stabbed," I said. "You told me she wouldn't be hurt."

"By me." Rhodes grinned. "Don't confuse me with God, Wakeland. My dick's too big for that."

"Other words, your promise isn't worth shit."

He looked at me like a parent at a nuisance child. "See that guy by the caddy corral?"

I hadn't. Behind us at a distance of maybe twenty feet was a well-tanned man in a charcoal suit. The outfit was a near match for the club's senior management, absent a nametag. The man wore snowboarding shades. The lines of his suit jacket were ruined by the bulge of a shoulder holster. Private security. I should have recognized.

Arm on my shoulder, Rhodes's tone stayed avuncular. "Before you beak off to me about my word, understand that Shep there had you clocked when you pulled in. He knows what you drive. More important to you, he knows what your lawyer friend drives. Shuzhen Chen. If I wanted, he could shoot you right now, front of all these upper-crust jagoffs. Guess how many of 'em would say they saw him do it?"

"Members privileges," I said.

"Fact is, I didn't have shit to do with what happened to Maggie. Not that I'll shed any tears over her, but I'm not your enemy, Dave. Your real enemy is you."

"That's true of everyone, so it's meaningless."

"Wrong. And you know that."

His grip hardened, tearing into my shoulder, seating me on the wheel well of one of the carts. My anger had briefly overshadowed my fear, but the race was competitive now. Rhodes looked around at the lush savage green of the course, the well-toned woman in the visor choosing her caddy, a pair of middle-aged men waiting for their cart. Happy people and obsequious staff.

"I was a caddy once, place in the Laurentians. Lotta old-time bosses used to come play. Calabrians and Sicilians, real Moustache Petes. Place'd throw Christmas and New Year's parties, and if you didn't have family commitments, you could make decent money. End of the night, any leftover food we could take. I never ate so good. These roast beef sandwiches, just thin-sliced meat on a butter roll. I'd bring home half a dozen, eat one a day till the roll was hard as petrified shit and the meat was going off. Still pretty good."

Rhodes cuffed me. Unlike Jeff's slap, this was administered by a practised hand, directly to the scab over the puncture mark he'd left before. His thumb traced over the injury with uncharacteristic tenderness.

"Stop tying your dick in knots worrying about Maggie Zito. You're not a kid anymore, Dave. Sock a little money away. Think long-term."

"I don't know how to do that," I admitted.

"Come work for me. There's things you do real well. I recognize talent, and I always reward hustle."

"Already have a job."

"Mine pays better," he said. "You can still do your little favours and try to get into that cute lawyer's panties. You want to fuck officers of the court, that's a whole lot easier with a membership to a place like this."

At no previous instant would I ever have considered his offer. I know the contours of my personality. What I crave above all is independence. The ability to plink out my own tune, however angular the melody and syncopated the tempo. Non-negotiable. I clung to that in moments of mania and defeat.

Rhodes stood over me, gripping my shoulder. He had spoken no untruth. My independence had done nothing to aid Maggie Zito or prevent her injury. It had harmed Jeff Chen and likely destroyed our business. My way had sent my sister to prison and infected Shuzhen with hopeless altruism. And I had little to show for it myself. A trail of damaged friendships, spurned opportunities, misery and death. The cost had been steep.

Amid the chaos and barbarity of the universe, a soul is a pretty inconsequential thing.

I shook my head, no, with more regret than defiance. Rhodes didn't seem surprised.

"I have to find the person responsible," I said. "Are you going to stop me?"

"So long as we both know I could."

I nodded.

As I left, I passed the man in the suit, who observed me until I cleared the gate. Of my meetings with Terry Rhodes this had been the least physically painful, but the worst nonetheless. I left with his voice in my head, and damned if it wasn't making a kind of sense.

FORTY-SIX

The *Rap Rider* was registered at Port Guichon in Surrey, much cheaper than mooring it within Vancouver waters. A thirty-foot Bayliner with twin Mercruiser engines, a cockpit that could seat twelve and a fully decked-out galley and living quarters. The Creels had bought her second-hand. She was due for maintenance, a servicing of the pumps.

The vessel hadn't been reported stolen, nor was Allison Creel declared a missing person. A temporary berthing at a marina would require a credit card as well as the name of the boat, the year and make, and contact information. But there were slips, private docks and hidden coves up and down the Pacific coast. The *Rap Rider* could be anywhere.

It could be nowhere, too. Boats capsize, founder, get swept away from shore. People, too. The Strait of Georgia was relatively calm and well-patrolled, but the western coast of Vancouver Island could be pummelled by waves from the open ocean. And if Allie turned the boat north, she'd encounter Arctic winds and temperatures. According to the harbourmaster, trouble came when inexperienced sailors expected cooperation from the weather.

"Thirty-foot's a dangerous size," the harbourmaster said. Harry Whishaw was retirement age, bald and wearing a Liverpool FC scarf beneath his rain slicker. "Big enough you're not feeling every wave. You get confident. But you can't fool the sea for long."

"What kind of distance could she travel?" I asked.

"Experienced sailor could take 'er to Mexico, easy. Zip right on down the coast. That's assuming she has a passport and enough cash."

"My sense is she's caught up in something less than legal."

Harry scratched his cheek. Razor nicks and a missed patch of white stubble. "Every year or two I read about some wannabe smuggler taking a boat down to Baja. They load up on coke or black tar, try to sail it back. Stupid."

"Why?"

"'Cause boats always need fixing," Harry said. "They're finicky and delicate birds. Second you pull in, you gotta justify being there, which guys like this don't wanna do. So that engine tick, that patch of rot in the hull, it never gets properly seen to. Soon enough they're stranded, just hoping the Coast Guard comes along."

"Let's say Allie Creel isn't an amateur, but not Captain Jack Aubrey, either."

"The way you do it, you relay," Harry said. "One boat travels up to Bellingham, Point Roberts, but doesn't cross. Then whoever's north of the forty-ninth, they zip out for pickup. Either you use buoys and a GPS marker, or just hand bomb the stuff one boat to the next. Depends on a lot of things—how much, how well you know your partners. Planes are another option. Hell, even drones."

"Any chance you could put the *Rap Rider*'s description out to other marinas?" I asked.

"Official or unofficial?"

"I'd appreciate first crack."

Harry looked at me with skepticism. "Sure, I can make some calls. Might be easier if you put up a case of Black Label to whoever spots her."

I told him there was a case in it for him if everything worked out.

"Everything working out is a pretty tall order," he said.

Briony had taken Maggie's kids home for dinner and bed. Shuzhen was alone in the hospital waiting room, working on her laptop. Her files and coffee mug took up the adjacent seats. She cleared a space for me.

"News?" I asked.

"Nothing good. Maggie's pulse dropped during surgery. They postponed a few hours. We still can't see her."

I ran a hand over the back of her neck, rubbing out some of the tension. Her skin was cold, goosebumped. We waited.

After a long silent interval, a nurse in scrubs came out of the operating wing, applied eye drops and wiped the corners of her eyes with a Kleenex. She picked up a phone and spoke in the cadence of a bearer of bad news. We eavesdropped. "We'll keep a good thought for her. All right. Of course. Any change at all."

Shuzhen interrupted the nurse's circuit back. "I'm Maggie Zito's counsel," she said.

A tired nod. "I'm sure the doctors will talk to you when they can."

"I'm her friend, too, and I've been here all day." Shuzhen's voice couldn't conceal the fatigue and enervation. "Please tell me what you can."

"It's an evolving situation," the nurse said. "The patient has a punctured lung, and her blood flow is down to sixty percent. Internal bleeding is common, but this is unoxygenated blood—very dark blue—meaning something nicked the pulmonary arterial path. We re-inflated the lung, but a fragment of whatever was used to stab her is still inside. That's being removed now by Dr. Chu."

"Once it's out and the bleeding stops?"

"It's still an awful lot of trauma for a body to absorb."

That wasn't the news Shuzhen wanted to hear, or the nurse wanted to deliver. We went back to our seats. Shuzhen absently picked up her laptop and shoved it into her case.

"This probably sounds silly to you," she said, "but do you know if there's a church nearby? One that's open late?"

"What denomination?"

"Doesn't matter."

"Well, it's short notice for me," I said. "But if your dowry's seven figures, the answer's yes."

A tired smile. "I'd just like to put in a word for Maggie. Couldn't hurt, could it?"

Christ Church Cathedral was near her apartment, the oldest surviving building in Downtown Vancouver. No service, but a choir was practising in the loft. A few people sat in pews at a distance from each other. Someone struck a chord on the organ and a full-throated note swept through the church.

Shuzhen approached the font, dabbed holy water, knelt and crossed herself. I stared up at the cedar planking of the ceiling, curved like a ship's hull. I felt out of place, kept waiting for the polite tap on the shoulder. Excuse me, sir, you're not supposed to be here. That said more about me than the place. Yet it was calming being there.

In the vestibule we passed a custodian sweeping the floor, humming along with the choir.

Church and then McDonald's. Shuzhen ordered a plain double cheese and fries. On the drive home she fell asleep and didn't wake until the Beast was bumping down the ramp of her building's parking garage.

Leaning on my shoulder in the elevator. "God, I probably stink real bad," she said.

"Awful," I said. She smelled of the hospital and long hours, of fast food and burnt coffee, hand cream and green tea. I could have enfolded myself in that smell.

In the apartment doorway we rushed to unclothe. My hands on the cool flesh of her back, the shoulders, unclasping her bra. The kitchen island cleared with a sharp wave of her arm. Hopping onto the cutting surface, kissing our way down.

The timing wrong, the pairing imperfect, but the need for communion overtaking us. Selfish and shameful and right.

Later, she wanted to swim. We ran bare-assed to the elevator, shrugging into our suits. I crabbed about in the shallows while she made her laps.

In the night I woke up feeling tears on my shoulder. A memory came to me: the two of us a decade ago, Shuzhen helping me pick out a suit for some corporate function. Taking her up to the observation deck at the top of Harbour Centre, looking out over the city. Two world destroyers surveying their domain, no idea what was headed their way.

FORTY-SEVEN

In the morning I heard the *Goldberg Variations* competing with the rain outside. Shuffling out of bed to find Shuzhen already dressed, tucking an umbrella into the front pouch of her rolling briefcase. Raindrops smeared the windows. I'd slept in.

"Not either of the Glenn Goulds," I said, setting water on the stove. "Don't tell me. Lang Lang?"

"Zhu Xiao-Mei."

"The odds of me getting that right were very poor, but you gotta respect the attempt." I rubbed sleep out of my face. "What are we up to today?"

"Court this morning," Shuzhen said. "Evidentiary hearing for another client."

"No news from the hospital?"

"No. Which is probably good, right?"

During the hours of waiting yesterday, the grain of an idea had sprouted. Maggie's motivation for killing the Stacks was supposed to be the death of her brother twenty years ago. To frame her, someone would have to know that history. Right now, I didn't.

"Do you have a file on Beau Zito?" I asked.

"Maggie's brother? I'll send it when I get to the office."

Shuzhen kissed me. I fought the urge to make an animal of myself. Duty first.

Hope is the last town out of the Fraser Valley en route to the Interior. To get there took an hour longer than I anticipated. Rush hour had ended, but that seemed to be the moment every semi-trailer and refrigerated van took to the road. Hope is also where *First Blood*, the original Rambo movie, was filmed. A carved wooden statue of Brian Dennehy greeted me from the lawn of Memorial Park.

I parked on the main drag, the Beast sticking out among the pickups and 4 × 4s, slotted between a print shop and a restaurant offering butter chicken and pizza. On foot, I passed chainsaw sculptures of prowling bears and sasquatches. A lot of the businesses catered to the highway trade. The police station was a blue gabled bunker on the southeast corner of town.

The civilian at the front desk was young and bright, a model of customer service. I asked them if I could speak to someone about the Zito file. They intercommed for a moment, the civilian relaying the nature of my request. Corporal Dhak would see me in just a minute.

It was more like twelve. I didn't complain. Corporal Dhak came out from the back, a trim South Asian woman in her early fifties. Her handshake was strong. Brian Dennehy would have appreciated that. I told her in detail what I was looking for.

"Beau Zito was my case, yes," Dhak said. "It's still open, so I can't tell you much."

"Could you show me where it happened?"

Dhak nodded. "Cost you the price of breakfast, though."

We crossed to the Blue Moose Cafe, where I bought a London Fog for myself and a flat white and raisin scone for the corporal. We wandered north.

"The town hasn't changed all that much in twenty years," Dhak said. "Busier, less overwhelmingly white. There was a rougher element back when I started, long-haulers that hung out at the bars or truck stops. But that's faded. We get the odd troublemaker from the Valley, but it's more or less peaceful."

The blue-green side of Mount Hope, which sheltered the town, did inspire a feeling of tranquility. We walked down Fourth, past the park near city hall, to an empty parking lot in front of a boarded-up shop. An old-fashioned diner was nearby, a carousel of pies in the window.

Dhak pointed at the derelict shopfront. "Liquor store at one time," she said. "Know what's going in now?"

"Where I'm from, the answer is always condos."

"Pot shop. A pot *emporium*. All things marijuana, available right before you get on a mountain highway with a steep shoulder and a hundred-klick speed limit. Real good idea, huh?"

A few feet back was the beginning of a residential street. Small white-trimmed houses in deep blues and ochres. The corporal swept her hand at the road.

"This wasn't paved at the time," Dhak said. "Sweeney's Roadhouse was over where the diner is. Lethally bad grub, a cold beer and wine next door. This is where they congregated. The Exiles, I mean."

"Beau Zito was in the diner, wasn't he?"

"Hitchhiking down from picking fruit in the Okanagan. Their altercation was around this spot. I remember the dirt was all agitated, as if it had been torn up. Then the parties separated."

"What was the scuffle about?" I asked.

"Perceived disrespect," Dhak said. "That was as much as I could ever find out. The people he was eating with were also seasonal labourers. Beau was well-liked and did his share of the work, but he had a temper and liked to mouth off about management. Chip on his shoulder. Didn't like being told what to do."

I could sympathize. "What happened after the argument?"

"Half-hour later, the bikers are still congregating. They see a pickup, someone being dragged behind it. Takes off too fast for them to do anything about it, though I'm sure they made a valiant effort." Dhak's tone suggested the case still frustrated her.

"How far was Beau dragged?"

"Not far. End of the block." She pointed and we strolled in the direction.

"The truck was going how fast?"

"Over the speed limit, from what the witnesses said."

"So the truck would have got here in seconds," I said. "Meaning Beau had been killed first."

"That's my guess, but hard to tell with a broken neck."

"Beau's sister is on trial for killing Budd and Jan Stack. Is it possible the Stacks were here at the time?"

"It's possible they came through, but I have no evidence of that."

I had pictures to show her of Budd and Jan. No recognition. Corporal Dhak squinted at my phone screen but didn't commit either way.

"I interviewed a whole bunch of bikers," she said. "Quite a sight in their vests and jackets. Some younger fellows with them, too. Prospects. I don't think anyone brought their wives."

"Were there photos taken at the crime scene?"

"Of course." Defensive, as if I'd questioned both her professionalism and the town's.

"Any of the photos show the crowd around the body?"

Dhak said she'd check and would meet me in an hour at the Blue Moose. I walked over to the library, a beige building in the same compound as a rec centre and curling club. I asked if I could look through the archives of the *Hope Standard*.

"It's all been digitized," the librarian said. Large purple frames, tattoos on his throat and hands. An aging punk with health care, I guessed, or the world's friendliest Russian gangster.

"I'm an analog guy at heart," I said. "Any chance I could look at the microfilm?"

He headed down into the basement to retrieve them. Eventually he returned with a cart, on which sat boxes of film. Six months' worth of the weekly *Standard*. The workstation was a computer with a microfilm reader attached. So much for analog.

I found the Thursday directly after the murder. Beau Zito, twenty-four, fruit picker, unidentified assailant. Brown or grey pickup. Then-Constable Sukhwinder Dhak called it a "heinous crime" that "demanded everyone's full cooperation." I wondered if this was the last time Dhak had used the word *heinous*. Probably not.

A follow-up story the next week added details about the dead man. The reporter had found a yearbook photo of Beau, young and with a teenager's proudly displayed moustache. He was smiling like a goof, not knowing the picture would accompany his obituary seven years later. The truck was now thought to be dark blue.

Maggie Zito was quoted as saying her brother was a good man and "whoever did this will get theirs."

I went forward a few weeks, but the coverage was thin. No new leads. Tips encouraged. A semi-trailer skidded off the Coquihalla the next week, sending a station wagon full of teenagers down the mountain. This fresh catastrophe consumed the paper.

Backwards now. Two weeks before the murder, a splash page showing the Exiles patch and rocker. MAYOR: RALLY EXPECTED TO DRAW "LOADS" OF OUTLAW BIKERS. A lock-up-your-daughters piece on the dangers the Exiles posed. Stay inside and don't panic.

The piece engendered several letters to the editor, some asking why the cops didn't arrest the bikers on sight. "They're telling us who they are by how they dress, for Pete's sake." Others spoke out against stigmatizing motorcyclists, ninety-nine percent of whom were unaffiliated. The letters accompanied a follow-up article that was more even-handed. BAD BOYS OR GOOD CUSTOMERS? MERCHANTS WEIGH IN. Restaurants and liquor stores praised the economic stimulation. The bookshop reported a loss of walk-in business. Premonitions of windows broken, quiet nights disturbed, hell descending on the town.

I'd come to Hope on the chance the person who killed the Stacks had been present for Beau's murder, maybe a part of it. That seemed less likely now, as I scrolled back to reread Maggie Zito's words. *Whoever did this will get theirs.*

Corporal Dhak was seated inside the Blue Moose, chatting to a woman she introduced as the mayor. I was gladhanded, asked what I thought of the town. I said I was having a much better time than John Rambo.

"Stallone actually enjoyed his time here," she said. "Stayed at a friend of mine's place."

There was nothing in Dhak's file about Budd Stack or his wife. Getting statements from the bikers had been like pulling teeth from a pissed-off buffalo. Some had refused to give real names; others gave obviously false ones. Donald Dee Duck. Joseph Camel.

One of the photos showed a forest of kickstanded Harleys in the parking lot I'd just walked through. The faces were hard to make out. But I knew Terry Rhodes by his silhouette. And the man next to him, holding a malt liquor forty, was Charles Corso.

I thanked the corporal and headed back to where I'd parked. Charlie the Priest had been in Hope the weekend Beau Zito was killed. Charlie would have been young then, eager to prove himself. What better way than to murder a man who disrespected the club? And if he got away with it, and later read the dead man's sister's threat, what would stop him from annihilating her as well?

FORTY-EIGHT

Heavy traffic on the way back to Vancouver. Six lanes threading down to one. Perturbing thoughts kept me company. Maggie's veiled threat in the newspaper. Charlie the Priest and a decades-old murder in Hope. And Terry Rhodes, always an X factor, who might have killed Beau Zito on a whim, or sanctioned it or simply enjoyed the spectacle.

Maggie and Briony would have been questioned about their brother's murder. The family always had to be ruled out. Necessary, yes, but what a feeling to have your sibling taken from you, then be asked to account for your whereabouts.

Maybe that was why I pulled onto the shoulder near the prison. It was also possible I'd been heading this way all along and just hadn't known it. Off the highway near Abbotsford, I drove down King Road to the fenced-off yard of the Matsqui prison. In a nearby compound was the Fraser Valley Institution for Women.

I didn't have an appointment, and they weren't going to let me see Kay today, security licence or no. Forms needed to be filled out, which would be processed in around two weeks. Then I'd be added to the approved visitors list. I could book a visitation after that, with twenty-four hours' notice.

"So two weeks plus a day and I can see my sister."

"*Around* two weeks. We process the forms as quickly as we can."

I filled them out on the dashboard of the Beast, passed them in and said I'd be back soon.

Shuzhen called me as the traffic on Highway 1 started to move. Over the speaker her voice sounded distant but hopeful.

"Maggie's been moved to a private room. Meet me at Surrey Memorial when you get in."

"Sounds like good news," I said.

"She's not worse. I guess that counts as good. What did you find in Hope?"

I outlined what I'd learned about Beau Zito's death.

"So Charlie the Priest was in Hope when the murder happened," Shuzhen said. "And his nephew Lloyd is the witness against Maggie. You think they set her up?"

"Very possible, but it could be any of them. Or any combination. Charlie the Priest and Lloyd and Allie, or Terry Rhodes and the Priest, or Rhodes and Rigger Devlin for that matter."

"Didn't Devlin fix your van?"

"That's right."

"Do you think—could he have—"

"Bugged the van? Unlikely. Between the motor and the stereo—"

"Not bugged, Dave. *Dave.*" Shuzhen's voice was sharp.

In the upper left corner of the windshield, the Devlins had attached a sticker. Next service in six months or 10,000 kilometres. I thought of Darlene Devlin talking in a low voice to the mechanic. Of the look of irritation and surprise on her husband's face when he spotted me in the shop.

I pulled into the parking lot of a White Spot and inspected the engine. The grimy original parts and the cleaner replacements looked in order. No superfluous wires connected to the battery. I checked around the dashboard, removed the stereo and looked behind.

No explosives. No hidden microphone or GPS. I flattened myself on the asphalt and crawled under the Beast, using the light on my phone to check the undercarriage.

Nothing. Clean. Or hidden so well I couldn't find it.

Never hurts to check.

Maggie wasn't conscious when I got to the hospital. We could see her through the window of a shared room. She had come through the second surgery. Her blood pressure had stabilized. She was breathing on her own.

I fetched coffee and junk food for Briony and the children while Shuzhen spoke with the security detail. The floor was locked down, the room guarded—just like with Lloyd Corso, I thought. Accuser and accused, both safe in hospital beds.

As the children ate, Briony stood tracing crescents on the floor with her heel. I asked if she remembered being interviewed after Beau's death.

"A cop from Hope drove down and spoke to me and Maggie, yeah."

"What was your sister's state of mind?"

"Shocked and horrified, of course. Same as me."

"And angry?"

"Maggie's always had a hair-trigger," Briony said. "She defends her family with guns blazing."

"In the paper she was quoted as wanting the killer to get theirs."

A manic smile, a chuckle. "That's the sanitized version. I'm sure my sis said way worse than that."

"Did Maggie ever look for who did it?" I asked.

"We phoned the Mountie station in Hope pretty regularly, if that's what you mean. At least for a few years. No new leads, they always told us."

"One of the bikers who drove by your house is named Charlie Corso. Charlie the Priest. He was in Hope around the time of the murder."

Her eyelids dropped and her expression grew distant. Briony hadn't resembled her sister all that much, but now I saw it, the same flush of anger at injustice. A ferocious rage she had learned to conquer and Maggie hadn't. Briony nodded for me to continue.

"Maybe the Priest was involved, and maybe he read that Maggie wanted revenge. If he ordered the Stacks' executions, he might have remembered your sister's threat and used her to cover his tracks. I wouldn't put this attack on Maggie past him, either."

"He should die."

She said this plainly, with no vitriol. A statement of obvious fact. Maybe of intent.

"I can't prove any of this yet," I said.

"Then you better hurry the fuck up."

We rejoined Shuzhen and the children and together we looked through the doorway. Maggie's nurse was arranging her cards along a side table. All the good wishes for health and a speedy recovery. The figure on the bed didn't stir.

FORTY-NINE

A morning of loose ends. For the moment, Maggie was safe in her hospital bed. The woman who stabbed her wasn't talking.

No word from the harbourmaster on the *Rap Rider* yet.

Allie Creel didn't have a great many friends. Her homeroom teacher remembered her as a vacant desk in class. Allie had been fired from a second-run movie house for doing coke in the washroom instead of selling popcorn. A waitress job ended when she flung a plate of hashbrowns at a customer. With her call centre job, she simply stopped showing up.

The closest I came to a genuine lead was a twenty-year-old single mother. She denied that she'd been in the pub the night Allie stabbed the waiter. Her expression told me otherwise. A clenching of the jaw at the mention.

"Look," she told me, "I don't hang with Allie anymore. I got a baby now. That part of my life—" She turned her head from the doorway of her parents' house, making sure her child was still in his high stool. "Allie would freak if she heard I was talking about her. She'd come here. I can't have that."

"Let's talk about someone else, then," I said. "When's the last time you saw Lloyd Corso?"

"But that's the same topic. Allie and Lloyd are close. He's just as crazy."

"Are they close enough she'd visit him in the hospital?"

"Allie doesn't think like that. About others."

The young mother was reaching a peak of fear and agitation. Her eyes pleaded for me to go.

"My last question is about boats," I said. "What do you know about the *Rap Rider* and where it might be?"

"A million miles away, I hope."

Her hand played with the chain on the door. I didn't move. Neither of us spoke. Realizing she'd have to give me more of an answer, she lowered her voice and gestured for me to lean closer.

"We used to go there when it was docked, to hang out and party. Allie's super into boats—she took some junior sea cadet course as a kid, could still do all the knots and shit. Her real father worked on a ferry before he ran out on them. We'd sit below deck and get fucked up and she'd talk about how next time her mom fucked with her she'd take the boat and leave, and how they'd never report it because she knew they were both stealing from work. Allie said with a boat she could make good money any time she needed."

"Doing what?" I asked. "Drugs?"

The young mother didn't know or wouldn't say.

At noon I parked outside of Bill Stoddard's office. There seemed no easy way to make him pay. If I kept hounding him, kept making a nuisance of myself—but that hadn't worked so far. I was running out of ideas.

The rent on the Wakeland & Chen office was five figures. The interest on our corporate debt was about the same. A lot of money to bleed out every month.

Being good at your job and loving your work didn't keep you from suffering for it. On the contrary, it made the ups and downs of a career feel all the more tumultuous. What Wakeland & Chen did had a value beyond money. I believed that absolutely. That didn't mean we could keep doing it forever. Why did everything in Vancouver feel so damn precarious?

As I was mulling over my options, a knock-kneed kid sidled up to the van. He was wearing a neon reflective vest, PRO-TEX SECURITY written on the badge above his pocket. He moved to read the licence plate, checked it against the info on his phone. Then double-checked. A regular Pinkerton.

I rolled down the passenger window and waited for him to speak.

"Um, hi. I'm with Pro-Tex? You actually can't go in the building?"

"Why, they institute a dress code?"

The Pinkerton frowned in confusion. "Mr. Stoddard didn't give a reason."

"What's your rate?" I asked. "Minimum wage, couple bucks higher?"

"Actually, right now, I'm on kind of a training wage?"

"So below minimum."

"Just till I'm trained."

"Would you like to sit down? You look beat."

His fingers moved for the handle before years of finely honed reflexives kicked in. Or he remembered his mom taught him not to climb into strange vans.

"I'm actually good," he said.

"Bill Stoddard didn't pay the last security company he hired. Begs the question who's paying you."

The Pinkerton studied his phone. He looked very uncomfortable.

"I get, uh, biweekly deposits," he said.

"Good job so far?"

"This is like my second day."

"Private security is probably not your calling," I said. "At best you'll be competent enough to earn your training wage, making the job a little worse. The world a little worse. A person should enjoy their work or at least be ethical about doing it. Don't you think? You don't have to answer right away. Run it through the computer back at headquarters."

Before I drove off, I told him to say hi to Bill Stoddard for me. The Pinkerton waved goodbye.

I'd already confirmed the movements of the Stacks on their last day, but lacking anything better to do, I did it again. The same busboys, valets, hostesses and ticket takers. Their information the same but now given begrudgingly. They were bored by it and by me. I tipped well.

There was something I'd overlooked in the lives of Budd and Jan. The dead couple were the solar force around which everyone else spun: Maggie Zito, Allie Creel and Lloyd Corso, Charlie the Priest. Budd and Jan. Never Jan alone. Had I missed something in her life, seen her only as collateral? Jan had owned businesses and amassed wealth, was as worthy a target as her biker husband.

I'd spoken to Jan's brother Junior McGuane and her sister-in-law Lori, her friends and neighbours and employees. Jan Stack was generous and monogamous and loved her home and supported charities and conservative causes. No torrid affairs, love children, embezzled millions or changelings locked in the family dungeon. A middle-aged white lady from Vancouver. Subtract the money, add a love of nickel slots, and Jan Stack could be my mother.

Shuzhen was preparing a continuance to postpone Maggie's trial. I met her at her office. We went for dinner at Kissa Tanto, Japanese-Italian food, then to the hospital. Maggie was conscious but sedated, not up to talking. The cards and flowers by her bed had multiplied.

On our way home I detoured through Granville Island. We parked near Sea Village and walked to the edge of the promenade that looked out over the float home community. Lights were on in the homes surrounding that of the dead couple. People inside.

We leaned on the railing, fingers intertwined. I stared at the dark vacant eyes of the victims' house and tried to think of what I was missing.

"Around Labour Day, Budd cancelled a flight with his brother-in-law," I said. "Booked and then no-showed. Paid him for the fuel. It's the only odd thing either of them did leading up to their deaths."

"Must have been business-related," Shuzhen said. "If it wasn't, Budd would have explained. 'Sorry I bailed, cracked my tooth,' or whatever. That makes sense, right?"

"Not enough sense." I mimed striking my head in frustration against the railing. "Nothing worse than knowing you don't know something."

"What was the purpose of the plane trip?" Shuzhen asked.

"Photography. Budd took pictures. He's no Jeff Wall, but actually pretty good."

"You sure that was the purpose?"

I waited for Shuzhen to elaborate.

"What if Budd hired someone else?" she asked.

"Another pilot?" I mulled that over and rejected it. "Junior seems insufferable, but he's experienced. And family. Budd would be booking himself a ticket to the Land of Marital Discord if he stiffed his wife's brother."

"Okay, but what if it wasn't a plane? Some other photography trip, like a boat."

The only boat that came to mind was the *Rap Rider*. Budd hiring the getaway vehicle of his own murder seemed a stretch. But I conceded it was possible.

"Let's speak to the McGuanes," Shuzhen said.

"I didn't get much out of them last time, other than grapefruit juice and vodka."

"But this time someone smart will ask the questions."

I didn't argue.

FIFTY

En route to Deep Cove I told Shuzhen what to expect from the McGuanes. She wasn't familiar with tiki culture and thought a salty dog sounded as thirst-quenching as warm bile. We parked close to the house, making sure we weren't followed or being ambushed. No music tonight. I didn't bother with the front door, simply led Shuzhen around the side. The gate was open.

Someone had redecorated the backyard with a small hurricane. The picnic table had been upended, its umbrella smashed and the Corona print canvas ripped from the ribs. The vinyl slats of the chaise had been punctured. Coals from the barbecue landmined the patio.

Junior McGuane was slumped in the Adirondack chair, a bong across his knees like the rifle of a sentry. He'd been staring at a spot on the fence. At once he shot out of the chair, rushing away from us, heading through the sliding door of the house.

"Away," he said.

I got a hand on the door and kept him from shutting it. As soon as he met resistance he folded, stumbling back into the centre of a very ordinary dining room. Junior looked at Shuzhen, confused.

"Can't," he tried to say, and began to blubber.

"Sit down, Mr. McGuane." Shuzhen guided him into a dining chair and filled a glass with water.

Junior's white hair was in tufts. His left eye was partially closed, an ugly mouse forming beneath it. The buttons on his Tommy Bahama shirt were torn, the seat of his tan shorts muddy. Someone had dropped him.

"Lori," he said, unfurling his story a word at a time. "Gone. They. Police. Can't."

I took a shot at translating. "Someone abducted your wife, beat you up and threatened to hurt her if you went to the police. That the story?"

He drank water, nodding into his glass.

"Someone you know?"

A head shake.

"More than one person?"

The start of a nod, then a shrug.

"You don't know how many," Shuzhen said, "but you saw one of them. That's really helpful, Mr. McGuane. What did the person look like?"

His mouth formed the first syllable. A W. "Woman."

"Okay, great. Did she look like me? How was she different or the same? Take your time."

"White," Junior said. "Tall."

"Real good. What colour was her hair?"

"Dark."

"Dark brown or black, or couldn't you say?"

"Brown."

"Long?"

"Yeah."

"Longer than mine?"

Nod.

"Did the woman have a gun?" I asked.

"Yeah." An effort to form the word, the memory of the experience washing over him.

A black eye like that would have taken at least an hour to swell. He'd sat there, panicking so much all he could do was stay still.

"It could be Allie Creel," I told Shuzhen.

I showed him Allie's high school picture. An ironic smile, hair in tight braids, acne. Junior nodded. "She looks different now. Except the eyes."

We forced him to drink a mug of herbal tea. Slowly Junior became less panicked, though panic never left him. I gave him a bag of frozen peas for the eye.

"Is this a kidnapping?" Shuzhen asked me. "I know the woman said not to, but shouldn't we phone the police?"

Under normal circumstances, yes—but what did that even mean? I tried to think of the last time anything had felt normal. "We need his side of things first," I said.

Junior's answers started off terse and negative. No idea why, no idea who. Whether lying or in shock, I couldn't tell. Instead, I asked him to take us through the event from the beginning.

"Just another night, really. Lori and I were listening to some Rachmaninoff, having a few rum rickeys. We still get along. We're each other's best friend."

"And then what?" I prompted.

"The gate creaked open a little, I thought by itself, and I went to close it. That woman was there. I remember thinking she looked young. That's about when she hit me."

"With the butt of the gun?"

"Think so. Somebody behind her, but I couldn't see too well. She grabbed my hair and told me get up. 'On your feet,' her exact words. I went back to the patio, and I guess she shoved me into the table 'cause I went ass over teakettle."

"What was Lori doing through this?"

Junior sloshed cold tea around his mouth to lubricate it. He spat it back into the cup. "My attention was on what the *gun* was doing. Lori, I think she just froze. The woman said something to her. 'Get your kit,' or maybe 'Get your shit.'"

"What did Lori do in response?" Shuzhen asked.

"I didn't see, but she moved, and they were leading her off, and one of them knocked over the grill. The woman told me to stay there. 'Don't say shit to the cops or anyone else.' They left, and I kind of crawled over to the chair."

From my vantage at the kitchen table I could see the length of the patio. I asked him to run through the story a second time. I tried to match action to location. The table on its side. The charcoals.

Shuzhen patted Junior's arm encouragingly. "Do you know what kit Ms. Creel was referring to?"

"Beats me."

"If Lori had time to pack just the essentials—medicine, things she absolutely needed—would you be able to tell if those items were gone?"

"Think so, yeah."

"Let's take a look."

While they did, I stepped to the gate and walked through the story. The second kidnapper had trailed the first, single file through the gate, letting Allie handle the husband. Was it likely that Junior McGuane hadn't seen this second person? A trained observer might have looked for details in the attack. But Junior wasn't accustomed to violence. I doubted he was lying.

No, the problem I had with the kidnapping scenario was Lori. There was no trace of her resistance. No dashing into the house to escape, no tending to her husband as he lay sprawled over the patio furniture. Lori might have been frozen by fear. But in that case, how did she calmly grab her toiletries and follow the kidnappers as if nothing was very much wrong?

The scenario was amiss. Lori was amiss. The whole damn case, from the moment I'd landed at YVR...

Shuzhen came back with Junior, saying Lori's toothbrush and vitamins and face cream were all there. If given a chance to pack an overnight kit, Lori McGuane would have taken those.

"Could 'kit' have meant your flight bag?" I asked. "Maps and navigation charts?"

"We use EFBs now," Junior said. "Electronic flight bags for all that stuff. Way less cumbersome. But yeah, I keep a bag with my iPad and licences, shades and a few snacks."

"Is it missing?"

He disappeared again. Shuzhen looked at me with puzzlement. Junior was a pilot—a skill that was always in demand for criminal ventures. Kidnapping his wife would give someone leverage, while leaving Junior free to file flight plans and ready the aircraft.

But to where?

Shuzhen's head shot around as Junior let out a note of surprise. He came back carrying a padded leather satchel.

"My flight bag is still here," he said. "But Lori's is gone."

FIFTY-ONE

Junior had taught his wife to fly years ago, taking Lori up for lessons that doubled as dates. They'd make short trips around the Lower Mainland, have a picnic or meal, then fly home. It was part of their courtship.

Lori was never a commercial pilot but was licensed for small craft. She didn't fly much anymore. Two or three times a year to keep her hand in or spell Junior when they travelled long distance.

"Could she be flying your seaplane?" I asked.

"The Piper? Yeah, she has spare keys in her kit. But Lori doesn't love flying at night. Upsets her tummy."

For a moment his face was wracked with simple domestic worry. Then the grave fact of the kidnapping overtook him.

"When was the last time you *know* she flew?" Shuzhen asked.

"Mexico. Last June. She and I traded off on the way down."

"And the way back?"

"Solo," he said. "Lori stayed a couple extra days to hang with Jan and Darlene Devlin."

"How did she get home, then?" I asked.

"Came back with them, I assume."

"But you don't know."

Junior shrugged. "Budd liked private charters. Have some champagne, a nice meal. For them the vacation started in the air."

"Did you carry anything back?" I asked. "This stays between us."

"I know what you're suggesting." Junior spread his hands in supplication. "If I was broke or desperate and someone asked me to run contraband, there was a time I'd consider it. But I'm too old and comfortable. And anyway, to make it worthwhile you have to strip out your plane."

"Could Lori have flown some other aircraft?" Shuzhen asked. "When you flew back alone, was her flight bag in the cockpit with you?"

He took the question seriously, trying to remember. "No it wasn't, actually. Lori took all her stuff, including her flight bag. I remember thinking that was weird, 'cause I had space for it, and with charter planes you're always hitting weight issues. 'Specially coming back, when everyone's loaded up on gewgaws and duty free."

"Phone the Devlins," I said. "Ask if Lori was on their charter."

He did, using the speakerphone. As Darlene Devlin's vodka-infused voice greeted us, Junior hit mute. "Should I tell her about Lori?" he whispered.

"No. Act like nothing's wrong."

He tilted his head and unmuted the phone. "Hey, Darlene, this is Junior."

"It's the transmission, right? It finally crapped out? I told you—"

"Actually this is kind of an odd question to ask. When you came back from 'Pulco, was Lori on your plane?"

"Why?"

Junior looked at us, helpless.

"Glasses," Shuzhen mouthed.

"Lori thinks she maybe left some sunglasses."

"Well, I wouldn't know," Darlene said. "The charter didn't work out so we all went back on separate flights. What kind of glasses did she lose?"

"Oh, just the drugstore kind. Thanks anyway."

Next we had Junior check his bank statements, and the balance on his credit cards. No charge for a ticket in June. Lori McGuane had come back from Mexico under mysterious circumstances and likely in the cockpit of a plane.

"Tell me about the day trip Budd booked with you," I said.

"How's that help get Lori back?"

"Understanding always helps." I didn't tell him that I suspected Lori hadn't been kidnapped so much as forcefully encouraged to make a repeat flight—maybe using the plane she and her husband owned.

"Well, Budd asked if I'd take him island-hopping, try out some fancy new lens. Take photos of the seals and stuff. I filed the plan, got the Piper all ready, and Budd flaked out."

"Could he have had an ulterior motive? Looking for something, maybe a boat?"

"Realm of possibility, I suppose," Junior said. "The Strait has a lot of islands with a lot of coves. Rum-runners used them during Prohibition."

"After which cross-border smuggling came to a complete halt."

His face formed a weak and bloodless smile. "Budd used to say if it was good enough for Seagrams, it was good enough for BC Bud."

Or heroin. Cocaine. Fentanyl. Guns or whatever else. If Charlie the Priest was bringing it in, and Lori had helped him...

Maybe Budd had considered using his brother-in-law's plane to help him find where the Priest had cached his stuff. Another thought occurred to me, which I didn't share with the pilot. Smuggling without the permission of the Exiles was punishable by death. If Budd suspected his brother-in-law, perhaps Junior's flight out to a deserted stretch of Pacific Northwest coastline was meant to be one way.

Junior confirmed that his Piper Cherokee was still in his hanger at the Abbotsford Airport, and hadn't been flown since Mexico. Finding this out consumed the last of his energy. He took a pill and crashed out on his bed.

There seemed to be too much to do and nothing to do. I found a box of unpalatable quinoa granola bars in the McGuanes' pantry. Shuzhen and I each had one. I told her what I suspected, starting in Mexico.

"Charlie the Priest sets up a deal in Acapulco to import something. Drugs, let's say, for the sake of argument. He's not kicking up to Terry Rhodes because he wants the money for himself. So he needs a pilot who's not one of the usual players."

"Lori is the sister-in-law of an Exile," Shuzhen said.

"True, it's a risk, Budd Stack finding out. Say the Priest is desperate. Say the shipment's on his doorstep and the plane is ready to go."

"And the pilot gets arrested or sick," Shuzhen said.

"They all vacation together, the top echelon guys. The Priest sounds out Junior about flying the load, maybe so subtle that Junior doesn't realize. But Junior says no. He's content. It's *Lori* that wants more. Maybe she has debts, or maybe it's a competitive thing. Keeping up with the Joneses, or the Exiles in her case. She tells her husband she's flying back with her friends, tells her friends she's on a different flight, and then flies the Priest's plane up the coast..."

Shuzhen nodded with enthusiasm, seeing where I was going. "...where it's met by Allie Creel and the *Rap Rider*. Mission accomplished, they think."

"That's exactly what they think. Weeks later and Budd gets suspicious, or is asked to get suspicious. There's new product floating around, or something about the flight gets back to him. His brother-in-law's a commercial pilot, Junior's got this plane, and he flew back alone."

"Would Budd really have killed him?" Shuzhen's voice was low, as if worried Junior would wake up and overhear.

"Killing family members is only a moral quandary if you have morals."

"So why cancel the photo trip?" Shuzhen answered her own question. "Because Junior is innocent. He didn't fly anything back, doesn't know anything, and all his flight logs are clean. And Budd doesn't suspect Lori because she's his sister-in-law and a woman."

"Sexism to the rescue," I said. "Budd is still snooping, though, and if he gets wind of Charlie the Priest's involvement, it's taxation at least, more likely a hollow-point to the skull."

"How does Maggie Zito fit in?"

I opened another quinoa bar, but the smell of stale grain and dehydrated cranberry killed my appetite.

"The Priest was in Hope twenty years ago, the weekend Beau Zito was killed. He might have even done the killing. In print, Maggie was quoted threatening retaliation."

Shuzhen leapt ahead of me. "So he enlists his nephew and Allie. Maggie's schedule he gets from her boyfriend Murray Fong. The weapons are tools from Maggie's own garage." Her hand dug into mine, fingers pressing into my knuckles. "Holy shit, Dave. Proving it, though."

I nodded. "Allie, Lori, the boat, the cargo. The more of those we can get hold of, the better chance to spring Maggie for good."

"But why kidnap Lori now?" Shuzhen asked.

"I don't know if Allie is still working for the Priest. Maybe their only connection was through Lloyd. With him out of commission, they're maneuvering around each other. Lori connects them, so she's a liability."

"So she's probably dead already."

"I think her time is very limited," I said. "Pilots are valuable, or else they would have killed her right away. My guess, the Priest needs Lori for one more flight."

"And then?"

I didn't have to say it, and didn't want to. Shuzhen looked at the patio debris, then at the steamer clock on the wall. We were already too late to stop one catastrophe.

FIFTY-TWO

Felix Ramos groused at being woken up at four in the morning, but it probably wasn't a unique experience. By the time I'd given him the address, he sounded more awake than I was. He'd be at the McGuanes' house in half an hour.

Shuzhen had napped fitfully on the couch. I washed my face, staring down my reflection, which seemed eager to tell me this half-assed quest was stupid and doomed to fail. That I wasn't a gunfighter, and that it would be better to write off Lori McGuane and turn this over to the authorities. Depending on one's definition of authority, that meant Deputy Chief MacLeish, or Terry Rhodes.

The problem was, I didn't trust either of them, their means or their morals, not with our lives. MacLeish would approach this with an eye toward his career. He'd protect Operation Eiger unless the evidence was overwhelming. I didn't have evidence like that. With Rhodes the result would be simple and savage. Burn everyone, kick the ashes and salt the ground.

That left Shuzhen and me, Junior McGuane and Felix. Assuming Harry Whishaw came through with the *Rap Rider*'s location, we could slip in, steal Lori back and hold Allie until the Coast Guard showed up. With Lori, the cargo and the real perpetrators, we'd have evidence even a police bureaucrat couldn't ignore.

Shuzhen called a car service to take her home. She'd visit the hospital and check on Maggie, right after taking a shower. "Hate wearing the same clothes two days in a row," she said.

"You get used to it."

"*Bums* get used to it, Dave."

She took a sample vial of Chanel from her handbag, dabbed her wrists, spritzed the air and walked into it. "Ought to keep the driver from rolling down all the windows."

Shuzhen kissed me goodbye, a moist peck with a touch of tongue to the teeth. At the door she paused.

"Don't make any moves without me," she said. "I'm serious."

I nodded. There was a time when feelings of protection would have made me do just that. Either I'd become a little more enlightened, or simply realized I needed all the help I could get.

"While I'm out," Shuzhen said, "I'm going to record a voice memo and send it to Nimisha. Everything we know. Just in case."

"Smart," I said.

"I'll bring my car. And a change of clothes for your stank ass."

Then she was gone.

I called Harry at the marina and left a message. Made toast and tea, sat and closed my eyes. When I opened them Felix was staring at me through the patio glass.

"The fucking nerve," he said. "You wake me so I can rush over here and find you napping."

A hockey bag was slung over his shoulder. Wordlessly he dropped it on the kitchen table and unzipped it. Inside, a pair of pump shotguns, boxes of shells and the hard plastic case of a pistol. Cuffs, zip ties. A pair of flash-bang grenades.

I wanted to crack a joke about this being overkill. But those were appropriate tools. Given how dangerous Allie was and the Priest's track record of carnage, we had to err on the side of slaughter.

"The Priest doesn't know you're helping me, does he?" I asked.

"No idea what he knows."

"And as far as your loyalties?"

"Terry Rhodes trusts you," Felix said. "I'm not gonna shoot you in the back. What else do you fuckin' want, a blood oath?"

Beneath the tough-guy nonchalance, he was probably as conflicted as I was. Charlie the Priest perched near the top of the hierarchy Felix had sworn allegiance to. Now the Priest was our target. Ambition and loyalty and maybe even a conscience all grappling to be heard.

Junior McGuane staggered out of his bedroom, scratching himself through his briefs. He looked at Felix with puzzlement and fear. "Don't I know you?"

Felix unpacked the hockey bag and didn't volunteer an answer.

"Shower and get ready," I told the pilot. "Book a flight plan that's elastic enough we can go around the Strait of Georgia."

"We're gonna get Lori back?"

There was no benefit in lying, but he didn't need to know how low the odds were. How many vectors would need to align. I left it at a nod, hoping I knew what I was doing.

We cleaned the barrels of the shotguns, loading them with twelve-gauge buckshot. The pistol was a SIG .45 that resembled the service weapon I'd once carried, briefly, before realizing I wasn't a cop. That had been a tough lesson. My preference was for revolvers and breech-loading long guns, things that fired fewer times but fired always, with few moving parts. Less to go wrong.

At the bottom of the hockey bag was a whetstone. Felix sharpened his pocket knife, then honed the two largest knives from the block on the kitchen counter. We had time, so he did the others, too.

"Comforts you, doesn't it?" I said.

He nodded, almost shy. "Reminds me of my dad. When we had the Chop House, he could do every knife in under two minutes, and we had a shit ton lying around. We used to time him."

"Mine showed me how to box," I said. "The basics, at least. How to not fall over or break your thumb on the first punch. Wrapping my hands for a workout."

A strong memory even decades later. My father smelling of coffee and rye whiskey and aftershave, the feel of the wraps tightening on my palm. He'd sit in a corner with a newspaper while I ran through drills or worked the speed bag.

"You any good?" Felix asked.

"Not anymore."

"What about back in the day?"

"The best."

"Really?"

"Heavyweight champ," I said. "Twice. That's why I'm sitting here with you."

That earned a laugh.

Harry returned my call at quarter after nine. "Thought sailors woke up at first light?" I asked.

"Young sailors, maybe. Wanted to earn my case of hooch before we spoke."

"Did you find the boat?"

"Two weeks ago she was berthed near Campbell River. Harbourmaster there is a chum of mine. She remembered seeing a scruffy-looking lady bringing supplies on board. Cleaning stuff, food, all sortsa shit. I had my pal do a little legwork. Did the lady buy anything at the boat shop, hardware store? Turns out she did. White and blue boat paint plus a pack of stencils."

"That's definitely worth the case," I said. "Thank your friend for me."

"Hold your damn horses," Harry said. "Your generation's got the patience of a dog with a stiffy. 'Cross from Campbell River is Quadra Island. I asked the marina on Quadra if a thirty-footer had berthed there recently, with a scruffy-looking lady aboard."

"And?" I didn't know Harry Whishaw all that well, but he seemed to enjoy the theatrical pause.

"A thirty-footer's been popping in regularly," Harry said. "Registers for the day only. The boat you're looking for is now called the *Bay Bride*, and she was there day before yesterday."

FIFTY-THREE

At ten the Beast rolled out of Deep Cove, carrying the three of us, the hockey bag and its arsenal stashed beneath the back bench with an old carpet thrown over it. Rush hour was finished. We cut a stately pace, sliding across the Second Narrows with ease.

Shuzhen would meet us at the airstrip in Cloverdale. An old friend of Junior's was fuelling the Piper. With luck we'd be in the air before noon, circle Quadra Island, spot the *Bay Bride* and then land at the marina. A seventeen-foot bowrider with duel outboards had been rented. We'd make our final approach in that. The plan was solid and adaptable—if an opportunity arose to catch the boat in the marina, or pin her between us and the open water, we could seize it.

If Allie Creel was a seasoned smuggler, she would have abandoned the boat or stolen another. The boat was the key to her. She felt she'd somehow earned it, that it was home. My guess was she'd brought the *Bay Bride* to the Lower Mainland yesterday, taken Lori aboard, and would hurry back across the strait to where she felt safe.

Whatever Allie lacked in planning she made up for in brutality and paranoia. The story Felix told of seeing Allie slash the waiter, the violence done to the Stacks—she was danger, and Lori was in her power. Anyone who got close would be at risk.

If we could bring our boat alongside hers using some sort of subterfuge. If we could overwhelm her suddenly and with undeniable force. And if the universe decided to take pity and spare us any last-minute cataclysms. And even then, the odds weren't very good.

The van was silent beneath the patter of oldies from the sound system. Muddy Waters and Pearl Jam, Heart and zz Top. Each of us lost in our own fears and limitations. Junior McGuane sat next to me, gripping the strap above the passenger door, uncomfortable with someone else at the wheel. In the back seat, Felix clasped and unclasped his knife.

We took the exit for the airstrip. Small planes filled the aluminum domes of the hangers, more tarped out on the grass beside the strip. An engine started, its drone high-pitched, like an oversized lawnmower. Shuzhen's Merc wasn't in the parking lot. We'd made better time and were early.

The Piper was in hanger three. Junior had final preparations to make. He took the hockey bag, stooping under its weight. Walking to the hanger he looked twenty years older. It struck me, in his long career as a pilot, he'd probably never flown under so much duress. I hoped Junior would rise to the necessity.

"More waiting," Felix said. "How do you stand it?"

"The sun is out. Birds are singing."

"And you're fucking with me again."

"I'm not," I said. "When you spend all your time thinking about the worst, you appreciate things differently. Everything's fragile and finite."

"Makes no kind of sense." Felix walked off to explore the main office.

I'd missed a call while driving. A number I didn't recognize with a local extension. Odds were, a telemarketing robot trying to pitch me some upgrade for my nonexistent lifestyle. I dialed, thinking it might be Shuzhen at the hospital with news.

Terry Rhodes's voice said, "Nice morning for a plane trip."

His voice threw off my equilibrium. I felt airborne already, struggling to keep my breathing even. "How'd you know?"

"One of my guys is with you."

"At the moment he's strong-arming a Coke machine."

"Well, kick him loose."

"Why?"

"*I said so* should be a good enough reason."

Without Felix, the plan of superior numbers and firepower seemed haphazard, foolish. "I need him," I said.

"You'll make do. Or you won't. Either way, this shit won't be tied to me or mine."

The call over. Felix had managed to dislodge a can of root beer from the machine. I told him the news and who the call had come from.

Felix sent the can barrelling toward the side of the building, exploding and landing in the grass to leak out.

"I don't know what to do," he said. "I mean I want to go. Fuck."

Hands on his neck, scowling at the dirt, at the sky. Appealing to the heavens.

"You need me to go, right? I could say you didn't give me the message."

"You could," I said.

"Rhodes would find out, though. He always finds out."

The prospect looked in genuine conflict. He'd been a kid when he pledged to the Exiles. In prison as a juvenile, he had little choice. But he did now.

"You're not a child," I said. "Make your choice and live with it, but stare at it straight. I can't choose for you."

THE LAST EXILE · 265

"You know I can't cross Terry Rhodes."

I didn't answer him.

"All right then." Felix forced himself to meet my gaze. "Good luck, Wakeland. Hope it works out."

I watched him walk off through the field, veering away from the buildings and the parking lot, away from the highway, toward no destination I could fathom. Growing smaller. A man alone in the deep green.

FIFTY-FOUR

The turboprop engine of the Piper Cherokee made a sustained ripple of mechanical flatulence, as loud inside the cabin as out. Painted canary yellow with baby-blue skids, the Piper had rolled out of the plant almost fifty years ago. From the scarring on the tan seat leather, the film along the glass and the mismatched wing flaps, the plane had reached middle age through hard duty. I hoped to be so lucky.

Junior McGuane's spirits improved in the cockpit. Muttering to himself, absorbed in the instruments, he taxied to the edge of the airstrip. Piloting an aircraft was something he knew and could control.

Without Felix there were no issues with weight. Shuzhen sat beside me in the back seat, dressed in leggings and an Arc'teryx jacket. She'd spoken to Maggie briefly. The injured woman didn't recall anything about the attack.

A good day for a flight, warm and cloudless. We broke from the earth. The Piper gained altitude and was soon soaring over the farmland of Delta, out of the mouth of the Fraser River. The water turned from grey turmoil to a smooth slab of cobalt blue.

Quadra Island was shaped roughly like a chicken leg with the thigh attached, floating just east of Vancouver Island. We'd skirt the drumstick of the bird, follow the shore north until we spotted the *Bay Bride*. Then break across the water to Campbell River, where we'd pick up our boat.

"What altitude should we aim for?" Junior asked through the headset. His voice sounded distant, like I was listening to him from a flight tower.

"Low enough we can make out the name."

"We'll be spotted, too."

An unavoidable risk. None of us were experts at aerial reconnaissance. A thirty-foot boat anchored somewhere within range of Campbell River would hopefully be easy to spot.

Shuzhen jabbed my arm, pointing. I leaned over her. "Orcas," she said, an enraptured look on her face.

I glimpsed nothing but a dark shadow along the water.

Houses had been built along the coast, some with private beaches or jetties. A fortune would be needed now to purchase such a place. An eight-figure rustic getaway.

A speck of white on a grey rock beach. Shuzhen directed Junior's attention to it. He cut over in a wide loop across the southeastern tip of the island. Driftwood in the water. An outcrop of arbutus trees provided a canopy for the white something, which had the general form of a ship. A glint of glass from a windshield.

"You have to circle," I told the pilot. "Make it look like a joyride, like you took some friends up."

"You want me to do stunts?" Disdain in his voice, as if I'd asked a world-class chef to reheat a corn dog.

"Just so it looks like we're goofing around and not spying," I said.

He course-corrected drastically, dropping the nose so the plane plunged toward the water. My stomach tried to climb my esophagus as we dropped. The water took on definition, each wave a distinct crest and wake. I grabbed Shuzhen's arm.

And just as sharp, Junior pulled the nose up. We began a steep climb. Teeth clenched, in case any vital organs tried to make their escape, I forced myself to scan the beach for the craft.

As we came around it revealed itself as a speedboat on a trailer, connected to a large white pickup truck.

"Not the *Bay Bride*," Shuzhen said.

Back we went. The plane made covering the shoreline easy. A beach fire—not them. A pair of women on the deck of a yacht—the wrong boat, the wrong crew.

Rounding the northwest coast of the island, Junior kept watch on the fuel gauge. I felt Shuzhen nudge me again and point, this time out my window. Anchored off the shore, a white thirty-footer. A tanned woman sprawled across a towel bearing the face of Tony Montana from *Scarface*. Dark hair, sunglasses, nude.

"Should I turn around?" Junior asked.

No need. The sunbather was Allie Creel.

The plane skimmed and dropped onto the waves near the marina. Junior motored up to the dock, climbed down and tied us off. I was glad to be on land, at least temporarily.

Deafened from the engine, we hauled the hockey bag with us, lunched near the water and tried to figure out our next move.

Option one: call in the Coast Guard. We spotted something suspicious on that boat, officer. Here's the location. Send someone with a badge to check it out. Allie Creel might surrender. She might also shoot Lori and break for the open sea. Or scuttle the boat, drowning them both. Scratch option one.

Option two: rip up and board her like pirates, freeing the damsel and plundering the ship. Without Felix, that was less appealing, the chance of casualties high.

Option three: do nothing. I tried to think of an option four.

"I could swim up to the boat," Shuzhen said. "Maybe get Lori without anyone seeing."

"You might be spotted, and there'd be nothing we could do. Plus we don't know who else is onboard."

THE LAST EXILE · 269

She nodded and bit her thumbnail, frustrated. "So what do we do then, Admiral?"

I checked the time. Shortly after three. Sundown would be close to eight.

"We cut over to Quadra and get within sight of the ship," I said. "We hug the shore. Not too close. We wait for seven, quarter past, when the sun will be at our back. Then we drive for her."

"And then what?" Junior asked. Now that we were out of the plane he seemed doubtful and anxious.

"Option four."

FIFTY-FIVE

The bowrider was called the *Hood*. Junior's friend had provisioned us with a case of Red Stripe in the galley, along with a bag of Cheezies. Once we were out of the harbour, Junior handed off the wheel to me. He uncapped a beer using the acrylic edge of the instrument panel.

"Settles the old nerves," he said.

I held a straight course to Quadra Island, then angled to port, running along the coastline, the boat jouncing as we cut across the waves. Shuzhen stood near the bow, her phone out, using the zoom to keep watch for the *Bay Bride*.

There she was, a bright white dab on the water.

The barking of harbour seals. Two dozen of them, marble-coloured, arrayed along the crags of the shore. Wishing us luck, I hoped. We held course.

When the boat was the size of a fist on the horizon, I slowed. We'd be featureless at this distance. I waved to Shuzhen and McGuane that it was time.

"We're going to be the Labour Day Holdovers," I said. "Loud dumb college kids whose classes don't start till next week. We're going to blast shitty music and burn an obscene amount of fuel jetting around at top speed. We won't get close enough to bother Allie, just close enough to become background noise. We'll hold beers. Junior, you'll wrap your T-shirt around your head so she won't recognize you. We'll be having a grand old time and then Something Will Go Wrong. Not enough fuel to get back, and then, beg your pardon, ma'am, would you mind towing us in?"

We fell to our respective jobs. I donned a baseball cap, unbuttoned my shirt and rolled up the cuffs of my jeans. Shuzhen shed her jacket and stalked the deck, taking shots of the water and birds, posing for selfies on the prow. Junior took the helm and let the throttle out, sipping from his bottle more often than I would have liked.

Auto-tuned dreck poured out of the overtaxed speakers—new-country laundry lists of American trucks now made overseas. Sad-boy Toronto hip hop. Teenage punk as carefully orchestrated as a Fauré requiem. It fit the image. I hated us already.

Junior steered with a drunk freshman's reflexes, pulling wild arcs, crossing against the grain of the water. As we zigzagged along the shore, we took turns crowing and letting out coyote yips. Fun, fun. If we were too obnoxious, the *Bay Bride* might lurch away. We'd have to pursue, and that would raise suspicion. Our obnoxious college kids would want their privacy, too.

I moved up to the bow and gripped Shuzhen around the waist. A couple of young lovers, not a care in the world. Her arm held the camera out and we grinned at it.

"Is Allie still sunbathing?" I asked over the noise.

"Can't see anyone."

"I'm going to bring the tools up."

She brayed laughter, blowing kisses, any tension masked by her performance.

I emptied the cardboard beer case and placed the .45 inside. Junior was on his third bottle, the empties lined up along the porthole. I filled one with water and brought it to him.

"Think of Lori," I said. He nodded, instantly sobered. I set one of the shotguns by his feet. "Don't pick this up unless someone's aiming at you."

"Think Budd ever did stuff like this?" he asked.

"Rescued someone?"

"No, the other."

"Probably not," I lied. Now wasn't the time for a re-evaluation of his brother-in-law.

At seven we stopped the engine, leaving only the music. Dinner hour. Every few minutes one of us would circle the deck, tossing an empty Red Stripe or whooping, dancing. When it was my turn I pissed off the side, finding I actually had to go.

The sun held out defiantly, only lowering to eye-level near eight. Junior pulled back the throttle and we churned in the direction of Campbell River. Abruptly he cut the engine, allowing it to sputter to a stop. Then ignited it again. Panicky landlubbers abusing a rental, too boozy and edible-mellow to care that this would show up on their parents' credit cards.

We turned gradually toward the *Bay Bride*. Waved. As we closed in I saw the sloppy paint job, the first two R's turned into B's, the last blotched over with primer. *Bay Bride* from *Rap Rider*. Blue plastic kayaks and other assorted junk cluttered the back deck.

"Hullooo!" Shuzhen called. "Ahoy or whatever! Yo, *Bay Bride*? A little help?"

Allie Creel ascended from the cabin, wearing a sleeveless Misfits tee and cutoffs. Squinting and saluting to shield her eyes.

"What's up?" she asked. Annoyed more than suspicious.

The skin on her forearms was freckled and peeling. Bug bites and stubble on her legs. Allie moved surefootedly amid the rubble on her deck.

Junior hunkered over the wheel. I stayed low, the shotgun held close to the deck, out of sight. I leaned my left arm and my beer on the gunwale. Shuzhen crossed to the portside as we came nearer.

"We got like zero gas," she said, pointing at me with a bottle. "Dumbass here totally cheaped out and now our fuel thingy's at zero."

"Not my fault," I whined.

Allie scrutinized the two of us, looked at the man at the wheel. The tinted windscreen prevented her from getting a good look at Junior. "You didn't notice you were low?"

"We're not like professional boat captains or whatever," Shuzhen said. Her voice took on the perfect rich-kid tone, frustrated and bored. "Could we maybe get a tow to Campbell River? We can totally pay you, like two hundred bucks?"

Allie looked at Shuzhen, wanting to say no. Turning down loud kids would only draw attention. She huffed out a big sigh.

"Toss me a line."

"That's like the rope, right?"

Shuzhen's first toss fell short, deliberately. We drifted closer and she gathered the rope, this time angling it up so it made the deck of the *Bay Bride*. I could see half-folded camping chairs, firewood, an axe—the boat cluttered with things Allie would need if she made camp.

"Saving our freaking lives." Shuzhen held up the beer case. "Please let me buy you a drink."

"Better stay aboard," Allie said. A pause while she generated an excuse. "I've got a really bad flu."

But the exuberant college kid was leaping over the gunwale already, landing on the deck of the *Bay Bride*. Shuzhen's fist popped out of the cardboard holding the pistol. At the same time, I snapped the shotgun up to level it at Allie.

"Surprise," Shuzhen said. "Like, totally."

FIFTY-SIX

Allie accepted the zip ties with the fatalism of the born loser. The universe had taken up arms against her from the moment of her birth. Even her family was in on the plot. And now this. Sure, tie my hands, what difference does it make? Life was never going to work out for Allison Creel.

"Want to tell us where Lori McGuane is?"

"Fuck you."

"Not even a hint?"

"Fuck you."

That childish petulance went hand in glove with a darting, coyote cunning. As we sat across from one another in the galley of the *Bay Bride*, Allie's eyes scanned for advantage. They lighted on the bench against the far wall, only briefly, then made a wide circle, looking everywhere but there.

The cushion of the bench she wasn't looking at lifted off. Inside among the ownership papers and junk was an emergency flare, a knife and a small radio. Allie never showed her disappointment.

The *Bay Bride* had been her home for a while. Food bits littered the floor, Ding Dong wrappers and crab legs, empty tins of Beefaroni. She'd put a foil container in the microwave, and the faint odour of burnt aluminum filled the galley. The scorched lasagna still lay in the overflowing trash.

Shuzhen searched the bedroom and the hold while I sat with the shotgun trained on Allie. At our range and in the confined space, I was more likely to club her with the stock than fire. We both knew this. Allie's eye twitched reflexively.

Junior McGuane waited onboard the *Hood*. Shuzhen took her time, searching the places a living person could be crammed. When that yielded nothing, she looked through the smaller compartments.

"Lori isn't onboard," she called, returning to the galley. "Is that good or bad news?"

I wasn't sure. Allie's response was predictable: "Fuck you."

"Let me double-check." Speaking for Allie's benefit, I told Shuzhen, "If she even raises an ass cheek off that bench, she means to kill you. Shoot her in the face."

The hostage flinched, eyes still closed.

I didn't doubt Shuzhen was right, and Lori wasn't aboard. My search was of Allie's personal spaces. Using one of Felix's knives, I slit the mattress and the pillows, checked the baseboards and the vents and the seams. In the bulkhead I found a jerry can with about a cup of fuel sloshing around the bottom. Sawing off the top revealed a vacuum-sealed brick of hundred-dollar bills. In the jumble of clothes around the bed, I found a wad of money in the same denomination. Maybe thirty grand in total.

Under the sink in the head was a porcelain tortoise. The top shell lifted off, revealing a collection of jewellery. A mix of pearls and pewter, silver and jade. And a large gold bracelet with an inscription.

To My Darling Jan
Still as pretty
As that night at the Roxy
Here's to forty more

I stepped out onto the deck and headed around to the transom. Junior gave a double-handed wave from the deck of the *Hood*, desperate for information on his wife. I didn't pause.

Raising the motors out of the water revealed a hollow panel to the left side of the housing. The screws were loose enough to remove by hand. Inside, a narrow trench, capable of holding several bricks or parcels, or possibly a human being. Empty at the moment.

"Anything?" Junior called. Another beer in his hand.

"Lori's not here, which probably means she's alive. I don't know any more than that."

"But shouldn't we—"

I headed back to the galley.

Shuzhen had traded the shotgun for the pistol. She held it two-handed, at a distance Allie couldn't close. The prisoner had her face on the table.

I placed the money and the bracelet where she could see them, rapped on the table. Allie opened her eyes.

"Why'd you kidnap Lori McGuane?" I asked.

"Why'd you fuck your mother?"

Sullen, enduring the world's conspiracy against her. I was tired of people like this. I felt a dozen centuries old. I slammed my palm into the table hard enough to leave a depression in the melamine. Allie's head jolted up but her expression didn't change.

"Did you kill the Stacks?"

"Sure. I killed everybody. Kill you, too."

"Who was your accomplice?"

"The pope and your mom. He ate her box after."

"Pointless, Dave," Shuzhen said. "Let's call it in."

She was right. We'd found Allie Creel, obtained evidence of her complicity in the murders. That information would aid Shuzhen's client. And none of us had been hurt. A good time to cash out. The McGuanes could fend for themselves.

Only they couldn't. Junior had helped us in good faith, and whatever Lori had done, she'd been threatened into this last part. Her best last chance was us.

"I found your secret compartment," I said to Allie. "You've been running drugs for Lloyd's uncle Charlie. Picking up cargo for him."

"Go fuck your sister with a mastodon dick."

"She's kind of a brat," I said to Shuzhen.

"Too much given to her by Mommy and Daddy."

"Y'all don't know shit about me," Allie said, seething. "Fought for every fuckin' thing I got—this boat, the money. Rigged fuckin' game, you're goddamn right I make moves. Got to."

"What kind of moves could a kid like you make?"

"Untie me, fuckin' find out."

"Are you a murderer, Allie?"

"A fuckin' soldier. Whatever it takes."

"Do you even know why the Priest had you kill the Stacks?"

Allie began to answer and caught herself, realizing we'd been winding her up. She spat at me. Her legs kicked out beneath the table. She uttered a long and inventive list of phallic substitutes my ancestors could employ. Shuzhen told her to shut up.

Junior was calling from the other vessel. We moved the prisoner onto the canopied deck.

"Where's Lori?" he asked. "Any news?"

He clambered onto the *Bay Bride*, moving with the precision of a man trying to prove he's not drunk. My fault for leaving him to fret on his own.

In the cockpit, I checked the GPS. The recent pinned coordinates were all in open water save for one. A cove to the north of Campbell River, along Discovery Passage. A beachfront property on Race Point Road, which fed onto Vancouver Island's main highway.

Cargo could travel to the mainland by ferry with little chance of detection.

"Could a plane like yours make it to Mexico with only one refuelling?" I asked Junior.

"If it had twelve-fives—twelve-and-a-half-gallon fuel tanks, plus full span ailerons."

"She'll be back tonight, then."

Rain had begun as the last of the sun disappeared. I looked at the others, lit by the boat's track lights and the instrument panel.

"As best I can figure, Allie here is part of a smuggling operation involving Lloyd Corso, the Priest and occasionally Lori McGuane. Stuff comes in from Mexico, not often but enough to be worthwhile. The Exiles don't know about this, but Budd and Jan found out. Or were going to."

"You don't know fucking anything," Allie said.

"The Priest's attempts to kill me weren't his best efforts—he couldn't use his familiar methods and people, couldn't risk having it traced back to him. Same with his move against Maggie, and why he let Allie into his operation at all." I held up a hand to quash Allie's objection to this. "My guess, the Priest is bringing in one last load tonight. Usually the plane drops the cargo in open water, or lands and they transfer it aboard. Then Allie sails it to his property on the island. Tonight, though, the plane is going to fly there directly."

"And Lori will be there," McGuane said.

I nodded.

"Why fly straight there?" Shuzhen asked. "Allie wouldn't have to go at all, then."

"Because his name is on the property here, and because this is the end. The Priest is desperate now. More important than the shipment is bringing all his co-conspirators together in one isolated

THE LAST EXILE · 279

place." To Allie I said, "From the start he meant to kill you. You must know that."

"Shut up." Allie leaned back on the weatherproof cushions, her forehead pelted by the rain.

"How else did you imagine this would end?"

I don't think the question had occurred to her.

FIFTY-SEVEN

In the dark we winched up the anchor and steered the *Bay Bride* toward the cove. The *Hood* bobbed behind us on its towline. Shuzhen steered, using the GPS more than her vision. No running lights.

Junior McGuane had gone from nervously quaffing Red Stripe to listlessly staring at his sneakers. I watched Allie Creel lean toward the seam of the upholstered seat and rake her cheek along it like a cat. Bent sideways, she glowered at me.

"What? Why you fuckin' staring?"

"Making sure you don't escape."

Allie raised her shoulders as high as she could. "How'm I 'sposed to do that tied up?"

"You're not," I said.

In truth, I was doing what I always did in the presence of incomprehensible violence: trying to comprehend it. Looking for murder in her face. What tics and mannerisms marked her as the killing type? But there was no killing type. Even the eyes, which seemed like dark tunnels terminating nowhere—a truck driver on a three-day haul could have the same dead-eyed glare.

I watched her anyway, hoping to be proven wrong. That murderers don't look like everybody else. That evil declares itself in the flesh, that it isn't simply part of our day-to-day. A thought too unpleasant not to test again and again.

I wasn't the only one observing.

"You and that chick," Allie said, inclining her head toward where Shuzhen stood. "The way you move around each other. Comfortable. I can tell you two fuck."

"Perceptive," I said.

"Yeah, I fucking am."

"What did you notice about Jan and Budd?"

"About who?"

Allie nodded, comprehending who I meant. A smile bloomed at one side of her mouth.

"She was worried about him. Worried for herself, too, and also kind of in disbelief. 'Can't be happening to me,' that sort of thing. Lying there bleeding. And then she looked up the stairs and I could just tell she was worried for him. Kind of beautiful."

"What did Lloyd think?"

A roll of the eyes. "Lloyd's soft. Puked in the kayak on the trip back to the boat."

"Did you know Lloyd came forward as a witness?"

"Better than saying he did it."

"But why frame Maggie Zito?"

"What the man wanted. Like I told you, I'm a soldier."

"Sure you are."

Allie righted herself with considerable effort. She blew a strand of hair out of her face. Leaning back, confident, bored.

"I've made a decision," she said.

"For Jesus? Good a time as any."

"For when I'm free. It was gonna be you. You first. But I think I'll make it her, so it happens in front of you. Bleeding out in your arms. How'd you like that?"

She wasn't blinking and her voice didn't raise to the tone of bluster. Doubtless she meant it.

"You're not a soldier or even a very good thief," I told Allie. "You're a sad kid with toys and emotional problems. You're to be pitied and locked away."

"Said what I'm gonna do. You watch. See if it doesn't happen just that way."

A pair of high white fluorescents lit up the beach and the small floating dock. A guide for the plane through the downpour. Half a mile offshore, the *Bay Bride* rolled over the surf, waiting.

Just after one we heard the engine. Saw the lights on the small aircraft as it slipped out of the clouds. A seaplane similar to the McGuanes' Piper, it curved neatly and floated parallel to the water before touching down. We watched the plane taxi to the dock. A figure lighted from the cockpit, though I couldn't make out if it was Lori McGuane.

The houses on the beach were dark. Someone stood close to the lights—shadows as this person met with the pilot. Only two of them. That was good. After a pause, the pair of silhouettes headed into the nearest house.

"Drive her right onto the beach," I told Shuzhen.

"That'll scuff the hull."

"We'll settle in small claims court later."

I fastened Allie's legs together, just to make sure she'd be immobile, then gagged her using a shirt from the floor. If the smell bothered her, she could take it up with her maid.

In shallow water now. The boat scraped on the sand and rocks. We'd come in at an angle, to the right of the fluorescents. I saw them now, square construction lights on tripods. They lit up a swath of rocky beach under beating rain.

Dropping down into the shallows, splashing my way to shore. The rocks were slippery and jagged. Shuzhen and Junior followed, our own little Juno Beach landing. The porch light in the house snapped on. Firewood under the awning, a horseshoe over the door.

Pebble and sand became soil and grass. At a natural rise in the landscape, I paused and held up a hand for the others to wait. I approached alone, resting the shotgun against the fence like I'd been taught to do while hunting, then slipped between the rails into the yard.

The planks of the porch accepted my weight with a silence I was grateful for. There was a window levered partway open. I knelt, listening. Voices male and female.

"That little bitch cracked him on the head. How'm I gonna explain it to Junior? 'You'll never believe it, hon, but I got away clean, and oh yeah, here's ninety thousand dollars?'"

"Don't explain, Lori. Sock the money away. The whole point of a rainy-day fund."

"I don't know if you've looked outside, but it's fucking pouring now."

I raised up to peer inside, catching a scent of burnt tobacco. Lori was pacing with a cigarette in hand. Dressed in a leather jacket, hair tucked beneath a Blue Jays cap. Her voice betrayed panic, the male voice reassurance.

"Hate flying at night. And where is she, anyway?"

"Allie always texts when she's close."

"So why isn't she close? I didn't want to do this—"

"I know, and Allie shouldn't have been so rough. A miscommunication."

"Whatever. Where's the little bitch at?"

Lori paused near the window and I dropped, leaning away from the sill. I heard hands on the glass.

"There's a boat out there," Lori said.

Time broke. That's the only way to describe it. Our movements were collectively sped up, yet our comprehension slowed to an oceanic pulse. In the space of one breath Junior McGuane saw his wife lit up in the window. Overjoyed, he called her name. Junior began crawling up from the ambush place, waving. Shuzhen moved to restrain him but he batted her away and lumbered toward the house, the wreckage of our plan strewn behind him.

I couldn't move.

Saw Lori in the doorway, stepping off the porch.

Saw her cringe as the figure inside the house fired into her back.

A soul-sick howl from Junior as he rejoined his wife on the beaten lawn.

From the porch, another bloom of venting gunpowder.

Lori dropping into her husband, hand on his breast, dragging him down with a mewl of surprise and shared agony.

The shooter told us to throw our weapons. I did. Shuzhen reluctantly followed suit. We were told to move closer together, to kneel down.

Junior McGuane sobbed noiselessly, unaware of anything but the dying creature in his arms. He didn't see Rigger Devlin hop down from the porch, walk close to him and fire.

FIFTY-EIGHT

Grunt work. I dragged Junior McGuane's body down to the beach, arms under the dead man's shoulders. Then scooped him and with considerable effort heaved him onto the deck of the *Bay Bride*. Soaked to the knee in the surf, my upper body gummy with blood.

I repeated the exercise with Lori, losing her shoe on the sand. After she was onboard, I retrieved the sneaker and lobbed it after her.

Rigger Devlin observed this with the barrel of the pistol snug against Shuzhen's spine. He wore a runner's thermal body stocking, gloves and a padded blue vest. The outfit looked ridiculous on him, screamed mid-life crisis.

"Nicely done," he said. "And now the plane."

The back seat of the aircraft had been stripped out. On the floor were a trio of large apple boxes, each piled with shrink-wrapped bundles. Each bundle contained thousands of flat cyan-coloured pills. Fentanyl, I guessed. They looked like dried lima beans.

Each box weighed forty or fifty pounds. The awkwardness lay in turning the box so it would fit through the door. I accomplished this, backing out onto the slippery wood of the small dock.

Rigger waved me over. His left hand brought out a set of keys from the vest pocket. He tossed them underhand into the box I carried.

"Behind the house you'll find a silver Subaru. Open the tailgate. Move Darlene's gardening junk onto the middle bench and load the boxes in the back. Gonna give you sixty seconds to do this and get back to me. You know what'll happen if you dawdle."

I nodded. Shuzhen looked at me with a beatific patience at odds with her ragged breathing. Trying to calm herself, to stay alert. Searching my face for signs of a plan I didn't have.

"Get moving," Rigger said. "One. Two."

I covered the uneven ground as swiftly as I could, discarding plans as quickly as they coalesced. *With an eight-round magazine—he used four on the McGuanes at least—or was it three?—what the hell did it matter when one was too many—*

The houses backed onto a cul-de-sac. A Subaru SUV was parked at the curb. I fumbled with the keys, got the right one, balanced the box on the gate while I transferred gardening shears and trowels to the back seat

could hide one up my sleeve—an improvised dagger—no, he'd be looking for that—

and shifted bags of mushroom manure. Then loaded the apple box, sprinting back.

"Fifty-two," Rigger was saying. "Fifty-three. And there he is. Did you shut the tailgate?"

Panting, I shook my head.

"Next time shut it. And go."

The second trip was easier. I was familiar with the dimensions of the box and the direction. But I stumbled stepping off the dock, sending one of the bricks of pills bouncing into a tidal pool. I bent for it, the box resting on my hip.

"Leave it," Devlin said. "Be more careful. Seventeen. Eighteen."

On the final trip I was breathing hard. I could hear the click in my bad knee as I goated over the rocks. Devlin told me to stop.

THE LAST EXILE · 287

"Breathe," he said. "You're doing fine. Almost done. When you load this last one, pour out the bags of manure over the cases. Spread it even. No plastic peeking out. Take the time to do the job right. Then lock the Subaru and come back."

I did as he instructed, tearing the bag open with my teeth, spreading it with hands numbed from exertion and cold.

The task complete, I came back to find the *Bay Bride* lit up and shoved off the beach. Shuzhen stood on the deck now. What looked like blood on her cheek. She'd resisted.

Behind her stood Allie Creel, grinning in lunatic triumph.

As soon as we were out of the cove, Allie reared back and struck Shuzhen in the mouth. Planting kicks as she lay on the deck.

"Stop," I said. "Please."

Allie looked at me and kicked again.

"Enough of that," Rigger said. "Take the wheel, Allie."

"Gimme the gun. I'll drop 'em both. You don't gotta worry."

"First put some distance between us and the house."

Allie took the helm reluctantly. As she turned the boat, I helped Shuzhen to her feet, squeezing her hand, trying to comfort her in an impossible hour.

Rigger Devlin was staring at the receding house.

"Charlie's place," he said to himself. "The Priest will have one hell of a time explaining this."

Before turning to us and the task at hand, Rigger's face showed quiet satisfaction. Not a cutthroat like the Priest or Terry Rhodes, but not simply the operator of a chop shop, either. Meticulous and even-tempered in his actions and all the more ruthless because of it.

I watched him gather the shotguns and Felix's hockey bag and lower them to the water. His was now the only gun.

"Lori first," he said to me. "Take off her other shoe."

"Wasn't she your wife's friend?"

"Don't talk." As I worked he added quietly, "Best friends. The Three Amigas, we called them. You should've heard them wailing over Jan. If Lori even suspected that was connected to her little flight…Over the side with her."

I watched as Lori hit the water, bobbing once, lost beneath the wake. The *Hood* still trailed us on its towline. Rigger directed me to take Junior's belt and shoes.

"You're planning on shooting Allie, too, aren't you?" I said this loud enough for it to carry to the cabin.

"Said no talking."

Silence from the helm. No change in course.

Junior McGuane was my chance. I couldn't deadlift him over the gunwale as with Lori. Instead I draped his arm over my shoulder, preparing to squat lift. Timed correctly, the pilot's body could serve as a shield, a weapon…

"Won't work," Rigger said, taking a step back and seizing Shuzhen by the throat. Jabbing the gun into her hip. "Just do as you're told."

So I did, straining as I took Junior's weight and leaned over the rail, watching him fall. The body trailed along the side until the prow of the *Hood* sucked him under. The rain had lessened and moonlight occasionally penetrated the clouds. The coastline had disappeared.

"Don't you want to know how we found you?" I asked.

"No." Devlin turned his head and called, "Allie. This is good."

The engine whimpered and went quiet. We slowed.

I didn't see what she hit me with, just a blip and I found myself sprawled on the filthy teak. Allie's sneaker punted my skull.

"Shoot her now," she said. "I want him to see."

"Is he out?" Rigger asked.

More kicking and prodding. I didn't respond. Couldn't.

"It'll take you both to lift him," Rigger said, prodding Shuzhen hard enough to elicit a groan. "Go help her."

"I wanted him to see," Allie said. "Wanted him to fucking watch."

"Then you shouldn't've clipped him, should you? He's out now, and I'm not waiting."

Neither in nor out. Nothing but a haze of colours, the reflective tape on the stairwell leading down to the galley. I felt underwater already, sinking lugubriously into the ancient dark.

"Each take an arm," Rigger said. "Work together and drag him up."

"You could fucking help, you know."

They expected Shuzhen to oblige as I had, to help Allie carry me over. Instead Shuzhen bent as if to do just that, only she lunged. Allie's attention was divided between me and her argument with Rigger. I heard the snap of broken cartilage. Allie howled in pain.

Their struggle was brief. A stampede above and around me, out of my line of vision. Rigger fired, not caring which of them he hit. Then a sudden quiet on the deck. The undulation of the boat on the waves. I felt their absence. Gone.

FIFTY-NINE

Rigger Devlin jabbed at the water with the gun, strafing the waves. The *Bay Bride* drifted and bobbed. From my vantage on the deck, I saw the pistol rest on the gunwale as Rigger peered over the side.

If there was a move to make, it had to be now, and it had to be decisive. Clear of mind. No trace of indecision. It had to be done with aplomb. I didn't think I could manage aplomb but grabbed for his wrist anyway.

My hands closed on the fabric of Rigger's sleeve. When his reflexives retracted the arm, pulling away and raising it off the gunwale, I sank everything I had left into forcing that wrist down, cracking it on the fibreglass edge. The gun clattered into the wake of the ship. Rigger snatched at it impotently with his free hand.

Infuriated, he stomped and chopped at me, trying to free the wrist. Nothing but to endure it. Do not take your focus off that wrist. Let him rip at your hair, throw punches at your head and neck. It's only a head, a neck. Torque that forearm. Beartrap it. Observe the way the elbow wants to flex and how it can't because you simply won't let it. Good. Now roll that arm the full three-sixty, all your weight behind it. Let Rigger Devlin roll with it, roll and scream.

A glint in my peripheral vision, an obelisk of dull metal. The wedge of the axe, gripped just under the head, striking me on the crown. Seconds gone. My grip gone. On my back. Rigger now several feet away from me.

Another lost moment. My eyes opened again. He was dragging the axe up, one-handed, hauling it over his head, staggering back to retain balance.

The wedge came down and I rolled left, heard the neat *thunk* of the blade chop into the deck. Rigger pulling at it, bracing it with his foot and dislodging it with a rocking motion. Like pumping water. The blade coming free all of a sudden, soaring up like a kite catching the breeze.

He rushed me, the axe extended fully over him, arcing down. A blow that would shear cartilage and snap ribs, lodge right in my chest like it had in the planks of the deck.

No stopping it, no time to evade. Rigger's face was contorted with animal fear. A wild man unaware of anything but the injured beast he had to kill to ensure his own survival. Kill and you're safe. Kill and you triumph once again.

Down came the arm, the axe following at the end of its long sway-backed handle. I kicked Rigger's knee, flopping out of the path of the stumbling man who'd committed an instant too soon. He lurched airborne following the swipe of the axe, landing on the top stair leading down to the cabin. Falling the rest of the way.

Crawling like an alligator, breathing as if the cool night air was running out. I pulled my body up to the top step and peered down. Rigger Devlin had come to rest with his leg on the bottom step. Unconscious, from the looks of it. The axe just as still.

For a selfish and dangerous moment I closed my eyes and stole deep chestfuls of West Coast oxygen, very grateful to be alive.

When I recovered, I eased my way down the steps to where Devlin lay. A finger under the jaw: still drawing his share of breath. An easy problem to solve. Seal up that nose and mouth. Or haul him to the rail and drop him, like Allie and Shuzhen.

But Shuzhen wouldn't want that. I could hear her telling me so. I begrudged Rigger Devlin his breath and told her all the reasons it was better if he stopped. She wasn't there to change her mind.

"All right, you win," I said, and tied him.

The stairs were harder to climb than to descend. On the deck I turned on the lights, scanning the water for signs of either Shuzhen or Allie. I saw nothing.

If I left the lights on, she'd come back. She'd have to. There was nothing else around.

A pale-pink strata of early dawn formed over the eastern horizon. I called Shuzhen's name, my voice growing hoarse, sounding self-mocking to my ears. The moon was a distorted stain of light over the dark rolling quilt of the strait.

I drew in the towline and stepped onto the deck of the *Hood*. Maybe she'd climbed aboard, was waiting for me. But no one was waiting for me.

"All those laps weren't for nothing," I said to the water. "What were you training for if not this? We won. Come back and let's celebrate. We'll order a bottle of something expensive and sip it on a patio somewhere. Sure the summer's over, and it could rain, and people might laugh at us sitting there. But the fall's the best time of year. And it's just starting. So come back, Shuzhen. Enough's enough. This is unfair. Come on now."

I leaned against the deck for a long while, pleading, making a fool of myself. The ocean didn't seem to mind.

SIXTY

"The Humane Society runs a kennel right inside here with us," Kay said. "We look after the dogs, groom and bathe them. A lot of inmates take courses on pet cosmetology. Don't laugh."

"No, that sounds great," I said.

Prison architecture reminds me of high school. The same ribbed metal roof, same brick walls painted cream or beige, the same reinforced doors with wood grain veneers. Hard to damage, easy to wipe down. Resilience, above all.

My sister wore the formless green T-shirt and pants of the institution. Her hair in a loose ponytail. Paler than she'd been before her conviction, a greater amount of gristle and sinew. But more or less the same.

"We prepare our own meals. Full kitchen and everything. I didn't cook this much when I was out."

Around us, other inmates were talking with their partners or children. One woman nursed in a corner.

"There's a conjugal wing," Kay said. "If you hear of any eligible bachelors."

I'd brought her some books. The Marilynne Robinson, which I'd finished. Seneca's *Letters from a Stoic*. A Regency romance by an author I knew she liked. I'd topped up her commissary account as well.

"So what about you?" Kay asked. "Heading back to Montreal?"

"No plans."

"Doesn't sound like you, Dave."

"The business is in dire shape," I said. "If I sell the flat in Montreal, and Jeff and I cut a deal with the bank, we'll manage but it'll be an uphill fight."

"You like uphill fights," Kay said.

I nodded. It felt good to see her, familiar. I knew the question I still had to ask, but couldn't voice it. Instead I asked about the dogs, about her pen pals.

"I got a note from Maggie Zito," Kay said. "She's up and around now. I don't think she knows how you did it, but she's grateful to be out. And she owes that to you."

"To Shuzhen," I said.

Kay nodded. Our time was nearly up.

"I'm a little worried," I began.

"About me?" My sister shook her head. "Nobody really messes with me. I'm getting through okay."

"What I worry about," I said, the syntax twisting the thought, "whether you being here is my fault."

The floor had been polished recently but bore fresh scuffs, problem areas that couldn't be buffed out. I stared at it, waiting for her answer. When I looked up, Kay was watching me with a mix of pity and scorn.

"Is that why you visited?" she asked. "To see if I'd say, 'No, Dave, you had nothing to do with this. It's all on me. My bad decisions. My bad luck.' You want me to tell you that so you can go?"

"If I'm at fault, I want to know. If there was something I could have done."

"You could've destroyed the evidence," Kay said. "Only you couldn't 'cause that's not who you are."

"Who am I?"

THE LAST EXILE · 295

Kay laughed. "A man who follows a code," she said, her voice taking on the dramatic flair of an old-time radio drama. "The hero who tamed this wild land, punishing evildoers wherever he went. Even when they're his own flesh and blood."

I put up my hands, defenceless from the charge. Kay stood and made the sign of the cross over me.

"The curse is hereby lifted," she said. "In the name of the father, the sister, and the holy whatever, you're hereby absolved of any wrongdoing."

I bowed penitently, nodded thanks.

"Not the only reason I visited," I said. "And I'll be back soon."

"Next time bring movies. I'm still working through the Criterions. If you can get me *Local Hero* or *Mississippi Masala*, I'd appreciate it."

"Not *The Great Escape*?"

My sister shook her head. "You're the one who tried to escape," she said.

Every day more of the heat seemed to be drawn out of the air. A blister of clouds formed over the city, shielding the North Shore mountains from view. A September sunrise in Vancouver was hard to beat.

I stood at the end of the short pier in New Brighton Park, waiting. Eventually I saw headlights. A black Lincoln Navigator pulled up to the stretch of curb across from the playground. Felix Ramos clambered down and held the door for Terry Rhodes.

The two crossed the wet grass. Rhodes was dressed in boots and jeans and a cardigan, Felix in jeans and a hoodie. Rhodes took a misstep and slid, grabbing Felix's arm for support. For a brief moment he looked frail.

When they reached the pier, Rhodes waited on solid ground while Felix frisked me. No nod, no recognition. His choice made, all feelings stowed away.

"Clean," he said to Rhodes, who stepped out onto the weathered boards.

In the water near us, a small tugboat guided a bulk carrier toward Viterra Cascadia Terminal. The distribution of labour between them seemed unfair.

"Presence of mind is a valuable fucking commodity," Rhodes said. A slight unkemptness to the hair, stubble on the jawline coming in whiter than before. Yes, he was looking older. Even Terry Rhodes would die one day.

"You mystify me, Wakeland. You baffle the shit out of me. By all appearances you've got the self-preservation skills of a prairie dog on a highway. Yet here you are."

Rhodes gestured at me demanding an explanation.

"Did Rigger Devlin kill Maggie Zito's brother?" I asked.

He shrugged, not denying it. "Who remembers ancient history? Rigger drove the truck, yeah. Hadn't earned the right to ride with us back then. Dragging that mouthy little wop earned him a few points toward his patch. Speaking of."

His hand thudded off Felix's chest with pride.

"Your boy here's earned his wings. Gonna come to the afterparty?"

"He's your boy," I said.

"Damn right he is. Now tell me about that two-faced chop shop sonofabitch."

"Rigger Devlin had Lloyd Corso and Allison Creel kill the Stacks. He was using Jan's sister-in-law Lori McGuane to smuggle fentanyl. Budd was close to finding out. Rigger made it look like Maggie did it because he knew you and the Priest would kill her before the truth could come out. He used the Priest's nephew and his place on the island to make sure you wouldn't suspect him."

Water poured out of the freighter's anchor wash. The tug moved on to other business. A congregation of seagulls settled along the shore.

"Rigger always was a crafty sonofabitch," Rhodes said. "Lloyd, though. Even as a kid, you told Lloyd he was a mailbox, he'd let a dog piss on him. How'd a guy smart as Rigger ever trust that little shit?"

"He found out Lloyd is an informant," I said.

"Bullshit."

"You don't have to believe me," I said. "But why else would Lloyd agree to testify against Maggie? It's the only way he could save his deal with the government and keep Rigger happy."

Rhodes struck the railing, sending reverberations over the water. The gulls took notice.

"All Rigger had to do was keep his head down and wait for you to kill Maggie. Then the whole thing would be wrapped up. And if Lloyd's testimony took out you and the Priest, so much the better for him."

"Guess I'm lucky to have a friend like you," Rhodes said.

He crooked a finger and Felix brought him a phone. Rhodes texted something. Then leaned over the railing and tossed the phone.

"So the plot against the king fails. I get Rigger, I get Lloyd, I get every fucking thing. Question is, Wakeland, what do you get out of this?"

"Left alone," I said. "That would be nice."

"You're in debt. Name a figure or tell me who owes you."

I imagined Bill Stoddard being visited by an Exiles collection team. An invoice from them wasn't something you could slick your way out of paying. Sooner or later, everybody pays.

"My debts are my problem," I said. "I can't take your money."

"You are a tough sonofabitch to pal around with," Rhodes said. "Something else, then. I hate owing people."

A smell came off the water, salt and sulfur, kelp and creosote. I looked at the constellation of lights near the top of Grouse Mountain.

"I need a place to live and I have no money," I said. "Know of any recently vacant homes I could lease? Maybe something close to the water?"

Rhodes shook his head in amusement. "If that's your price," he said. "How you gonna square this with your conscience?"

I couldn't. But the float home was empty and I had nowhere of my own. One more crooked land deal wouldn't matter all that much, especially with no actual land involved. The city was built on crooked land deals, after all. A whole continent of stolen real estate, floating on the dead and dispossessed.

Before we parted, I asked what would happen to Rigger Devlin and Lloyd Corso.

"Don't worry about them," Rhodes said. "These things have a way of sorting themselves out."

SIXTY-ONE

For three days I worked to strip out the furniture from the Stacks' float home. When it was empty, I cleaned the place top to bottom—or stem to stern. The decks needed scrubbing, the bedroom and hallways needed paint, and the wall of the shower stall needed tile and grout. I wasn't sure yet what I needed, so I kept busy.

Every task removed one more trace of the prior occupants and how they died. Budd Stack's photos came down, but the hallway seemed bare without them. I re-hung two of the black and white nature shots. That looked all right.

In the storage I found a case of Beaujolais. Each night when I finished work I sat on the upper deck with a glass, listening to Jason Molina or Margo Price. A wretch in torn jeans and a paint-stained shirt, alone with a two-million-dollar view.

Maybe I shouldn't have told Terry Rhodes that Lloyd was an informant. It didn't seem to make a difference. When Operation Eiger broke, Rhodes and Charlie the Priest were served with multiple indictments. The case would take years to see through.

One afternoon I spied Maggie Zito and her kids walking along the seawall. Maggie moved stiffly, a hitch in her step. This aggravated her son. He tugged at her arm to go faster. Maggie's daughter was balancing on the railing, content to idle.

I could have called to her, invited them aboard to see the place. Could have asked how she was doing. For a woman who'd been stabbed in the heart, Maggie seemed just fine. I was the one in no shape for visitors.

But I got one anyway. On the third night, Shuzhen stopped by.

She'd gone into the water and started swimming, intent on putting distance between herself and death. Only when she paused to turn back, she could no longer see the *Bay Bride*. The current was taking her in and she didn't fight it.

Shuzhen woke up on the beach not far from where we'd landed. She staggered to the nearest house and called it in. Then she waited for search and rescue to locate the boat, to notify her that I was alive.

A crisis like that, you'd expect it to draw lovers closer together. At first it had. I'd never been so grateful to see someone, to hold her to me. I believe Shuzhen felt the same.

And yet in the past few days, I hadn't seen her. We traded odd texts at strange hours of the night. *Glad we're still here. Me too.*

Now she crossed the foyer, carrying a travel case. She freed George Eliot, giving the cat the run of the house. Shuzhen joined me on the deck. The cat promptly flung herself at the screen door, causing it to tremble.

"My roommate's not coming back," she said. "I told her I'd find George Eliot a proper home."

"Is that what this is?"

A breeze came off the water. Shuzhen and I kissed. I told her the mattress I'd ordered hadn't arrived yet. Deck chairs and wine and a sleeping bag were all I could offer.

"Pretty empty," she said.

"I'm in no hurry."

Through the fabric of her jacket I could see her shoulder blades trying to diffuse tension. "You heard about Rigger Devlin, right?"

A corrections officer had found him in his pretrial cell. His shirt knotted around his neck. No note.

"Guess I don't know how to feel," Shuzhen said. "I mean, I know he tried to kill us. But it sort of feels like, instead of saving Maggie, all we did was swap her out for him."

A glimmer of apprehension, one I didn't want to feel. Something had been damaged between Shuzhen Chen and I. I'd been close to having it all—the job and the home and the woman. Somehow I'd missed my shot. The realization hurt like a knife in the side.

"I have a trial coming up in the oil fields," she said. "Husband shot by an abused wife. I'll be up north for a while working on her defence."

"Weekends you'll be back?"

"Not at first. We'll see."

That grim humour that so often accompanied pain. What was it she'd said to me all those years ago? *I could maybe wreck your life.*

"This is an awful big space for one person," I said.

"Why I brought you George Eliot."

Shuzhen moved close and allowed herself to be kissed. I tried to cling to her. She took my hands, squeezed them, moved them down to hang between us.

"Good night, Wakeland," she said. "Welcome home."

After Shuzhen left I filled my glass and sat cross-legged on the deck, staring at the broken shards of moonlight on the water, the slink of traffic across the bridge, allowing myself to feel the full weight of her absence. Welcome or not, sweet or not, home.

ACKNOWLEDGEMENTS

A series owes so much to so many people, not least the readers. If you've checked out the other Wakeland novels, I hope this one lives up. If this is your first, please give the rest a shot. They have their moments. In either case, your support means the world.

All characters are fictitious, all errors mine.

I'm indebted to my agent Chris Casuccio at Westwood Creative Artists.

To Anna Comfort O'Keeffe and the entire team at Harbour, with special thanks to editor Derek Fairbridge and publicist Fleur Matthewson. A terrific group of people to work with.

Thanks to Josh and Gab for the French lessons, and to Lisa Jean Helps for the legal consultation. To Charlie Demers for the sawdust remark and Compline, Andrew Nicholls for the knuckles research. And to Nick Wells for the comment about St. Paul's.

Thank you to Robert Burns and Kim Rossmo for the shoptalk.

Thanks also to the great bookshops at home and abroad for their support. Thanks to Naben Ruthnum and Kris Bertin, Gorrman Lee and Dennis Heaton, Iona Whishaw and Janie Chang, Chris Brayshaw and the Pulp Fiction Staff, Mary-Ann Yazedjian and Book Warehouse, and my family.

Above all, this is for Carly.

ABOUT THE AUTHOR

SAM WIEBE is the author of the Wakeland novels, one of the most authentic and acclaimed detective series in the Pacific Northwest, including *Invisible Dead, Cut You Down, Hell and Gone* and *Sunset and Jericho*. His other work includes the bestselling *Ocean Drive*. He lives in New Westminster. For more information, visit samwiebe.com.